Before Sierra had time to realize what was happening, Ben tackled her,

and she found herself with a hundred and eighty pounds of lean, hard male sprawled on top of her. Not an entirely unpleasant predicament, she decided.

"This is all so sudden," she said. "After all, we've only just met."

"Shh!" His solid chest heaved against her breasts, and when she squirmed beneath him, he pinned her even more firmly with his body and forced her to lie still.

Despite appearances, it suddenly became clear that she was the only person present who found this situation arousing. "Was that a bullet that just came through here?" she asked mildly.

Ben nodded, a wild gleam in his eyes. From her vantage point, Sierra could see a faint, puckered scar on his forehead that had been hidden by his dark blond hair. And she began to wonder just what else this man was hiding from her....

Dear Reader,

With all due fanfare, this month Silhouette *Special Edition* is pleased to bring you *Dawn of Valor*, Lindsay McKenna's latest and long-awaited *LOVE AND GLORY* novel. We trust that the unique flavor of this landmark volume—the dramatic saga of cocky fly-boy Chase Trayhern and feisty army nurse Rachel McKenzie surviving love and enemy fire in the Korean War—will prove well worth your wait.

Joining Lindsay McKenna in this exceptional, action-packed month are five more sensational authors: Barbara Faith, with an evocative, emotional adoption story, *Echoes of Summer*; Natalie Bishop, with the delightful, damned-if-you-do, damned-if-you-don't (fall in love, that is) *Downright Dangerous*; Marie Ferrarella, with a fast-talking blonde and a sly, sexy cynic on a goofily glittering treasure hunt in *A Girl's Best Friend*; Lisa Jackson, with a steamy, provocative case of "mistaken" identity in *Mystery Man*; and Kayla Daniels, with a twisty, tantalizing tale of duplicity and desire in *Hot Prospect*.

All six novels are bona fide page-turners, featuring a compelling cast of characters in a marvelous array of adventures of the heart. We hope you'll agree that each and every one of them is a stimulating, sensitive edition worthy of the label *special*.

From all the authors and editors of Silhouette *Special Edition*,

Best wishes.

KAYLA
DANIELS
Hot
Prospect

Silhouette Special Edition

Published by Silhouette Books New York

America's Publisher of Contemporary Romance

To Chris:
modern-day prospector,
human alarm clock,
and world's greatest brother.

SILHOUETTE BOOKS
300 East 42nd St., New York, N.Y. 10017

HOT PROSPECT

ISBN: 0-373-09654-2

First Silhouette Books printing February 1991

Printed in the U.S.A.

Books by Kayla Daniels

Silhouette Special Edition

Spitting Image #474
Father Knows Best #578
Hot Prospect #654

KAYLA DANIELS

loves to travel and has visited every state but one. She has lived in Alaska, California, Alabama and New Orleans' French Quarter. Kayla wrote this book while living in Hendricks, Minnesota, where she learned how to square dance, met some distant branches of her family tree and drank about ten thousand cups of coffee up at Irene's Cafe.

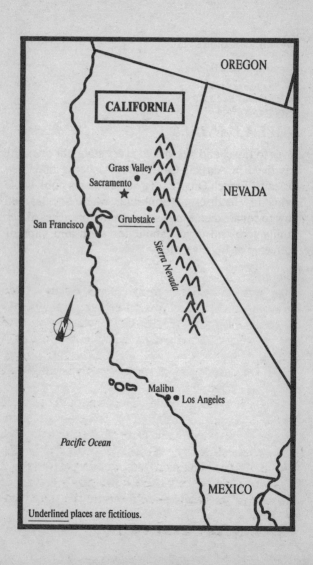

OREGON

CALIFORNIA

NEVADA

Grass Valley

Sacramento

San Francisco

<u>Grubstake</u>

Sierra Nevada

Malibu
Los Angeles

Pacific Ocean

MEXICO

<u>Underlined</u> places are fictitious.

Prologue

Sabotage.

The word ricocheted through Ben Halliday's brain like a zinging metal ball in a pinball machine. But the red warning lights on the instrument panel in front of him were flashing a far more ominous message than *Tilt*!

And the danger alarms ringing in his head weren't part of any game.

As Ben struggled to maintain control of the crippled Cessna 210, he forced himself to choke back his outrage, his sense of shock and betrayal. Resisting the urge to curse himself for one careless, possibly deadly mistake, he focused completely on the desperate task at hand: coaxing the small plane down gently enough so that maybe—just *maybe*—he'd survive the crash landing.

He'd only have one shot at it.

With lightning-quick expertise, he scanned the cockpit instruments, automatically noting the rapidly dwindling altitude and air speed. Below him the jagged, snowdrifted peaks of the Sierra Nevada loomed closer and closer, like jaws growing wider and wider just before they swallowed him up.

Ben's stomach lurched sickeningly along with the Cessna. He shoved in the throttle, counting on the increased power to provide more lift. The sputtering engine increased its loud, whining protests, but—as far as Ben could tell—with no effect on the aircraft's relentless downward plunge.

With sweat-slicked palms, he pulled gradually yet firmly on the yoke, trying to bring up the plane's nose and increase the wings' angle of attack. The craft began to yaw wildly from side to side. Ben pumped the rudder pedals, but he might as well have tried to stamp out a forest fire with his feet. Wrestling with the unresponsive controls was like riding a bucking bronco, except that in this case the ground was a long, *long* way off.

"Come on, baby," he urged through gritted teeth. "Stay with me . . . come on, you can do it."

Beads of sweat crawled down his temples as he battled to achieve exactly the right balance. He had to keep the Cessna's nose up, yet at this sluggish speed he couldn't nudge the wing angle too high without sending the plane into a stall.

Ben stole a quick peek at the ground, then wished he hadn't. He was close enough now to make out the individual pine trees that studded the slopes with their sharp green spikes. Swallowing, he choked back the coppery taste of fear rising in his throat. Once he gave in to panic, he'd be a goner for sure.

Adrenaline surged through his bloodstream. Every nerve and muscle in his body was stretched taut with effort, as if he were part of the plane itself and could keep it aloft with his own physical strength.

But all too quickly the rugged landscape approached. Then, to make matters worse, a strong updraft buffeted the doomed Cessna as it veered over a steep drop-off below. The wind currents tossed the plane around as if it were made of paper. Ben pitched forward into the windshield, striking his head with a blow that left him dazed.

He shook his head to clear away the fog. Despite the dizzying stench of gasoline fumes filling the cockpit, he forced several deep breaths into his lungs. Ignoring the sticky warmth he felt oozing down the side of his face, he grappled with the controls, forearm tendons corded like steel cables with the strain.

He darted his eyes to the ground again. Hopeless as it seemed, he had to pick someplace to set this baby down—a highway, a meadow, a damn *parking* lot, for God's sake.

"Fat chance," he mumbled. Where in this forbidding, mountainous terrain was he going to find a place flat enough even to *attempt* a landing? As he scanned the ground ahead, all he could see were more mountains, more stream-filled ravines, more of those damn tall pine trees waiting to impale him....

Wait a second.

Ben's frantic, searching gaze snagged on a break in the trees up ahead. Some kind of open field, perhaps?

Or another deep, rocky gorge gaping up at him....

Gingerly he turned the yoke to the left, praying the ailerons would respond and bank the plane in the direction of that opening.

They didn't.

"Figures. Well, why should *they* work when nothing else does?" Ben growled.

But using every scrap of his considerable piloting ability, he was able to cajole enough of a response from the disabled controls to steer the aircraft more or less toward the clearing.

Now the plane was skimming over the tops of the snow-dusted trees, so close that Ben could see the individual needles. His heart thudded in his ears, drowning out the tortured gasps of the engine.

"This is it . . . this is it," he muttered, chest heaving, head throbbing, muscles tensed to the limit.

For a few moments, time slowed to a glacial crawl as he neared the break in the trees. He was committed now to this course, and if the opening turned out to be another canyon . . .

"Hurrah!" he crowed hoarsely when the most beautiful sight in the world crept into his field of vision. The snow-covered, boulder-strewn ground below was hardly the ideal landing spot, but at least it was roughly horizontal.

Ben's burst of triumph vanished as quickly as it had exploded—because the plane was traveling much too fast. Because the controls were virtually useless.

Because, in all probability, Ben Halliday was about to die.

A maelstrom of emotions churned through him: rage, frustration, regret and, finally, an aching sadness.

"I'm sorry, Ma," he whispered. "You counted on me, and I let you down."

He yanked back on the throttle as the plane skidded over the clearing, but he was still going too fast . . . too fast . . . the field wasn't wide enough . . . the trees ahead were too close. . . .

At the last instant the engine sputtered one final cough and died, and a white roar of silence filled Ben's ears as the thick, prickly trees reached out their branches to snatch him. . . .

Either the whole crash was over incredibly quickly, or Ben had blacked out on impact. In any case the next thing he knew, he was opening his eyes and squinting cross-eyed at a dense canopy of pine trees overhead.

He didn't know how long he'd been out cold, but one fact was certain: he had to get away from the plane before the fuel tank exploded. The mangled interior of the cockpit was barely recognizable. Ben grasped the edge of the opening where the door had once been and tried to heave himself upward.

"Ow!" He let loose a stream of curses as a javelin of pain shafted up his left leg. Moving more cautiously, he rested his weight on his right leg and shoved. Perched on the threshold of his wrecked Cessna, he paused, gasping with effort and agony.

The letter.

Damn it, he had to get that letter. No matter what the cost.

Without hesitation he turned and crawled painfully back through the crumpled cockpit, searching for his coat. He had to find it. The letter was in one of its pockets.

Concentrating on the search, aware that with each passing second he was in greater danger of being blown to smithereens, Ben allowed one small, detached corner of his brain to take inventory of his injuries. From the stabbing in his chest that accompanied each breath, he figured several ribs were broken. His left leg was a virtual dead weight whose excruciating pain sent waves of nausea through him. Something was wrong with his head, but whether this was from the earlier blow or from the crash, he couldn't tell.

There it was! He spotted a corner of his coat wedged under a tangle of glass and metal. Panting, he tugged and cursed until the coat tore free. With shaking hands he fumbled through the inside pocket to make sure the letter was still there. Crimson drops plopped onto the tan suede.

Clenching the letter between his teeth, Ben scrabbled his way back to the gaping hole in the other side of the cockpit. His brain registered a tortured, recurring sound, but it wasn't until he'd clambered out of the plane and dragged himself to the nearest stand of trees that Ben realized the groans were erupting from his own chest.

For a moment the agony was so great, he thought he'd pass out. But he had to hang on for a while longer, just long enough to hide the letter.

Because as sure as day followed night, Quentin Jericho's henchmen wouldn't be far behind him.

Ben propped himself on his elbows and stuffed the letter inside his shirt.

Then the plane exploded.

When Ben came to, he was sprawled some ten feet away from where he'd been before. An eerie orange glow bathed the landscape, and the loud snapping of burning glass and metal punctuated the steady roar of the flames.

Ben's face felt hot, as if he had a bad sunburn. But the scorched feeling was a caress compared to the red-hot pokers jabbing the rest of his body.

In a sudden panic, he grabbed his chest. Thank God. The letter was still under his shirt.

Refusing to surrender to the pain yet, he lifted his head to scan his surroundings. He needed a rock, a hole in a tree—*someplace* where he could stash the incriminating piece of paper.

As he raised himself onto his elbows, a galaxy of black dots peppered his vision, and gray, cottony mist swirled through his brain. "No, damn it," he muttered, clenching his teeth. "Not yet... not yet... gotta hang in there... just until... until I can hide the..."

The next time Ben opened his eyes, he was gazing up at the homeliest face he'd ever seen. Even through the fading daylight and gently falling snow, he could make out widely spaced eyes beneath a drooping straw hat...enormous nostrils...big pointy ears...and breath that would wilt skunk cabbage.

Ben blinked, shook his head to clear his pain-blurred vision, then blinked again.

Now, what the hell was a mule in a straw hat doing way up here on this godforsaken mountain?

Chapter One

"Listen to this, Charlemagne. 'Your mother misses you very deeply. Of course, she doesn't say it in so many words, but I know that your stubborn persistence with this reckless escapade weighs heavily upon her heart.'"

Sierra Sloane thrust the letter in front of Charlemagne's eyes. "Do you believe this? Wait, wait—it gets better. Listen."

Charlemagne chewed placidly on a mouthful of weeds and listened.

"'Naturally your decision to throw away a promising career for the sake of some wild-goose chase has been a big disappointment to me, as well. I know you and I have had our differences in the past, Sierra, but I beg you to think of your poor mother's feelings, and please reconsider your impetuous decision, which I know was made in a moment of sentimental weakness.'"

Sierra mashed up the letter and flung it back over her shoulder. "What a bunch of baloney!" She paced back and forth across the campsite, shaking her chestnut curls in exasperation. "For one thing, I know darn well that Mother is the one person in the world who sympathizes with my decision. She'd do the same thing herself if she could."

She scooped up the crumpled paper and shook it in front of Charlemagne's nose. "Do you know what this is?"

Charlemagne didn't reply.

"I'll tell you what this is. This is Daddy's latest scheme to drag me back to Los Angeles and that corporate oppressor of the human spirit they call Sloane Enterprises." She flung her arms wide in a dramatic gesture of helplessness. "What is this now? Plan A? Plan B? C, D or E? Good heavens, I've lost track by now. We could be all the way up to Plan Z, for all I know."

Charlemagne yawned sympathetically.

"Wanna know what I think of this latest scheme of his? I'll show you." With brisk determination, Sierra snatched up a dozen rocks lying around the campsite and pushed them into a rough circle.

"Thinks he can pull my strings by making me feel guilty, does he? I'll show him what I think of his sneaky tricks," she muttered, tossing handfuls of sticks and brush into the circle of stones. Rummaging through the saddlebags draped over a branch of a nearby tree, she found her pieces of flint and crouched down by the makeshift hearth.

"I'll show you what this letter's good for," she announced, tossing the crumpled wad down with disdain. "Kindling! How 'bout a nice fire, Char? I kind of fancy pancakes for breakfast this morning, don't you?'' She clinked the pieces of flint together again and again, her tongue protruding with concentration.

"Looks like we might be in for a storm today, anyway. Look at those dark clouds heading this way! A fire will feel real good...if I can just...get it started...."

Clink. Clink. Clink.

"Yup, looks like summer's nearly over, Char. Feel that wind! Why, I can practically *smell* autumn in the air!" Clink. Clink.

"Come on, one little spark...one measly little spark..."

Clink.

"Oh, hell." She tossed the flints aside in disgust. "Well, even if I *had* gotten a spark, it's probably too windy to start a fire. I'd never get a flame going in this gale."

Sierra pushed herself to her feet and tucked the flints back into the saddlebag. Wind whipped her hair into her eyes as she scratched behind Charlemagne's ears. "You gonna be okay if the weather gets a little rough?" she asked. "Here, let's make sure your hat's tied on tight. Wouldn't want it to blow away." She slapped the mule affectionately on his flank. "Looks like a good day to stay inside," she said, scanning the western horizon, where she could already see distant flashes of heat lightning.

She slung the saddlebags over her shoulder and headed for the tent, which was pitched at a rather lopsided angle. "Hmm," she muttered, studying the tent critically, her eyes darting to the fast-approaching storm.

She fished her rock hammer from one of the saddlebags and skirted around the tent, pounding in the stakes more securely. "Guess that'll have to do," she said finally as the first spatters of rain hit her shoulders.

Inside the tent she tossed her gear aside and collapsed cross-legged onto her sleeping bag. With a sigh she reached into a plastic bag and scooped a handful of nuts, raisins and sunflower seeds into her mouth.

"Yum, yum," she mumbled, chewing mechanically. "Trail mix for breakfast." She sighed. "Again."

Raindrops tattooed against the tent, increasing in force like the rat-a-tat-tat of a snare-drum crescendo, individual beats merging into one steady, deafening stream of sound. Sierra shivered, though the air temperature was fairly warm. For the first time since leaving Los Angeles two months ago, she was keenly aware of her isolation. Not that she was lonely or anything. Just . . . alone.

A huge gust of wind screamed up the mountainside and slammed into her tent. Sierra flinched. Drawing her knees up close to her chest, she huddled with her arms wrapped around her legs as the storm howled outside.

Somewhere very close by, she heard an ominous creaking noise. Then another. And another.

"Uh-oh," she said.

Ben tugged the hood of his gray rain slicker up over his head and hunkered down behind a tangle of brush. Peering at the campsite, he nodded with satisfaction. This was the place, all right. He'd recognize that mule anywhere.

Now the only problem was how to make sure the old prospector was alone. The fewer people who saw Ben, the better. He'd had a devil of a time tracking down Caleb Murphy without drawing any attention to himself. He hadn't dared ask anyone in town where the old miner was camped out these days, for fear of leaving behind a clue for one of Jericho's goons.

Ben shifted uncomfortably as the ghost of his months-old injury gnawed at his leg. He'd never really believed before that the weather could affect a person's aches and pains, but ever since he'd risen early this morning and sniffed rain in the air, his left leg had been acting up again. He'd hoped today's hike would banish the stiffness, but the throbbing from his thigh down to his calf had only grown worse. Gritting his teeth, Ben willed himself to ignore the pain as he'd learned to do during those long months of physical therapy.

Well, he could live with pain, but he wasn't sure how long he could stand the maddening wetness creeping beneath his collar and into his boots as he crouched below the dripping trees. And the fierce wind, though not cold, lashed through his slicker and combined with the dampness to make him even more miserable.

Maybe he was being overly cautious. Chances were Murphy was alone inside that tent, anyway. Why not simply saunter over and knock on his door—or his tent flap, as the case might be?

The prospect of shelter from the sodden outdoors was a temptation Ben couldn't resist, even though the tent didn't look like much of a shelter. Murphy must have put it up in an awful hurry, by the unsteady looks of it. Well, any port in a storm, Ben thought as he levered himself painfully to his feet.

At that moment a ferocious gust of wind shoved him toward the tent. But before he'd taken three steps, Ben froze and watched in astonishment as the entire tent seemed to expand like a balloon and then collapse.

Even more amazing were the muffled cries that emanated from inside the tangled folds. Amazing not only for their highly inventive profanity, but also for the fact that they were uttered in a high-pitched voice that Ben couldn't imagine coming from the grizzled prospector's vocal chords.

After watching the helpless thrashing for several moments, he decided to risk tweaking Murphy's pride by coming to the rescue. He loped across the campsite and tried to find the tent's opening—not an easy task with all the wild flailing going on inside.

"Hold on a second! Don't move—you're only making matters worse! I've got it— there!" Ben hoisted the tent opening and peered inside to find himself face-to-face with the most exasperated, the most adorable female he'd ever seen.

It was hard to say which of them was more startled.

The woman's enormous, thickly lashed eyes seemed to fill her face. Rich, brown eyes flecked with gold— eyes a man could lose himself in if he wasn't careful. Unruly reddish brown curls framed her heart-shaped, pixieish face, which glowed fiery pink at the moment from her frustrated efforts to free herself from the collapsed tent.

Her cheeks grew even redder as she absorbed the surprising fact of Ben's appearance, and her lips parted as she sucked in a little gasp of air.

His eyes darted immediately to those lips—full, rosy lips that were a strangely seductive contrast to her otherwise delicate features. Suddenly he was awash with the overwhelming urge to taste those lips, to explore her mouth with his own and discover what other delicious surprises she might have in store.

The unexpected flood of desire caught Ben off guard, coming as it did after months of recovery and rehabilitation when his only physical craving had been to escape the pain. For a moment he forgot his soggy feet, his aching leg and the purpose for his presence.

Then a droplet of water plopped onto the tip of her pert nose. She blinked and tossed her head. The defiant uptilt of her fragile chin showed another intriguing contrast. "Who the hell are you?" she demanded crossly.

Ben rocked back on his heels. "What kind of welcome is that? I'd expect a little more gratitude from someone I just rescued from the clutches of a man-eating tent. *Woman*-eating, I should say."

"I didn't need your help. I was doing perfectly fine without you."

"Oh, really?" Ben chuckled. "If I hadn't come along, you'd still be trying to find your way out of this tent. But if you'd rather I left you to your own devices—" He made as if to leave, dropping the tent flap to the ground.

"No, wait!" She scrambled out of the toppled tent. Pushing back her damp curls, she bit her lower lip and studied Ben for a moment. "Look, I'm sorry," she said finally, sounding as if those words didn't pass her lips very often. "You took me by surprise, that's all." Then a sheepish grin teased the corners of her mouth. "I guess I was kind of embarrassed about my tent falling down." She stuck out her hand. "Sierra Sloane."

He grasped her hand, then did a double take. "Sierra?"

"As in Sierra Nevada. That *was* going to be your next question, wasn't it?" she asked, peering mischievously at him from beneath rain-spangled lashes.

"You've been asked that a few times before, I take it." Her slim fingers nestled cozily against Ben's palm.

Reluctantly he released her hand. "You've certainly come to the right place, with a name like that."

"Hmph. I know people who'd disagree with you," she said, throwing back her head with a defiant gesture he was already coming to recognize.

Her remark raised another question. What the devil was this gorgeous *young* woman doing way up here in old Caleb Murphy's tent? Ben scanned her slim figure from the muddy tips of her worn leather boots to the frayed collar of her plaid shirt. She barely came up to his shoulder. Now that he took a closer look at her, he realized how young she really was. Hardly more than a teenager, he'd guess, despite the undeniably womanly curves her disheveled garb couldn't disguise. Her fresh-scrubbed complexion with its faint dusting of freckles across her nose made him think of a high-school cheerleader. Peaches and cream. Apple-pie wholesomeness.

So what the hell was she doing mixed up with a man four times her age?

"Why are you glaring at me like that?" she asked suspiciously, propping her hands on her hips.

"How old are you, anyway?"

Her dark eyebrows shot toward the sky. "What are you, the census taker?"

"Humor me."

"I'm twenty-eight, not that it's any of your business."

Okay, so Caleb Murphy was only *three* times her age. Still, Ben scowled at the images that flitted across his imagination. But she was right. Sierra Sloane's dubious personal life was none of his business. He had a far more vital matter to worry about. "I'm looking for your, uh, companion," he said, inspecting his fingernails.

Her forehead wrinkled in adorable confusion. *"Who?"*

Ben licked his lips. "You know." When it became obvious she *didn't* know, he glanced around helplessly, then jerked his thumb over his shoulder. "I'm looking for the guy who owns that mule. Fellow by the name of Caleb Murphy."

Whatever reaction he'd expected, it wasn't the odd mixture of sorrow and surprise that swept over her face like the storm clouds overhead. She swallowed, and Ben could have sworn the moisture in her eyes had nothing to do with the rain.

"What do you want with Grandpa?" she asked with a slight quiver in her voice.

Ben's jaw dropped. "Grand— You mean, the guy who wanders around the mother-lode country looking for gold? Caleb Murphy? He's your grandfather?"

"Was."

"I beg your pardon?"

She brushed a hand across her eyes, then met his gaze with sad resignation. "Grandpa died almost three months ago," she said evenly, despite a slight trembling of her lower lip.

"Oh, no. Oh, my God." An icy chill swept over Ben. How on earth was he going to get the letter back now? And without that letter, he'd never be able to even the score, to see justice done. All his hopes, his plans, his promises threatened to collapse around him in ruins, like the windblown tent.

Then he noticed Sierra's face and cursed himself for being an insensitive jerk. "God, I'm so sorry," he said, taking one of her hands between his. "I had no idea— I mean, the last time I saw him, he was fine."

Her eyes lit up like a sunrise. "Were you a friend of Grandpa's?"

"No...not exactly. But I did meet him once."

Her hopeful interest faded. "Oh." Shrugging, she started to turn away, then stopped when she realized her hand was still imprisoned between Ben's. They both looked down, met each other's gaze, then quickly averted their eyes again.

"Oops." Ben released her hand.

Sierra backed away slowly, then knelt to the ground and began pawing through the tent folds. "I'm sure sorry you came all the way up here for nothing," she said over her shoulder.

Ben rubbed his forehead. What to do now? After everything he'd been through, he couldn't simply give up. Maybe Sierra had come across the letter in her grandfather's things; maybe Caleb had mentioned to her where he'd hidden it.

The trick would be extracting the information from her without revealing too much. Not that Ben didn't trust her; his instincts told him that Sierra Sloane was someone you could count on. But until that letter was safely back in his possession, the less Sierra knew, the better.

Bitter experience had taught him that where Quentin Jericho was concerned, too much knowledge could prove fatal. Once before, Ben had made the mistake of underestimating Jericho's ruthless power. It had nearly cost him his life.

He didn't intend to make the same mistake again.

Ben knelt beside Sierra. "If I offered to help fix the tent, would you bite my head off?"

She laughed. "I might," she replied, "but I'd wait till we had the tent back up to do it."

* * *

Much as she hated to admit it, Sierra was grateful for her unexpected visitor's help. Not that she couldn't have put the tent back up by herself…eventually. But by that time the storm would probably have blown over.

She watched him covertly as he pushed the flap aside and crawled inside the tent to join her. When he tugged off his rain slicker, she got her first good look at him. And suddenly her two-person tent seemed like very close quarters indeed.

The vibrant, male presence that filled the tent sprang from a far more basic source than his six-foot frame, button-straining chest and thickly muscled thighs. Some raw, masculine essence of the man himself seemed to burn up all the oxygen in the tent so that Sierra had trouble catching her breath. Whoever this friend—*acquaintance*—of Grandpa's was, he made all the other men Sierra had ever met seem like pale imitations of the real thing.

She guessed him to be in his early thirties, although her initial impression had been of a man a bit older. Faint creases of what looked like past suffering etched the corners of his eyes and mouth, but did nothing to diminish the bold attraction of his ruggedly carved features. In fact the physical evidence of endured tragedy merely enhanced his appeal. Here was a man who had been tested to the limits and survived.

Rain had seeped inside his slicker hood, plastering a damp fringe of sandy blond hair to his forehead. His eyes, which had appeared slate blue against the backdrop of gray clouds, were a deep cobalt when he returned Sierra's appraising glance. Hastily she busied herself searching through her meager cache of supplies.

"Hungry? How about some trail mix? Beef jerky?"

He slicked back his wet hair. "I don't suppose you've got a pot of coffee stashed away in those saddlebags, have you?"

His husky, baritone voice set her nerves purring. "Hmm, no. I tried to light a fire earlier, but I couldn't get a spark off the flint. Guess it was too wet," she added, omitting the fact that it hadn't been raining at the time.

"Ever hear of matches?"

She snorted. "Grandpa never used matches. He said, why fuss with man-made gadgets when nature provides something just as good?"

Her visitor scratched his head and regarded her with amusement from beneath his sandy eyebrows. "Seems to me you might have got that fire started if you'd used a match instead of banging a couple of rocks together. Or are you on some kind of Girl Scout wilderness survival trip?"

"Don't be ridiculous. Aha!" She pulled a silver flask from the saddlebag and waggled it in front of him. "Now you're going to be sorry you laughed at me."

"I wasn't laughing at you," he said, reaching forward to accept the flask. "I'm trying to figure you out, that's all. But I guess I should introduce myself first. Ben Halliday."

This time when their hands clasped, an odd current of awareness and acknowledged attraction seemed to flow between them. A tingling sensation traveled across Sierra's fingers, up her arm and down her spine. She suppressed a delicious shiver.

"So," she said brightly, "how do you know—*did* you know—my grandfather?"

Ben wiped the top of the flask with his shirt cuff, then tilted his head back and took a swig. Fascinated, Sierra watched his Adam's apple bob up and down. He shuddered and smacked his lips. "Boy, that hits the spot on a day like today."

His fingers brushed hers as he handed back the flask. Without thinking, she took a hefty gulp of whiskey. She might as well have swallowed lighter fluid.

Ben slapped her on the back. "You okay?" he asked, the twinkle in his eye belying the concern in his voice.

Sierra gasped for air, her vision blurred by a film of tears. "Hoo, boy, that stuff is strong!" she coughed, struggling to regain her lost dignity.

"Not your usual brand?"

She threw Ben a haughty look. "It was Grandpa's favorite. And mine, too. It just went down the wrong way, that's all." How she wanted to wipe that amused grin right off his mouth! Or better yet, kiss it off. . . .

"You and your grandfather must have been pretty close," Ben said. His amusement had vanished, and in his casual tone, Sierra detected a hint of wary curiosity. "When I, er, ran into him that once, I didn't realize he was dragging a granddaughter around these mountains."

"Oh, I didn't live with Grandpa," she explained. "At least, not since I used to spend my summer vacations with him when I was a kid."

Ben arched his eyebrows in surprise. "Then how on earth did you wind up living way out here all by yourself?"

"I'm not by myself. I have Charlemagne, don't forget."

"Charlemagne? Who's th—oh, you mean that mule?"

Sierra had to stifle a giggle. The poor man looked confused, to say the least. Confused...but cute. "Charlemagne doesn't know he's a mule. Sometimes I forget that myself."

Ben took another swallow from the flask. "Okay. So how did you and *Charlemagne* end up together?"

Sierra played with a frayed thread on her shirtsleeve. "When Grandpa died, he left me everything he owned. I was ready for a change in my life, so I left Los Angeles and came up here to carry on where he left off." She shrugged. "End of story. At least the short, condensed version."

"Someday you'll have to tell me the long, unabridged version," Ben said. His crooked smile sent a rush of warmth and exhilaration coursing through Sierra's bloodstream, more potent than a shot of whiskey. "You're not really trying to make a living by panning for gold, are you?"

The note of disbelief in his voice was an all-too-familiar echo of the skepticism she'd heard from her family, friends and co-workers ever since she'd announced her intentions a few months ago. Despite her resolution to ignore the scoffers, Sierra's defensiveness flared up.

"My life-style may be somewhat unconventional, but it's certainly not some wild-goose chase, if that's what you're thinking."

"I didn't mean—"

"Have you checked the price of gold lately? The forty-niners who mined this area in the last century took the easiest-to-get-at deposits, but they left behind plenty of gold that simply wasn't cost-effective to extract. However, the current high price of gold, combined with advances in modern technology, now makes it economically viable to go after what's left over. A lot of the old abandoned mines are being reopened."

Ben studied her, probing his cheek thoughtfully with his tongue. Then he said, "But you're not taking advantage of modern technology. You're still using a mule and a gold pan, just like the old forty-niners."

"Just like my grandfather," she shot back. "He managed to make a living that way, and so can I. What was good enough for him is plenty good enough for me."

Ben leaned forward, intending to point out the illogic of Sierra's reasoning. Then he noticed the scarlet flush staining her cheeks and the stubborn set of her jaw. Maybe this was one of those times when discretion was the better part of valor.

He drank another leisurely swallow of whiskey and handed back the flask. From what he'd seen so far, Sierra was completely out of her element up here in the wilderness—a babe in the woods chasing some crazy dream because of her misguided devotion to her grandfather.

Ben understood better than most that kind of devotion. He sympathized completely with Sierra's loyalty to a lost loved one's memory. After all, that same brand of loyalty was the driving force that had sustained him through those agonizing months of recovery after the accident. It was the motivation that propelled him out of bed each morning, that had led him to track down Caleb Murphy and brought him instead to this unexpected encounter with the old man's intriguing, impossible granddaughter.

But Ben suspected Sierra's quest for gold sprang from a more complex source than sentimentality. Unless he missed his bet, she was searching for a lot more than precious metal.

And for some inexplicable reason, Ben wished he were going to have the chance to learn more about her. The woman was a mass of contradictions: one minute she was spouting off cost-effectiveness projections, and the next she was scorning plain old matches as some kind of newfangled nonsense.

With an almost wistful hunger that unsettled him, Ben longed to explore the mystery of Sierra Sloane, to dig for answers to the questions that stirred his curiosity. But he had a quest of his own to pursue.

And until he'd seen justice done, he couldn't spend time on detours, no matter how lovely or provocative.

He found Sierra's efforts to squelch her annoyance with his skepticism rather endearing. She took a dainty sip of whiskey, coughed, pushed back her tangled russet tresses and pasted a resolutely polite smile on her face. It was easy to see she was sick and tired of all the flack people had given her lately. "So," she said, "you haven't told me what brings *you* to these parts. What business did you have with Grandpa?"

Here was where Ben had to tread very, very carefully. He had to come up with a plausible excuse for seeking out Caleb Murphy without creating an obstacle course of lies that would trip him up later. He hadn't yet figured out how he was going to wangle that letter out of Sierra, and he wanted to leave as many options open as possible.

Vagueness, that was the key. If he gave elusive enough replies, she couldn't pin an inconsistency on him if he later decided to change his story a bit. Telling her the truth was not an option, of course. What chance would a woman who couldn't light a campfire or stake a tent properly have against Jericho's thugs?

And they'd show up sooner or later—Ben would bet his life on that. Jericho had to suspect Ben had hidden the letter somewhere near the crash site, since it wasn't in his possession after he was airlifted to the hospital in Sacramento. Of course, there was always the chance the letter had been destroyed in the wreck. But that wasn't a chance Jericho could afford to take. And once he found out Ben had returned to this area, he'd dispatch a couple of his goons to retrieve the letter and get rid of Ben. Permanently.

Unfortunately they wouldn't be the kind of fellows who'd have any scruples about eliminating anyone else who might know the contents of the letter. Which was why Ben had to be especially careful not to involve Sierra any further than absolutely necessary. No matter what the price, he would never endanger one curly hair on her gorgeous head.

So he had no choice but to lie to her instead.

"I'm a reporter," he said.

"Oh, really? What paper do you write for?"

Names of various California newspapers shuffled through his brain. Too risky. With his luck Sierra would be related to the editor or something and instantly know he was lying. "Actually I'm more of a free-lance writer. I write for whatever magazine will buy my articles."

"And you came up here to write a story about Grandpa?"

"Yes, that's right," he said quickly. "Your grandfather was quite a colorful character. I wanted to include him in an article I'm writing about modern-day prospectors."

Sierra propped her chin on her fist and studied Ben. "Must be kind of hard to take notes for an article without a tape recorder or a pencil and paper or something."

Was he imagining the suspicious glint in her eyes? Or was she truly puzzled by his lack of journalist's equipment? Whichever the case, Ben realized he'd have to watch his step around Sierra Sloane. She might be a hopeless dreamer and a charming klutz, but she was sharp as a porcupine quill.

"I wasn't planning to interview your grandfather today," he explained. "I didn't think I'd track him down so quickly. I only arrived in Grubstake last night," he added, naming the small town about ten miles away. "I decided not to lug my tape recorder up here until I was sure I could find him."

Sierra continued to scrutinize Ben as if she thought his story was full of holes. He could hardly blame her. What did a cassette recorder weigh, a couple of pounds? His excuse sounded lame even to his own ears.

It was almost a relief when the bullet whizzed through the tent.

Chapter Two

Before Sierra had time to realize what was happening, Ben tackled her. The back of her head hit the ground with a thud, and she found herself with a hundred and eighty pounds of lean, hard male sprawled on top of her.

Not an entirely unpleasant predicament, she decided. Especially when that lean, hard male wore a sexy scowl with kind of a wild gleam in his eye. "This is all so sudden," she said. "After all, we've only just met."

"Shh!" He pressed a finger across her lips. His solid chest heaved steadily against her breasts, but apparently Sierra was the only person present who found this arousing. When she squirmed beneath him, Ben pinned her even more firmly with his body and forced her to lie still.

"Was that a bullet that just came through here?" she asked.

Ben nodded briefly. His head was cocked to one side, like a wild buck alert to danger. From her new vantage point, Sierra could see a faint, puckered scar about an inch long up near his hairline. Previously it had been hidden by the dark blond strands that swept across his forehead. She wondered what other things Ben was hiding from her.

Like, why he was so jumpy, for example. "Look, this has been very enjoyable," she said, "but I'm ready to get up now. I want to go recommend a good marksmanship school to that hunter out there."

"Are you trying to get us killed?" Ben demanded in a hushed voice, his lips barely an inch from hers.

Sierra's pulse picked up speed. She swallowed. "I assure you, that's the farthest thing from my mind," she murmured, unable to tear her gaze from his dark, compelling eyes.

"Good." His breath was a heated caress against her mouth. The tantalizing scent of whiskey teased her nostrils. "Stay here," he ordered quietly, "and stay down until I get back."

Naturally she ignored him, scrambling into a sitting position the instant he pushed himself off her. "Where are you going?" she whispered.

"Now, look!" Ben turned back from the tent opening and jabbed a warning finger at her. "For once in your life, will you please take someone else's advice? Somebody out there is trying to kill us."

"Oh, pshaw."

"Damn it, Sierra—"

"Okay, okay." She held up her hands in surrender. "Go to it, Rambo. I'll play the damsel in distress, if that makes you happy."

The final look Ben fired at her was far more murderous than any possible gunman lurking outside, Sierra decided. On hands and knees, she scooted across the tent and nudged the flap ever so slightly aside so she could watch Ben.

To her surprise he seemed to have disappeared. She had to admit he was pretty good at this cloak-and-dagger stuff. She didn't believe for a minute that he was really a journalist—not unless he'd been a foreign correspondent in a war zone or something. But that didn't make sense, either. You didn't go from dodging bullets and guerrilla attacks to writing human-interest stories about quaint old prospectors.

Maybe he was a Green Beret or an antiterrorist commando. He *did* have that mysterious scar on his forehead....

A sudden rustling in the brush across the clearing caught her attention. A muffled shout reached her ears, followed by the crack of a gunshot. Charlemagne brayed loudly.

"Ye gods, Char! Are you all right?" Sierra dashed out of the tent and rushed to the mule's side. Anxiously she ran her hands over his flanks to inspect him for injuries, but Charlemagne seemed to be all in one piece.

Sierra turned as Ben emerged from the trees, one arm in a choke hold around the neck of a stout, potbellied man with a walrus mustache and a wild haystack of snow white hair. His other arm held a shotgun pointed at his captive's back. "Hold it right here," Ben growled. "You're going to answer a few questions before I turn you over to the sheriff."

Sierra folded her arms. "Oh, very impressive, Mr. Halliday. You've just captured—singlehandedly!—the most-dangerous, most-wanted desperado in these here parts.'' She shook her head. "My, my, Sourdough Pete in person. I imagine there's quite a reward on his head. I believe he recently escaped from a senior citizens' home in Sacramento, didn't you, Pete?''

"That's right, missy.'' The prisoner pushed a pair of cracked spectacles up the bridge of his nose. "And I ain't goin' back, d'you hear me?''

The shotgun wavered a little in Ben's grip. "You— you know this character?'' he asked.

"Sure do. Pete's an old friend of Grandpa's. His children had him declared mentally incompetent and committed him to a nursing home. But old Pete outsmarted those attendants, didn't you, Pete?''

Pete bobbed his head up and down. "O' course, none of them was *armed*," he said, turning around to give Ben an accusing look.

"Congratulations.'' Sierra rocked back and forth on her heels, smiling sweetly at Ben. "You've just managed to overpower an eighty-three-year-old man with a hearing aid and a heart problem.''

Ben quickly unwrapped his arm from around Pete's neck and stepped back. "He *did* shoot at us," he mumbled, grinding the heel of his boot into the ground. "And he fired at me again when I jumped him.''

"'Twere only bird shot, sonny!'' Pete glowered indignantly at Ben while he dusted off the sleeves of his dirty red windbreaker.

"I'm sorry.''

"What's that? Speak up, boy!''

"I said, I apologize! I thought you were—well, never mind. I was only trying to protect Sierra.''

"Whoa, there—hold on! Don't try to blame this on me. I told you it was just some hunter with bad aim. No offense, Pete," she added hastily.

Pete's chest swelled up like a bullfrog's. "Danged gun barrel's outta whack," he said, snatching the shotgun from Ben. "That's why my shot went wild. I was aiming for a squirrel in that tree just past your tent there." He spat a brown stream of tobacco juice on the ground, narrowly missing Ben's boot.

Personally Ben thought Pete's poor shooting had more to do with the nearsighted squint behind those smudged spectacles. But he figured he'd stomped on the old man's pride enough for one day. Not that his own pride was in such great shape, either. The merry sparkle in Sierra's eyes showed how close she was to bubbling over with laughter—at Ben's expense.

Damn it, why did he so hate making a fool of himself in front of her?

Never mind. He couldn't afford to be overly concerned with her opinion of him. This scare with the shotgun had only served to remind Ben of the urgency of his task. He had to retrieve that letter without letting Sierra know what he was after. And he had to do it fast.

As far as he could see, he only had one course of action: make a play for her. Wine her and dine her. Sweep her off her feet.

Winning Sierra's heart and her trust would be the quickest, surest way to get that letter back.

Any normal, red-blooded American male would have drooled over the prospect of cozying up to such a sexy, alluring woman. But the idea left Ben cold. Cold—and disgusted with himself. He'd never deliberately taken advantage of anyone before, and the thought of cold-bloodedly seducing Sierra left a bitter taste in his mouth.

Unpalatable though it was, deceiving her was his only choice.

He forced his lips into an imitation of a smile. "Hey, how about letting me make this…misunderstanding up to you? To both of you. Let's head back into town, and I'll buy you each a big steak dinner."

Ben could see Sourdough Pete's indignation warring with his appetite. "Well," he said, scratching the three-day growth of white stubble on his cheeks, "I reckon that's the least you owe us…." His appetite won. "Sounds good to me," he announced, slapping his hands on the round paunch overhanging his belt. "How 'bout you, Sierra?"

Her suspicious gaze was riveted on Ben. "It's nearly ten miles to town," she said. "Seems kind of far to walk just for one dinner. Especially in the rain."

Ben studied the sky. "Looks like the weather's clearing up. Besides," he said, pointing at the tent, "I noticed you're kind of low on supplies. You'll need to go into town soon, anyway, to stock up." Mentally he crossed his fingers, praying that for once Sierra wouldn't argue with him simply to be ornery.

He found an unexpected ally in Sourdough Pete. "Come on, missy. I got me a hankerin' for some steak, and you could use a little more meat on your bones, too. You're too dang skinny." He winked at Ben. "In my day, when you grabbed a woman, you had somethin' to hold on to."

Sierra rolled her eyes. "Of all the chauvinistic twaddle I ever heard—oh, all right, Pete. Stop mooning at me like some poor starving refugee. Although I don't see why *I* need to come along."

"Why, to keep us menfolk in line, ain't that right, sonny?" Pete slapped Ben on the back with a blow that sent him staggering forward a step. He winced at the sudden jolt of pain that shot up his leg. "Who knows what trouble we might stumble into without a pretty little gal around to keep us on our best behavior?"

"Hmm. I don't know, Pete. My presence doesn't seem to have kept Mr. Halliday out of hot water so far." She cast Ben a saucy grin as she sauntered across the campsite. "I sure hate to take this tent down, after all the trouble it took to put back up."

Watching the sassy sway of Sierra's copper brown curls, Ben shook his head and wondered what the hell he was getting himself in for. He still hated himself for what he planned to do, but as a reluctant grin tugged at the corners of his mouth, he began to think that romancing Sierra Sloane might turn out to be...well...kind of fun.

If she hadn't been so desperate for a bath and a nap, Sierra assured herself, she would never have agreed to let Ben rent her a hotel room in Grubstake. Be Beholden To No Man had been her grandfather's motto. On the other hand, didn't Ben owe her a favor after nearly scaring her and Charlemagne half to death this morning?

That was Sierra's rather groggy reasoning, anyway, as she peered with bleary disgust at her reflection in the bureau mirror. Ugh. Sure couldn't call that nap a *beauty* sleep, she thought, trying to rub out the creases embedded in her cheek by the chenille bedspread. She'd collapsed on the bed the second the hotel-room door had slammed shut behind her.

Despite two months of trekking around the mountains, Sierra still wasn't quite in the peak condition required for a four-hour hike—even if it *was* downhill most of the way. Her thrice-weekly visits to a trendy Beverly Hills health spa apparently hadn't been enough to tone her body into a lean, mean, fighting machine. And now her cushy urban life-style was catching up with her. Muscles groaned in aching protest as she lowered herself gingerly into a tub of scalding hot water.

She closed her eyes with rapture as she slid into the steaming, piped-in, purified water. "Isn't indoor plumbing wonderful?" She sighed. "Not that I'd ever admit it to anyone. Look! Soap! Full of perfumes and artificial colors and all sorts of nasty chemicals. And I don't have to worry about polluting any pristine mountain streams." Stretching her legs, she poked her feet out of the suds and wriggled her toes in ecstasy.

After luxuriating in her bath for as long as possible, Sierra pushed herself stiffly out of the tub and grabbed a towel. A thick, plush, terry cloth towel that made her pink skin glow with pleasure as she vigorously rubbed herself dry.

Even yanking a comb through her tangled damp curls was a treat. Washing hair while camping out wasn't the easiest of chores. She rummaged through her dirt-encrusted duffel bag, tossing clothes over her shoulder to fall like autumn leaves on the floor, the bureau, the bed.

Thank goodness she'd had the foresight to keep one respectable outfit from her previous life. She inspected herself in the mirror, lips pursing in satisfaction at the flattering fit of her dark green corduroy jumper. A bit wrinkled perhaps, but otherwise presentable. The short-sleeved, yellow sweater she wore underneath added just the right jaunty touch of color.

She bent over as if to touch her toes, shaking her hair wildly, then flinging her head back. As she fluffed the springy curls with her fingertips, she couldn't help wondering how Ben Halliday would react to the sight of the new, improved Sierra Sloane.

Then she scoffed at her own reflection. She'd given up all that phony stuff, hadn't she? All the games, the concern for appearances, chewing her nails over what other people thought of her. The only person she needed to impress was herself. Not some alleged journalist who'd seen a few too many action adventure movies.

Still . . .

She licked her lips to give them a glossy sheen, then pinched her cheeks to flame them with color. Ben Halliday was up to something—of that she was positive. And if a little good old-fashioned flirtation would help her discover what it was, where was the harm? She could bat her long lashes and wiggle her hips as well as the next woman.

Sierra scuffed her feet into a pair of slightly battered sandals, then gave herself a smoky, half-lidded look in the mirror. "Ben Halliday," she breathed huskily, "you don't have a chance."

Flickering candlelight . . . dry red wine . . . soft music crooning in the background. The hotel dining room was the perfect setting for a romantic evening with a beautiful, desirable woman, Ben thought.

Except for the definitely *undesirable* presence of one tobacco-scented old prospector, happily devouring a

ten-dollar sirloin and regaling Ben and Sierra with the
tale of his escape from the nursing home.

"Then, in all the confusion I snuck outside and just
walked right off. Them security folks were too busy
tryin' to stop the food fight to even notice me."

Ben drummed his fingertips on the white tablecloth
and slid his gaze across the table to watch Sierra watching Pete. The shimmering candle flames danced across
her features, casting mysterious shadows that made her
eyelashes seem even longer and thicker, highlighting the
smooth arch of her cheekbones and the sleek hollows of
her face. In the dim candlelight, her skin took on a rich
golden hue, and her dark hair glinted with hints of
copper. The wine in her glass swirled and sparkled as if
she clutched a fistful of rubies. When she lowered the
glass, her lips glistened with moisture. Almost in a
trance, Ben ran his tongue over his lips.

And it wasn't Sierra's wine he imagined tasting.

He'd hardly recognized her when she'd bounced
down the staircase into the hotel lobby an hour ago. As
she sashayed toward Ben, his admiring glance had
traveled from her coy smile to the soft swell of her
breasts to the slender curve of her waist. Her jumper
clung enticingly to her hips before draping around the
best pair of legs he'd ever seen.

Gone was the hoydenish, jeans-clad tomboy, replaced by a *very* feminine, *very* alluring woman. Still as
fresh faced and impudent as ever, but with an overlay
of sophistication and confident self-possession Ben
hadn't noticed before.

His intense fascination with this previously unsus-
pected aspect of Sierra's personality surprised and
alarmed Ben. After all, he was supposed to play the se-
ducer, not the seducee in this little melodrama. *He* was

supposed to set *Sierra's* pulse racing and palms sweating, not vice versa.

That was the plan, anyway. The plan did *not* include long walks on the beach or nights before a blazing fire or houses with white picket fences. Ben didn't have time to waste daydreaming about an impossible future.

Let's get this show on the road, he scolded himself.

Beneath the table he slowly inched his boot toward Sierra until he encountered resistance. He deliberately nudged her foot, not enough to dislodge it, but enough so that his meaning would be unmistakable.

Oh, she was a cool one! Her rapt attention to Pete's story never faltered, at least not on the surface. As Ben stroked his toe back and forth across the arch of her sandaled foot, an outside observer would never guess what was happening under the table. Ben bolted his glance to Sierra's face, willing her to turn from Pete and meet his eyes so he could send her visual confirmation of his message.

She propped her chin in her hand, otherwise appearing to ignore Ben. But he was getting to her, no question about it. A tiny vein fluttered in her temple, and he was almost certain her breath had quickened. Ben focused every volt of his mental energy on transmitting over and over again a very succinct, very explicit telepathic suggestion.

Good. He could almost swear a rosy flush was spreading up Sierra's neck and flooding her cheeks. He edged his other boot forward and imprisoned her foot between his.

Now the corner of her mouth curled upward in the beginning of a smile. "How on earth did you manage to start a food fight in the nursing-home cafeteria?" she asked Pete. A cool customer, all right. Ben could barely detect the slight quaver in her voice.

Relishing the memory of her well-shaped, slim calves, he slid his boot languidly up past her trim ankle.

"Piece of cake," Pete replied around a mouthful of baked potato.

"That easy, huh?"

"No, I mean that's how I started the food fight. See, we was having pineapple upside-down cake for dessert that day, and—" With a clatter, Pete dropped his knife and fork onto his plate. "Say, what in tarnation is movin' around down there, anyhow?" He shoved back his chair and peered beneath the table.

Hastily Ben yanked his feet back.

"I coulda swore I felt something nosin' around down there," Pete said with a puzzled frown. "It was startin' to crawl right up my leg, in fact. Didn't you feel it?" he demanded of Ben.

Ben drained his wineglass and shrugged. "Not me, Pete." He picked up his silverware and attacked his steak, feigning sudden hunger.

"How 'bout you, Sierra? Didn't you feel it? I wonder if this here hotel don't have rats or somethin'."

"Gee, Pete, I didn't notice anything. Maybe it was a stray cat. Must have taken quite a liking to you." Sierra tore a dinner roll in half and buttered it. "Of course, I suppose it *could* have been a rat of some kind." Her voice vibrated with mirth. Ben sensed her mocking scrutiny as he popped a forkful of steak into his mouth and tried to chew innocently. Why was it that now, when he longed to be inconspicuous, Sierra shone her attention at him like a spotlight?

It was just like her to act so contrary.

"Hey, I've got a super idea," she said, snapping her fingers. "Why don't you interview Pete for your article?"

Ben lifted the wine carafe and refilled their glasses, grateful for the abrupt change of subject. "My article?"

"You know. Your magazine article," Sierra replied, bestowing the word "magazine" with a sly emphasis that gave Ben the eerie impression she could see right through his journalist's charade.

"Oh, *that* article. Sure, I could do that. I guess." The last thing Ben wanted was to squander precious time with Pete while he should be concentrating on Sierra.

She bit into the buttered roll and chewed thoughtfully. "I mean, it seems a shame for you to go back empty-handed. Pete's been prospecting these mountains nearly as long as Grandpa did. I'm sure he could provide you with plenty of colorful anecdotes."

"I'm sure he could." With a sinking feeling, Ben absorbed Sierra's satisfied smirk and the eager expression on Pete's face. He was trapped. No way was he going to avoid "interviewing" Sourdough Pete for his nonexistent article.

He spent the rest of the meal with his boots firmly planted under his own chair, chewing mechanically while he tried to think up a way to get Sierra alone after dinner.

Surprisingly help came from an unexpected quarter. As the waitress was clearing away their dessert plates, Pete stretched his arms above his head and yawned loudly. "Mmm-*mmm*, that was mighty tasty apple pie. I'm kinda tuckered out, though. Guess I'll go get me some shut-eye." As he tugged off the napkin tucked into his shirtfront, he gave Ben a broad wink.

Good grief, the old-timer was trying to play matchmaker! Ben instantly felt ashamed for not giving Pete enough credit. The old man's courting days might be long past, but he obviously hadn't forgotten what it was like to have a chaperon hanging around.

The poor guy was probably desperate for company. Shut away in an institution by his own relatives, wandering these lonely mountains in a vain search for gold and glory...no wonder he'd seemed so eager for an evening of companionship.

Ben cleared his throat. "Say, Pete, you don't have to leave right this minute, do you? I thought we'd have some brandy with our coffee."

As he rose creakily to his feet, Pete dismissed Ben's suggestion with a wave of his hand. "Naw, it's way past my bedtime, sonny. Besides—" he bent low near Ben's ear and spoke in a loud whisper "—three's a crowd." Then he slapped Ben on the shoulder and sauntered out of the dining room, drawing curious stares from the tourists clustered around other tables.

Ben had half risen when Pete left, and as he settled back into his chair, he shook his head. "Quite a character," he said to Sierra. Then another thought occurred to him. "Say, where's he going to sleep, anyway? He turned down my offer to get him a hotel room, and he doesn't exactly look like he can afford one."

"Save your money," Sierra said, tasting the coffee the waitress had placed in front of her. "Pete hates sleeping indoors. He told me that was the worst part about being in the nursing home. He likes to be able to look up and see the stars when he wakes up at night."

"Then where's he going to—"

"I expect he'll unroll his sleeping bag out back of the hotel and bed down right next to Charlemagne." She smiled distantly, as if recalling some scene Ben wasn't privy to. "Those two are kind of fond of each other."

"You've known Pete a long time, I take it." Ben sipped his own coffee, relaxing for the first time that evening.

"Oh, sure. He and Grandpa go way back, so he was always around when I'd come to visit."

"And where did you come to visit your grandfather *from*?"

She ducked her eyes, studying her coffee for a moment before replying. "Los Angeles."

"Does your family still live there?"

"Uh-huh."

Sierra had turned strangely silent, not at all like her usual loquacious self.

"Brothers and sisters?" Ben prodded.

"Nope."

"And what did you do for a living before you started panning for gold?"

She glanced at him sharply, as if suspecting him of poking fun at her. Then she shrugged, tracing the rim of her cup with one finger. "I worked for a large corporation. I guess you'd call me a junior executive type. You know—staff meetings, profit-and-loss charts, power lunches—the whole rat race."

Ben set his cup down with a noisy clunk. "You?" he asked incredulously. "*You* were a corporate executive?"

Her old defensiveness returned. "Why is that so surprising?" she asked. "Don't you think women are capable of making it in the business world?"

Ben held his hands up in protest. "Hey, I never said that. It's only that . . ." I can't quite picture *you* making it in the business world, he thought, leaving the rest of his sentence unspoken. He didn't want to make Sierra any madder at him. "Somehow I can't picture you sitting in an office all day," he finished instead. "You seem more the outdoor type." A blatant lie. He was willing to bet Sierra had never camped out in her life before embarking on this crazy adventure of hers.

But his response seemed to mollify her. "Yes, well, I couldn't picture myself working in an office for the rest of my life, either. Then, when Grandpa died..." She paused for a moment and gave a quick little sigh before continuing. "It made me examine my own life, question the choices I'd made. Somewhere along the way I think I'd sort of lost sight of the person I was meant to be."

"And who *is* that person?" Ben asked gently, surprising himself with the sincerity of his own question.

"Sometimes I think—and then other times, I—" She broke off with a trickle of laughter. "Maybe I'm not sure of the answer myself," she admitted with a sheepish grin. "But in his will Grandpa left me everything he owned. It wasn't much, I guess. Except for Charlemagne, of course."

"Of course."

"But somehow it meant more to me than all the stocks and bonds and money-market accounts in the world. Because it was everything he had. And he left it all to me. Even though in recent years I neglected him."

"Neglected him how?"

"Oh, you know. After I got to be a teenager, the idea of hanging out with my grandpa didn't seem 'cool.' I had better ways to spend my summer vacations. And then college came along, and then my job... well. You get the picture."

She plucked absently at a thread in the tablecloth. Ben covered her hand with his. "Sierra."

She looked up, startled.

"Your grandfather knew how much you loved him."

Her eyes misted with tears. She looked away, across the room. "I hope so," she said in a soft, shaky voice. "Oh, boy, I sure hope so."

Now Ben thought he understood what had brought this city girl to these rugged mountains. She wasn't searching for gold; she was searching for a way to make up for the past.

Ben squeezed her fingers. "Come on. Let's go for a walk."

She threw him a wobbly smile. "I'd like that."

Outside, the night was balmy, but the faint scent of burning leaves infused the air with the unmistakable snap of autumn. Summer hung on stubbornly, reluctant to surrender its grip on the season.

Somehow Ben hadn't got around to releasing Sierra's hand, and they strolled slowly toward the edge of town, fingers intertwined. Sierra's nerves were humming pleasantly, as if Ben's touch were sending a low-grade electric current singing through her body. Her skin tingled with anticipation. She had a hunch that something exciting was going to happen before this evening was over.

She'd been aware of Ben's impatience during dinner. With secret delight she'd sensed how eager he was to get her alone. Well, that fitted right in with her own plans. Ben had lied to her about his reason for seeking out her grandfather—of that she was certain. So she would be completely justified in using all of her feminine wiles to coax the truth out of him, wouldn't she?

A delicious shiver ran through her at the prospect.

"Chilly?" Ben asked, sliding his arm around her shoulders and drawing her closer.

She snuggled next to him. "No, I'm not cold," she replied a little breathlessly. "It's pretty warm out tonight, isn't it?"

"Warm for late September, that's true. But real fall weather is just around the corner." As they passed through an amber circle of light cast by a street lamp, Sierra could see the concern written in his face. "What will you do when the weather turns cold?"

"Wear warmer clothes, of course."

"What about when it snows?"

"Probably build a snowman."

He squeezed her arm. "Come on, Sierra. You're a city girl from sunny southern California. Surely you don't intend to camp out all winter, do you?"

"My grandfather—"

"I know, I know. Your grandfather did it, and so will you." In the darkness she heard Ben sigh. "Don't take this the wrong way, but are you sure you know what you're doing? Do you have any idea how harsh the winters can be up in these mountains?"

"You sound like you're speaking from personal experience," Sierra said lightly, trying to sidetrack him before they got into another argument. Fighting about her plans for the winter was definitely *not* on tonight's agenda.

"My parents were from Grass Valley, about an hour's drive north of here."

"Is that where you grew up?"

Ben shook his head. "My folks moved to Los Angeles when I was a baby."

"Is that where you live now?"

He hesitated. "That's right."

"What about your parents?"

Ben was silent for so long, Sierra began to wonder if he'd heard her question. Finally he said, "My father died when I was six. Ma passed away early this spring. She'd moved back to Grass Valley a few months before her death."

She turned abruptly, stepping in front of him and placing her hand against his chest. "Oh, Ben, I'm so sorry."

He covered her hand with his; she could feel his heartbeat thumping beneath his shirt. "I guess we've both lost someone we loved recently," he said in a gruff voice.

"Yes." Sierra drew back, and they continued walking. She'd only meant to change the course of the conversation, not put a damper on it. Casting about for a cheerier subject, she pointed to a ramshackle false-fronted building across the street. "That used to be the newspaper office back in the gold-rush days. And see that brick foundation over there? That's all that's left of the old jail."

"You seem to know this town pretty well."

"Oh, I spent lots of time in Grubstake when Grandpa still owned the hotel."

Ben stopped dead in his tracks. "Your grandfather owned the hotel?" His forehead was furrowed in amazement.

"The very one we're staying in."

"But I thought he was—I mean, didn't he always—"

"He didn't start mining until I was about ten. My mother used to help him run the hotel, and then after she got married and moved away, he had a hard time managing without her. I think maybe he sort of lost the heart for it, too. He missed my mother a lot."

"Is your father from around here, too?"

"No. He and Mom met when he was a guest at the hotel. I gather it was quite a whirlwind courtship, and then as soon as they were married, he dragged her off to Los Angeles."

Ben chuckled. "I presume your mother didn't look at it quite that way."

"Well, maybe not. But I know she never got over being homesick for these mountains. That's why she named me Sierra."

"Lucky for you she didn't grow up in the Adirondacks."

She giggled. "Or the Alps."

"Or the Ozarks."

"Or the Himalayas."

"I don't know—Himalaya Sloane." Ben tapped his chin thoughtfully. "Has kind of a nice ring to it, don't you think?"

"You must be tone-deaf."

They had reached the end of town. Sierra led Ben through a small wooded park, steering them past redwood trees and picnic tables, into a clearing where a deserted bandstand loomed against the dark horizon.

"Race you!" she called, dropping his hand and sprinting off.

"Why, you—"

The words drifted to Sierra from far behind. Then she heard the thud of Ben's footsteps, increasing in volume as he chased after her. Her hair flew back over her shoulders; she tossed her head and laughed with exhilaration. Adrenaline pumped through her bloodstream, and she ran faster, but Ben caught up with her just before she reached the bandstand. She heard his steady panting, the rustle of denim, the crackle of leaves and twigs—all growing closer until she felt the heat radiating from his body and smelled the arousing masculine fragrance of sweat and soap.

Then Ben's arms captured her from behind—strong, muscled arms that pulled her back against his heaving chest. Sierra tried to wrestle herself from his grasp, and as his laughter blended with hers, his straight white teeth flashed in the moonlight. Golden strands shimmered in his hair, while his eyes were hidden in shadow. His labored breathing was warm against her cheeks, the scent of wine adding to her sense of intoxication.

"No fair!" she cried. "You cheated!"

"*Me?* You're the one who had the head start!" Slowly Ben's indignant grin faded, replaced by an expression of such sober intensity that Sierra wondered what was wrong.

Then he raised his hand to cradle the side of her face and bring her mouth closer to his. His lips feathered across hers, light as a moonbeam, stirring to life something wild and free inside her. As the deepening heat of their kiss melted his restraint, Ben's mouth grew more ardent, more insistent. When at last he claimed her lips with total, reckless passion, Sierra wrapped her arms around his neck and hung on for dear life as a sudden flood of rapture engulfed her.

Her last coherent thought was that her plan was going remarkably well.

Chapter Three

Ben had nearly forgotten what it felt like to kiss a woman, to hold her in his arms and smell her hair and taste her mouth. First he'd been completely focused on his recovery from the crash. Then his determination to even the score with Quentin Jericho had pushed his interest in women onto the back burner. It seemed like years since the last time he'd allowed himself to revel in such sensual pleasures.

But if his memory served correctly, never before had a simple kiss stirred such deep, intense longing inside him.

He dragged his mouth from Sierra's lips and sought the lush, soft curve of her neck. Her hair brushed against his face, and he inhaled deeply of its floral fragrance. His lips found the pulse beat in her throat, and as he nuzzled her with lazy enjoyment, he felt the vibrations of her satisfaction purring through the slender column of her neck.

When he claimed her mouth again, her lips opened eagerly to admit his exploring tongue. She tasted like apples and sugar, as soft and textured as velvet. Her tongue curled languidly around his, and as she snuggled closer to him, the hardened peaks of her breasts pressed against his chest, arousing him with another unexpected surge of desire.

Something stone-hard and frozen inside Ben began to thaw. The emotional leash with which he'd restrained himself for so long loosened slightly, releasing a raging hunger. Not only hunger for the physical delights of Sierra's body, but also a craving for something he couldn't quite identify—some deeper satisfaction that had eluded him in all his previous encounters with women.

Drawing back for a much-needed breath, he studied her kiss-swollen lips...the way starlight glittered in her burnished curls. Her heavy-lidded eyes gave her a sultry, come-hither expression that made her even more desirable.

"God, you look beautiful in the moonlight," he said in a gravelly voice. Sierra's dark eyes flared, glinting like obsidian. "And everywhere else, for that matter...." Ben's last words were swallowed up as their lips reunited in another searing, hungry kiss.

Ben was sliding his hands along the sides of her breasts before he fully realized what he was doing. Through his passion-fogged senses, he noted Sierra was offering no protests, no resistance to his increasingly bold caresses. In fact she seemed as eager to continue this reckless insanity as he was.

Which was why he stopped.

Tiny lines of puzzlement gathered at the juncture of Sierra's brows. Her lips glistened with the moisture of his kiss, unsettling Ben even further.

It wasn't her smoldering gaze or her bruised-looking lips or her seductive, womanly curves that got to him. It was her basic sweetness, her charming klutziness, her innocent abandon. It was that faint dusting of freckles across her upturned nose, damn it!

How could he deliberately seduce this adorable, enchanting, and all-too-willing victim?

It was too easy. Like taking candy from a baby. Ben would never be able to live with himself if he cold-bloodedly manipulated her to get the information he needed.

On the other hand, maybe he was kidding himself. There'd been nothing cold-blooded about their embrace. In fact Ben's blood had pulsed hot through his veins during their kisses. The last thing on his mind in those wonderful, all-too-brief moments had been the letter he had to retrieve.

So why did he feel like such a cad?

Maybe it had something to do with the confused, slightly hurt look on Sierra's face.

"I'm sorry," Ben said, holding her by the shoulders at arm's length, exerting every scrap of his willpower not to bundle her back into his arms again. "I got a little carried away." He chucked her tenderly under the chin. "You're an awfully sexy lady, you know. And almost impossible to resist. Forgive me?"

The hurt and confusion smoothed from her face, to be replaced by a thoughtful, almost assessing expression. "Sure." She shrugged. "Nothing to forgive." She stepped back and jammed her hands into the pockets of her jumper. "You didn't exactly hear me screaming for the sheriff, did you?"

"No, but still..." Not for the first time in their short acquaintance, Ben wished he could peer behind those big brown eyes and see the wheels turning around in that logic-defying brain of hers. She had a way of studying him that made Ben restless and fidgety, as if she were measuring him against some standard by which he was doomed to fail.

He wasn't used to unfavorable comparisons. He'd been a straight-A student in high school, on the Dean's List at Stanford, then a rising corporate wunderkind with a seemingly limitless future.

He'd been Quentin Jericho's protégé, his right-hand man, his fair-haired boy. Until he'd discovered the evil secret in Jericho's past. The secret that had sent Ben's father to his death and ruined his mother's life.

The secret that Ben had sworn by his parents' memory to avenge.

But first he had to find the letter he'd entrusted to Caleb Murphy after Jericho had engineered his plane crash. The letter spelled out the secret in Jericho's own handwriting. Exposing its contents to the public would destroy Jericho's reputation, his political influence, his corporate empire.

Which was how Ben found himself in this incredibly awkward situation with Murphy's granddaughter.

"It's probably a bad idea, anyway," Sierra said.

"What?" For one confused, alarmed instant Ben thought she'd been reading his mind.

"For us to get involved with each other, I mean."

"What makes you say that?"

She propped her hands on her waist. "What about your journalistic integrity? Your objectivity? I'd hate to be accused of undermining the cornerstone of democracy by subverting the American free press.''

"Sierra, what the hell are you talking about?"

She threw up her hands in exasperation. "Your article, remember? You might be tempted to give my late grandfather's story special treatment if you and I became . . . close."

"I hardly think one slanted fluff piece on modern-day gold miners will threaten the foundations of freedom."

"Oh, so you *don't* think it's a bad idea for us to get involved?"

"No. Yes! I—it's not that simple." Ben rubbed the back of his neck and paced to and fro, staring unseeing at the ground.

Sierra sauntered to the bandstand with an outward calm she was far from feeling. Her knees felt wobbly as she sat on the edge of the concrete platform and swung her legs back and forth while she studied Ben.

Though she'd rather endure unspeakable torture than confess it, Ben's kiss had unnerved her far more than she cared to admit. Well, not his kiss, really, but the disturbing surge of desire it had sent cascading through her. Now that the heavenly sensations rippling through her body had receded, Ben's kiss had left Sierra a bit shaky, with a faintly seasick feeling in her stomach— like a hangover after a bottle of champagne.

She was used to being in control of her life and her emotions. With the previous men in her life, she'd always had the upper hand somehow. They'd been perfectly nice men, with perfectly nice careers and perfectly nice manners. They'd sent her flowers and candy, and one had even hired a violinist to serenade her outside her window one night.

They'd made all the right moves, yet something had been missing—some crucial element that could turn her giddy and breathless and make her forget caution and propriety and all the other restraints that had gone rushing from her head the instant Ben Halliday's lips had captured hers.

This roller-coaster, out-of-control feeling was new to her. And she wasn't sure if she liked it. Despite what her father would have called her "impetuous impulses," Sierra had never allowed the whims of fate to rule her existence. Even her decision to throw away her career to follow in her grandfather's footsteps had been entirely logical—from Sierra's point of view, anyway.

But for one insane, passion-crazed moment tonight, she'd been ready to throw caution to the wind and recklessly follow wherever Ben led her. Thank goodness at least one of them had had the good sense to slam on the brakes!

Why, then, did she feel like cursing whatever had stopped Ben instead of feeling grateful?

Under cover of darkness she secretly studied his profile, admiring the craggy angles and solid lines visible in the dim light from the moon. A swatch of hair swept across his forehead above the rugged outline of his features. As he continued his pacing, his wide shoulders and solid chest seemed to displace the night air like the prow of a mighty ship cresting through the ocean. Sierra's glance lingered on his narrow hips, then strayed down his long, muscled legs. At once she saw something she hadn't noticed before.

"Hey, you're limping!" she exclaimed.

Ben halted in his tracks. He looked up at Sierra, then down at his left leg as if he, too, had been unaware of the slight dragging motion. "Oh, that."

"You must have sprained your ankle earlier, while I was outracing you to the bandstand."

His teeth flashed white as he smiled. "No, that's not it. Although I'm sure that didn't help."

As he hobbled toward her, Sierra frowned with concern. "How did you hurt your ankle, then?"

She felt the bunched muscles in his shoulders as he transferred his weight to his arms and lowered himself next to her. A slight hiss as he released his breath was the only clue that the movement had cost him pain.

"Old war injury," he said.

Sierra regarded him skeptically. "*What* war?" she asked. "Or were you drafted in the eighth grade, perhaps?"

Ben chuckled. "That's what I like about you," he said. "Well, *one* of the things I like about you. You make me laugh." Then he paused, and Sierra could almost feel something bleak and bitter settle over him. "I haven't laughed a whole lot lately," he said finally in a distant, musing voice.

"Why not?" she asked softly.

Ben shrugged. "My mother's death hit me pretty hard, even though I knew she was dying. Then right after her funeral, I was in a plane crash."

"A plane crash?" Sierra's voice rose to an astonished squeak. "My God, what happened?"

Ben jerked away slightly, as if he'd caught himself saying too much. "It was nothing. I mean, the plane I was flying had mechanical problems. I was the only one on board."

"So that's how you hurt your ankle?"

He shrugged again. "Not my ankle. More like my entire leg."

"Is that where this came from?" Without thinking, Sierra lifted her hand to Ben's forehead to touch the scar that was invisible in the darkness. Startled, Ben met her gaze. As her fingers brushed against the faint ridge of flesh, his eyes flickered with some mysterious emotion that made her shiver. For an instant they were connected by more than physical contact, as if their souls had reached out and found each other. But the brief encounter was too intense, too revealing. As they both instinctively withdrew, the moment passed.

Sierra pulled back her hand as if scalded.

Ben swallowed. "Yes," he replied in a thick voice, "that's where the scar came from, too."

"Guess I'm not too observant. I—I didn't notice your limp before."

"It comes and goes. Some days I hardly notice the discomfort, while others..."

"Your leg must have been pretty badly injured if it still bothers you after all this time."

He made a dismissive motion with his hand. "It could have been worse. At least I'm alive to complain about it."

"I haven't heard you complaining. Did you find out what caused the mechanical problems with your plane?"

"No." He said the word quickly, then pushed himself to his feet. "The plane was almost completely destroyed in the crash. There weren't many clues left to piece together. Come on, I'd better get you back to the hotel." He held out his hand to help Sierra to the ground, releasing her as soon as she was on her feet.

As they walked back to the hotel, a prudent three feet apart, Sierra was more convinced than ever that Ben was lying to her. His answers to some of her questions had been evasive, and he'd been entirely too anxious to change the subject when she'd asked him about the plane crash.

Maybe she was being overly suspicious. After all, nearly losing your life was a pretty traumatic experience. Was it any wonder he didn't care to dwell on the matter?

But what about his flimsy claim to be a journalist? Some sixth sense told Sierra that Ben's real reason—whatever it was—for seeking out her grandfather was somehow connected with the crash.

She stole a sidelong glance at Ben's face as they passed beneath a street lamp. As they stepped off the curb, he winced, and a crazy protective instinct flooded her. Something very bad had happened to Ben Halliday—something besides his mother's death and his own brush with mortality.

The knowledge sent a pang of distress through Sierra. She hated the idea of Ben's suffering any harm or sorrow, and the realization startled her. She'd only just met the man, for heaven's sake. So why should his happiness and well-being suddenly be so important to her?

Nevertheless, her concern for him was a fact Sierra couldn't deny. Ben would never admit he needed help from her or anyone else, of course. He was like Sierra herself in that regard. But why else would he be hanging around, plying her with food and wine and maneuvering to get her alone if he didn't want something from her?

And tonight, when he could easily have taken advantage of her rapturous daze, Ben had proven that he was after more than the obvious quarry.

Being needed was a rather new sensation for Sierra. Her life had been filled with competent, powerful, self-sufficient people who might love or respect her, but didn't exactly *need* her.

Her grandfather had been the exception. But she hadn't realized until it was too late how much the old man had missed her, how important her visits had been to him.

She'd let her grandfather down. But she'd be damned if she'd let down Ben Halliday.

Which made her more determined than ever to pry the truth out of him.

Ben sprawled in a tangle of bed sheets, hands locked behind his head, counting the knotholes in the beamed ceiling and trying to shake off the melancholy that clung to him like fog.

It was the green vase that had started it all. The tall, cut-glass vase on the hotel bureau, brimming with yellow and red chrysanthemums, glinting like emeralds in the sunshine that streamed through the window, had captured Ben's attention the instant he'd opened his eyes this morning.

His mother had owned a green vase exactly like it.

And seeing that identical vase first thing upon awakening had brought it all back to Ben: his mother's final illness...the moment she'd reached for his hand just before drawing her last breath...the shock of stopping by her home just before the funeral and finding the place ransacked.

The green vase had been shattered to smithereens. Everything in his mother's house had been flung open, torn apart, dashed to pieces. Or so it had seemed to Ben's stunned, horrified eyes. He'd known that in the city, burglars often scanned the obituaries, breaking into a home while the grief-stricken family was at the funeral. But here in peaceful, small-town Grass Valley? And what kind of burglar would wreak such systematic destruction without actually taking anything?

His mother's jewelry and silver were scattered on the floor, but hadn't been stolen. It didn't make sense—until Ben knelt to the floor to pick up the wooden clock that had always rested beside his mother's bed.

How many times near the end had she begged Ben to keep the clock after her death? "Always keep it running, so its ticking will remind you of me, even when I'm gone," she'd urged him time and again.

As he picked up the clock, its face cracked, a corner chipped off, Ben noticed it had stopped. Through his grief and bewilderment, his mother's plea echoed in his ears.

Maybe the clock wasn't broken; maybe the batteries had only run down. With shaking fingers Ben pried off the back of the clock.

And found the letter.

He'd understood so much after reading it, like why his mother had made such a big deal about the clock, knowing Ben would eventually have to change the batteries and would find the folded-up letter. He understood that Quentin Jericho's men must have ransacked the house, and why Jericho was so anxious to find and destroy the letter. And he understood at last the air of sorrow that had surrounded his mother as far back as he could remember.

Ben had assumed she'd never got over his father's death, and that was true in a way. But her unhappiness had another source: the secret she'd kept all those years, the secret revealed in the letter, the secret that—in death—she'd finally entrusted to Ben.

With mounting horror Ben had stood in his mother's bedroom and realized how long and how much she'd endured for his sake. It didn't take a genius to figure out that Jericho had purchased Margaret Halliday's silence with her son's future.

Jericho's outward generosity toward the family of his former business partner had been nothing more than a bribe to keep the ugly truth hidden. Jericho had paid for Ben's education, sent him on summer vacations to Europe, launched him on a promising career—all in exchange for Margaret Halliday's silence.

What kind of pain had it cost her, seeing Ben's gratitude and affection for the man who had destroyed his father? How much did she suffer every time she heard Ben refer to "Uncle Quent"?

Even now, months after his mother's death, the guilt still pierced Ben like a knife in the gut.

He had to make it up to her. He had to avenge his father's death by using that letter to destroy Jericho. He'd sworn it on his mother's grave the day of her funeral.

Memories of that horrible day swarmed around Ben's head like a flock of vultures. Right after finding the letter, he'd stormed to the funeral service and practically dragged Jericho outside the church to confront him. Having seen the damning evidence with his own eyes, Ben was still hoping against hope that Uncle Quent could produce a perfectly logical explanation for the whole thing, that he would somehow show Ben how this sordid revelation from the past wasn't what it appeared to be.

Instead Jericho's eyes had flared with shock when Ben informed him what he'd just discovered. His florid face had drained of color seconds before a hooded, sly expression crept across it, telling Ben everything he hadn't wanted to know.

In retrospect, of course, Ben had blown it by losing his cool. If he hadn't rushed to confront Jericho in a blur of pain and outrage, Jericho wouldn't have left the funeral, ostensibly to avoid any further scene with Ben. Jericho wouldn't have had a reason to sabotage the plane that Ben took off in immediately after the funeral. And the letter would have made it safely from Grass Valley to the news media in Los Angeles, instead of turning into some kind of time bomb, hidden God knows where, posing a threat not only to Ben, but also to Sierra now.

Ben's rash actions had nearly cost him his life, and might very well have cost him his only chance to avenge his parents. He wasn't about to make the same mistake again.

He pulled the pillow over his head, trying to bury the guilt, the grief, the anger. He needed cool, logical reasoning to succeed. He'd have to shove his emotions aside and sort them out later when all this was over. Better focus on something else, he decided.

Like how soft and sexy Sierra had felt last night, wrapped in his arms, returning his kiss with a fiery passion that made his loins throb to remember.

With a groan Ben rolled over onto his stomach and tugged the pillow even tighter over his head. But he couldn't smother the memories that tormented him, arousing his body and twisting his heart. In front of his squinched-shut eyes, he kept seeing Sierra's face—those limpid, trusting eyes, that spatter of freckles across her pert nose, her mischievous, alluring smile. How could he even consider seducing her to get that letter back?

How could he avoid it?

Did he even *want* to avoid it?

Now that he'd touched her, kissed her, Ben found himself craving more…much more. His hands clenched reflexively as he relived the brief moment when he'd cradled the provocative swell of her soft breasts—right before his self-loathing had forced him to stop. Was he any better than Quentin Jericho, using people, taking advantage of their weaknesses to further his own selfish aims?

Cursing under his breath, Ben flung the pillow across the room and peeled himself out of bed all in one fluid movement. If only his feelings for Sierra were that simple. Unfortunately his desire for her sprang from a far more complicated source than his quest for revenge. He admired her spunk, even if she wasn't exactly a wilderness-survival expert. He relished her tart wit, even though she frequently aimed it at him.

And he was touched by the vulnerable side that she tried to conceal behind her stubbornness and self-assured bravado.

But he couldn't afford to be detoured by such distractions. He had to learn to ignore them, the way he'd learned to ignore pain. Ben tested his leg gingerly as he hobbled to the shower. What the hell had possessed him to chase after Sierra last night and risk reinjuring his leg?

"Don't answer that," he warned himself in a sleep-rusted voice. Thank God his leg seemed better this morning. No more romping around like some high-school kid chock-full of hormones. The seduction of Sierra Sloane would proceed in an orderly, *adult* manner, with emotions tightly harnessed and Ben's underlying goal firmly planted in his brain at all times.

As he lathered his chest under the stinging, hot needles of water, Ben began to feel more like his old self. Was it any wonder he'd been so overwhelmingly attracted to Sierra? After all those months of rehabilitation and therapy, when his only physical craving had been to escape from the pain, his first encounter with a pretty woman was bound to be rather intense. All that sexual energy, all those urges bottled up for so long—no wonder he'd been swamped by a tidal wave of lust when the dam finally broke.

Thus reassured that Sierra wasn't *really* some kind of sorceress, Ben rolled up the cuffs of a fresh blue chambray shirt, snapped his watchband around his wrist and stepped into the corridor, pulling the door shut behind him. Whistling softly, he strode past several rooms and rapped smartly on Sierra's door.

He ran his fingers through his still-damp hair as he waited. No answer. He knocked again, then tried the doorknob. Locked. He pressed his ear to the door, listening for the rush of the shower, but all was quiet. Either Sierra was a very sound sleeper or she'd beaten him downstairs this morning.

Sourdough Pete was spread-eagled in front of the fireplace when Ben entered the lobby. Behind the front desk Addie Winslow, the hotel proprietress, was frowning.

"Tilt it a little to the left, Pete. No, no—the left! That's it. Hmm." She poked on the glasses hanging by a gold chain around her neck and studied the framed landscape critically.

Pete's cheeks turned a boiled lobster color as he strained to hold the large painting in place over the mantel.

"I just don't know. Try moving it a little to the right." She pulled off her glasses and said, "I can't tell. What do *you* think, Mr. Halliday?"

"I think I'd better give Pete a hand before he hurts himself," Ben said, stepping quickly to the fireplace and relieving poor Pete of his burden.

"Oh, my word, I didn't realize...Pete, I'm so sorry." Addie bustled around the desk and took Pete by the elbow, helping him into a chair. "Can I get you anything? A glass of water?"

"Naw, I'll be all right, soon's I catch my breath."

Ben suspected the old prospector was rather enjoying all the solicitous attention from the widow Winslow.

"Now that you mention it, I guess some water might be nice," Pete croaked in a weak voice. He winked at Ben as Addie hurried off, patting her tidy bun of gray hair and tsk-tsking her way out of the lobby. "Mighty fine figure of a woman," Pete said, shaking his head with admiration after Addie's plump, disappearing form.

Ben chuckled. "You old rascal."

"That's what women like, sonny—rascals." He shook a crooked forefinger at Ben. "You'd best remember that advice, if you hope to get anywhere with young Sierra."

"What about Sierra?" Addie's eyes were bright with interest as she returned with Pete's glass of water.

Ben sighed inwardly. The last thing he wanted was a public discussion of his love life. "I'll hang this painting for you, Addie," he said quickly, "if you've got a hammer and nail."

But Addie was not so easily sidetracked. "I've got them right here," she said, reaching behind the desk and handing Ben the tools. "Sierra sure grew up to be a pretty young thing, didn't she?"

"Mmm, very nice," Ben mumbled noncommittally around the nail held between his teeth. He positioned the painting once more.

"She was always such a lively one. I remember how she used to hang around here when her Grandpa Caleb still owned this hotel. Why, one night when all the guests were asleep, she set little paper cups of water over every square inch of the upstairs hallway so that folks couldn't get out of their rooms in the morning without squishing them."

"I'll bet *that* was good for business," Ben muttered.

"Then another time she rigged all the window shades so that when you pulled them down—"

The rest of her fond reminiscence was drowned out by the pounding of Ben's hammer. "How's that?" he asked.

Addie cocked her head from side to side. "Perfect," she announced. "Thank you ever so much, Mr. Halliday." But her matchmaking was merciless. "I've often said, what Sierra needs is a nice, stable young man— someone who'll steady her down a bit without putting a damper on those high spirits of hers."

Personally what Ben often thought Sierra needed was a keeper.

"Of course, she's got to be careful who she gets involved with, considering who her father is. A girl in her position has to watch out for—oh, what's that word, Pete? Not gold diggers..."

"Her father?" Ben asked.

"Gigolos," Pete supplied.

"Yes, that's it, gigolos."

"Who *is* Sierra's father?" Ben repeated.

"As I said, a girl like Sierra—her father?" Addie's forehead wrinkled in surprise. "Why, Maxwell Sloane, of course. Yes sirree, with all that money—"

"Sierra's father is Maxwell Sloane?" A cold prickle like the stab of a thousand sharp icicles crept up the back of Ben's neck. "*The* Maxwell Sloane? Founder of Sloane Enterprises? The man they call *Midas* Sloane, whose touch turns any business venture to gold?"

"Why, yes, that's right. So you can see why that young lady has to be mighty careful about who she gets tangled up with, but I know that when the right young man comes along . . ."

Ben didn't hear the rest of Addie's prediction. His mind was reeling with the implications of what he'd just learned. The knowledge had hit him like a two-by-four right between the eyes, leaving him dazed.

The unpleasant truth was that if he succeeded in making Sierra fall for him and then broke her heart, he'd end up with *two* rich, powerful men determined to kill him. Because Maxwell Sloane was bound to put a price on the head of any man who trifled with his little girl's affections.

Menacing as that prospect was, it somehow didn't disturb Ben as much as the discovery that Sierra had lied to him.

Which was ridiculous, considering that Ben had also lied to her. But *he* had a good reason. What possible motive could Sierra have had for hiding this mind-boggling piece of news?

Ben had thought he knew her. He'd thought they were becoming . . . well, friends or something. She'd told him about her grandfather. She'd shared her sadness and regrets, and in return Ben had opened up to her, revealing more of himself than he'd intended.

His resentment was completely unreasonable. Sierra owed him nothing—certainly not honesty, not after the way he'd already deceived her. But Ben couldn't help feeling a little... hurt. His reaction was unfair. And stupid. But there it was.

In as casual a tone as he could muster, Ben asked, "Speaking of Sierra, do you have any idea where she is right now? I need to discuss something with her."

Pete cleared his throat, disguising what sounded suspiciously like a chuckle. Addie threw him an I-told-you-so glance, then smiled benevolently at Ben. "Why, yes, as a matter of fact I happen to know that she's over at the general store, stocking up on supplies. She mentioned it to me on her way out this morning, in case someone—" she gave the word a slight emphasis "—came looking for her."

"Well, er, thanks," Ben said. "Guess I'll go find her, then."

"You do that, sonny. And remember what I said." When Ben blinked uncertainly, Pete mouthed the word "rascal."

"Oh, yeah. Right." Ben gave Pete a two-fingered salute as he backpedaled out of the lobby. "Well, see you both later."

Pete tugged on one end of his mustache as if trying to rein in a smile. Addie beamed after Ben like warm sunshine.

Ben wished he were anyplace else on earth.

He spotted Charlemagne about halfway down the street, wearing that goofy straw hat and tied up to a fire hydrant. As Ben approached, the mule raised his head, then snorted with supreme disdain. "Good morning to you, too," Ben grumbled. He whisked open the door of the general store and collided with Sierra. Boxes and bundles flew everywhere.

"Hey!" she shouted. "Oh, it's you. I should have known."

Ben knelt next to her. "Sierra, we have to talk."

"Heavens to Betsy, those have got to be the most ominous words in the English language." She reached for a packet of instant-soup mix. "Aren't you even going to help me pick this stuff up?"

"Later." Ben felt something moist and cold nuzzling the nape of his neck. "Damn it." Without looking around, he batted away Charlemagne's nose.

"Looks like somebody got up on the wrong side of the bed this morning," Sierra said cheerfully, scooping up a box of biscuit mix.

Ben grabbed her wrist and pulled her to her feet, knocking her packages to the ground again.

"What's bugging you, anyway?" Sierra demanded as he dragged her beyond the range of Charlemagne's wet, inquisitive snoot.

"I'll tell you what's bugging me," Ben said through gritted teeth. "Why didn't you tell me that your father is one of the wealthiest men in the world?"

Chapter Four

"Oh, that," she said.

"Yes, *that*. How could you neglect to mention your father is Maxwell Sloane—*Midas* Sloane, head of Sloane Enterprises, financial genius, adviser to presidents—"

"I didn't think it was important," Sierra replied, shrugging.

Ben's jaw dropped. "You didn't think it was—"

"Important," she repeated. "Now, would you mind letting go of my wrist? You're cutting off the circulation in my hand."

Ben released his grip, but kept staring at her, feeling as if he'd been hit by a bombshell.

Sierra rubbed her wrist and shook her fingers rapidly up and down. "What a relief! The feeling's coming back. Maybe I'll play the violin again, after all." She looked up and paused. "I don't see what you're getting all bent out of shape for,'' she said. ''What difference does it make who my father is?''

''I thought you were—I thought we—it's just that— oh, never mind,'' Ben finished gruffly. Sierra's genuine puzzlement had deflated his indignation like a sputtering balloon. She was right; he was overreacting. Not mentioning her illustrious heritage had struck Ben as strange at first, as if she were deliberately concealing the truth. On the other hand, even after their short acquaintance, he could see it would be extremely out of character for Sierra to proclaim herself as Maxwell Sloane's daughter to every person she met.

And Ben wasn't about to reveal the other source of his consternation: that Maxwell Sloane would undoubtedly use his vast resources to punish the man who broke his daughter's heart.

Well, he'd have plenty of time to worry about that later. Right now he had to mend some fences. ''I guess I *was* making too big a deal out of it,'' he said, giving Sierra a sheepish smile. ''I was kind of stunned, that's all. Come on, I'll help you pick up your groceries.''

As he knelt to the sidewalk and began to hand Sierra boxes and packets, he could feel her inquisitive eyes boring into the top of his head. Before her simmering curiosity could boil over into a big splash of questions about his sudden change in attitude, he forestalled her with a question of his own. ''I assume that large corporation you told me you worked for was Sloane Enterprises?''

Sierra took the package of pancake mix he handed her and tucked it into one of the saddlebags slung over Charlemagne's sagging back. ''Yep.''

''And how did your father react to your recent . . . change in life-style?''

She snorted. "Don't ask." Then she answered him, anyway. "You wouldn't believe all the nonsense I've had to put up with since the day I announced I was turning in my key to the executive washroom."

"He thought you were making a mistake, did he?"

"A mistake?" Sierra rolled her eyes. "Hardly. More like I'd gone temporarily insane. He thought I was throwing my life away, casting shame and ridicule upon the hallowed name of Sloane, not to mention letting him down personally. My father had given me everything, and I was flinging it back in his face. That's the way *he* sees it, anyway." As she spoke, lines of strain creased her forehead, and her voice grew taut with barely repressed emotion. It was obvious her father's scorn and disappointment had wounded her deeply.

She must love him an awful lot, Ben thought.

He retrieved the last stray box of powdered milk and handed it to her, noticing her flushed cheeks and compressed mouth. As she turned to fasten the buckle on the saddlebag, she tossed her curls and straightened her back with a slightly defiant movement. The sight of her fragile, determined shoulders wrestling with the weight of the world strummed a tender chord inside Ben. When Sierra looked up at him again, her dark eyes glistened, and he had to curb the overpowering impulse to sweep her into the comfort of his arms and banish her troubles with kisses and caresses.

Their eyes met for only an instant before she ducked her head in obvious embarrassment. Her cheeks flamed even more brightly as she mustered a weak smile. "My father's tried every trick in the book to lure me back to L.A. First he threatened to disinherit me. Then he tried to bribe me with a big promotion and a new Mercedes. His latest ploy was the old guilt routine—trying to convince me that my mother cries herself to sleep every night because of me. Ha! He should know better than to try *that* one."

"Why is that?"

"Because Mom's the one person on earth who actually sympathizes with the choice I've made. She loves these mountains, and misses Grandpa as much as I do. Mom understands me." Sierra let her breath out in a long sigh. "I only wish my father did."

Ben reached over and grazed her cheek with the back of his finger. "He'll come around someday."

"Not him. Why, he's as stubborn as *I*—well, let's just say he's pretty darn stubborn."

Ben's eyes twinkled. "I know exactly what you mean." If Maxwell Sloane was half as obstinate as his daughter, the man could give lessons to mules.

He'd spoken in an amused tone and was startled by the sudden flicker of uncertainty in Sierra's expression. Then the color drained from her face, and confusion clouded her eyes. She fell back a step.

"Sierra—?" Ben moved toward her, but she twisted deftly aside, eluding his outstretched hand. "Sierra, what is it? What's wrong?"

She busied herself untying Charlemagne, allowing her hair to fall forward and curtain her face. "Nothing. Nothing's wrong. I've got to go, that's all. There's gold in them thar hills and all that."

"You mean you're leaving? Now? But why? I thought we could—"

"Come on, Char. Quit nibbling on Mr. Halliday's collar. We've imposed on him enough as it is. Say goodbye and we'll be on our way." She tugged on the mule's rope.

"Sierra, what the hell— ow! Damn it!" he shouted as Charlemagne trod unceremoniously on his right instep. Limping, Ben trailed them down the dusty street. At the rate he was going, he'd be lucky to have one good leg left by the time this adventure was over.

He caught up with them at the corner, planting himself directly in Sierra's path so that she had little choice but to stop. But he couldn't force her to meet his eyes. She stared stonily over his shoulder as if he weren't there.

Ben felt her slipping away from him, as if the warm rapport they'd established were rapidly disintegrating beneath their feet. He was desperate to reach her, to pull her back before it was too late. And he was honest enough to admit it wasn't just because Sierra was his only way of getting the letter back.

He gripped her shoulders. "Sierra, whatever I've done, whatever I've said, I didn't mean to upset you. I'm sorry. I want to make things right between us." He swallowed. "Won't you at least give me a chance?"

Her eyes darted back and forth as if she were closely observing some internal struggle. Ben held his breath. At last she looked at him, but her shuttered glance was hardly reassuring. "Okay," she said. "Maybe we *should* talk." She shrugged his hands off her shoulders.

"How 'bout if I buy you breakfast?"

"I'm not hungry," she said, contradictory as always. "But I wouldn't mind some coffee."

"Great."

"I'll meet you at the cafe across the street in fifteen minutes."

Ben's relief evaporated. "You're not going to skip out on me, are you?"

The gaze she sent him was cool and assessing. "No," she replied slowly. He would have felt a lot better if she hadn't added, sotto voce, "Not yet, anyway."

As he watched her tow Charlemagne back toward the hotel, Ben scratched his head, damned if he could figure out why all of a sudden Sierra was treating him as if he had the plague or something.

He was worried. Because it was starting to dawn on him that perhaps even more than the letter was at stake here.

"That rotten, no-good, lousy sneak," Sierra muttered as she tied Charlemagne to the back-porch railing of the hotel. She hoisted off the saddlebags and dumped them onto one side of the porch. Then she kicked them for good measure.

Now that her daze had worn off, she was furious. Anger, after all, was easier to cope with than hurt.

All the puzzle pieces had started falling into place when Ben had made that remark about knowing how stubborn her father could be. Well, what he'd actually said was that he knew what she meant about her father. But that little slipup was like an innocent-looking piece of yarn, unraveling Ben's whole story once Sierra's mind started plucking at it.

She'd insisted on fifteen minutes before meeting him for coffee because she needed time to organize and assemble all the bits and pieces, all the clues pointing to the inescapable conclusion that Ben Halliday was a conniving, low-life skunk.

The whole scheme was so obvious now, she felt like a fool for not recognizing it before. And if there was one thing Sierra hated, it was feeling foolish.

She scooped up a couple of fallen apples from beneath the tree she'd climbed and played in as a child. Absently handing one to Charlemagne, she reviewed the incriminating points.

First was Ben's suspicious claim to be a journalist. She hadn't believed *that* part for one minute, which was some consolation, anyway. He hadn't come to find Grandpa; he'd been looking for *her* all along. And at last she'd figured out the reason why.

Then there was all his phony concern. Did she know anything about panning for gold? What about wilderness survival? What was she going to do when winter came?

Sierra mimicked Ben's questions in silent disgust. Charlemagne, chomping lazily on his apple, seemed to be doing the same thing.

At last she understood Ben's reluctance to reveal any of his personal history, although she *had* pried out the informative nugget that he was from Los Angeles. That fit neatly in with the rest of it. He'd practically admitted knowing her father, hadn't he?

Sierra plopped herself down on the edge of the porch and banged her feet viciously back and forth. She'd fallen for Ben's smooth, sweet-talking charm hook, line and sinker. But now she understood his flattering interest in her...why he'd pursued her so relentlessly over mountain and stream.

Ben Halliday was nothing but a cog in her father's latest scheme! He'd been hired to romance her, to seduce her back to Los Angeles and the safe, secure, deadly dull boardrooms of Sloane Enterprises.

He was getting paid to sweep her off her feet.

And he'd damn near succeeded, too. Thank goodness she'd seen through his masquerade before it was too late.

Then Sierra's indignation faltered; her stomach gave a sad, sickening little lurch. She handed Charlemagne the other apple. Her triumph ebbed, leaving a bitter taste in her mouth and a weariness in her heart. She closed her eyes. "Darn it," she whispered. "I really liked him."

Then her eyes flew open, and she whipped her head around guiltily, making sure no one had overheard her confession. The only witness crunched his apple and pretended he hadn't heard.

Sierra shoved herself to her feet, dusted off her derriere and shook her curls out of her face. Doing her best to stoke up a furnace of outrage, she marched toward the cafe, heading for the showdown.

She found her opponent seated in the back booth, poking his fork through a pile of congealed-looking scrambled eggs. He rose halfway to his feet and beamed at her approach, but Sierra could see worry lurking behind those treacherous blue eyes.

Good. Let him suffer.

She lowered herself primly across from him. "Coffee, please," she told the waitress.

Ben leaned forward. "Sure you don't want some breakfast? The food here's terrific."

"No. Just coffee." Sierra glanced disdainfully at Ben's meal. How would he know how the food tasted when all he'd done was push it around his plate?

She gazed idly at her reflection in the metal napkin holder until the waitress set her coffee down and refilled Ben's cup. Ben gulped his coffee as if it were liquid courage. Setting the cup down, he gave Sierra a little half grin, twisting his mouth to one side in a boyish kind of way she'd once found rather endearing. Resolutely she steeled her heart against his perfidious, endearing expressions.

Ben cradled the cup between his palms. "So," he said brightly, "are you going to tell me why you're so mad at me?"

Obviously he'd decided to brazen this out by feigning complete innocence. The low-down rat. Well, the old charm routine wasn't going to work this time.

Smiling sweetly, Sierra let him have it with both barrels.

"I know who you are and what you want," she said.

Ben's hands jerked, sloshing coffee over his fingers. As he pried a wad of napkins from the holder, Sierra could see his devious brain working fast and furiously. His face was pale, making his shifty eyes seem even bluer than usual. Obviously she'd been right about him.

Yet the knowledge gave her no satisfaction.

When he'd mopped up the last puddle of coffee, Ben met her laser-beam gaze. "I'm not sure what you mean," he said.

"Quit playing games, Mr. Halliday. The jig is up. The party's over. The fat lady sings."

Ben gaped at her, then burst out laughing. "You know, in my entire life I've never met anyone even remotely like you."

"No? Well, I've met plenty of men like you, unfortunately. Men who'd do anything for money, like lying, like pretending things they don't feel, just because my father—"

"Hold on a second," Ben interrupted. "You mean to tell me you think I'm after your money? That I'm some kind of fortune hunter? For God's sake, I didn't even know who your father was until this morning!"

"You expect me to believe that, after you let it slip that you know how stubborn my father can be?"

"Huh?"

"Don't play dumb with me. I saw through your charade from the beginning. Free-lance journalist, my foot! How come I've never seen you carrying so much as a pencil? Next time my father hires you to do his dirty work, I suggest you bring along the appropriate props!"

Ben blinked. "Dirty work?"

"Oh, please. You want me to spell it out? Fine." Silverware went flying as Sierra swept back her hand in a dramatic gesture. "My father hired you to lure me back to Los Angeles. He paid you to pretend you were interested in me, to make me fall for you so that I'd follow you back to L.A. Don't try to deny it," she said, raising her palm when Ben's mouth fell open. "I've heard enough of your lies." She leaned across the table, so that her face was mere inches from his. Her voice dropped to a husky, dangerous whisper. "I only have one question, Mr. Halliday. Exactly how far did my father expect you to go? What if your hollow words and meaningless kisses weren't enough to sway me? Were you supposed to make love to me as a last resort?"

Ben moved his face even closer, so their mouths were nearly touching. "That's three questions."

Sierra snapped her head back. "Very funny." She slid out of the booth. "We'll see how funny it is when you report back to my father empty-handed. He doesn't accept failure too well." As she made her way down the aisle, she flung over her shoulder, "But of course, you already know that."

She heard Ben scramble after her and felt the curious stares of the other customers. Holding her head high, she sailed out of the cafe and was halfway down the block before Ben caught up with her. He must have slowed down to pay the bill.

His boots thundered on the sidewalk until he fell in step beside her. "Sierra, this whole idea is crazy! You can't possibly believe all those things you said back there."

She stopped dead in her tracks. Ben stumbled, trying to halt his momentum. "I don't hear you denying any of it," she said. But oh, how she wanted to....

He wiped his forehead, looking ill at ease. Glancing up and down the street, he shifted his weight from foot to foot. "Okay," he said finally. "Maybe *some* of it's true. I said *some* of it," he added, dodging in front of Sierra to prevent her from walking off.

She pressed her lips together, partly in disgust, partly to keep from crying. "If you admit *that* much, how do you expect me to believe anything else you say?"

"Because—because...damn it, Sierra!" With a groan of exasperation, Ben seized her by the shoulders, yanked her against his chest and kissed her. Hard.

For an instant she nearly surrendered, so stunned was she by the swiftness of his embrace, so stirred by the passionate intensity of his kiss. It would be so easy to melt into his arms, to lose herself in the magic spell he wove around her. Desperate to believe that Ben might truly care about her, she could almost forget all the evidence to the contrary.

Almost. But not quite.

Sierra sucked in a deep breath. Then she stomped on Ben's foot.

"Ow!"

She jumped back a prudent distance, observing his painful, puzzled wince with satisfaction. "I'd rather kiss a snake," she announced, wiping off her mouth with the cuff of her sleeve. "Although, come to think of it, that's exactly what I just did."

With that, she gathered her indignation around her and swept off down the street, holding her head high. She could only pray that Ben, hopping up and down on one leg, couldn't see her knees wobbling.

Ben sat at the bar of the Paydirt Saloon, nursing a Scotch along with his sore foot. Drinking before noon wasn't his usual style, but ever since meeting Sierra, he'd found himself doing a lot of things he'd never thought he would.

Like lying to people. Like using people. Like letting himself be distracted from his quest by haunting memories of the hurt in Sierra's blazing eyes...the unyielding, unforgiving uptilt of her chin...that darn spattering of freckles across her adorable nose.

With a muffled groan Ben drained the contents of his glass and studied his reflection in the ornate, gilt-edged mirror hanging behind the bar. How had he landed in such a mess, anyway? He, who'd always been so firmly in charge of his destiny, who'd always relied on logic, honesty and hard work to achieve his goals.

Somewhere along the path to this particular goal he'd jettisoned his honesty. Then he'd discovered that logic wasn't a particularly useful quality when dealing with Sierra. And now his hard work seemed about as pointless as running a marathon on a treadmill.

As he crunched on his ice cubes, giving up was the furthest thing from his mind. Ben Halliday was no quitter. But the thought of another skirmish with Sierra was positively overwhelming.

"Ready for another one?" The bartender was mopping the carved mahogany bar top with a white towel. "You look like you could use one."

"You're right about that," Ben said, digging into his pocket. "But no, thanks. Gotta keep my wits about me." He tossed a couple of bills onto the counter.

"Gotcha." The bartender winked. "Woman trouble, huh?"

"Trouble doesn't begin to cover it. Trouble would be a Sunday-school picnic compared to—ah, never mind." Ben slid off the bar stool, wincing as he landed. He took a couple of tentative steps, then decided his foot was sufficiently recovered to carry him off in search of Sierra. With a final nod to the bartender, he traipsed across the sawdust-covered floor and pushed through the swinging saloon doors.

The dazzling sunshine nearly blinded him after the bar's gloomy interior. He stepped gingerly along the sidewalk, then, with long-practiced skill, switched off the faint pain signals reaching his brain. His brain had other matters to wrestle with right now. Like figuring out what clever, plausible, totally fabricated story he could tell Sierra to get himself out of the doghouse.

For one instant Ben considered coming clean with her—telling her the truth about the letter and the reasons he'd sworn to destroy Quentin Jericho. Just as instantly, he rejected the idea. He was more determined than ever to shield Sierra from any dangerous knowledge that would provoke Jericho to harm her—or worse.

The thought of Jericho so much as breaking one of Sierra's fingernails filled Ben with such molten, white-hot anger that he had to pause for a moment to clench and unclench his fists and gulp several deep lungfuls of air. By God, if Sierra suffered so much as a stubbed toe because of Jericho or any of his men, Ben wouldn't be satisfied with exposing Jericho for the ruthless villain he was. He wouldn't be satisfied with seeing Jericho behind bars.

If Jericho hurt Sierra, Ben would kill him.

The realization was startling and unsettling, yet so unshakable, so crystal clear that it seemed as much a part of Ben as his own name. But for the time being, he didn't care to examine too closely the reasons for his fierce protectiveness. Because doing so might force him to admit that Sierra already meant more to him than the quickest route to that letter.

By the time he entered the hotel lobby, he still hadn't figured out how to explain and justify his deception to her. Obviously that feeble journalist pretense wasn't going to work anymore—if it ever had. Did he have any choice but to let Sierra keep believing this wild theory that her father had hired Ben to woo her back home where she belonged?

He spotted Addie Winslow behind the front desk, her gray head bent over an open ledger. Speeding up his pace, Ben hoped he could whiz right by without getting snagged into a conversation. He liked Addie, but her bright-eyed curiosity and eager matchmaking were about as welcome as quicksand right now.

When she glanced up over the tops of her spectacles, Ben gave her a brief smile and a quick little wave as he plowed ahead toward the staircase.

But Addie was not so easily bought off. "Hello, Mr. Halliday, I was just wondering—oh, Mr. Halliday? Mr. Halliday?"

With a sigh Ben withdrew his foot from the bottom step. "Yes, Addie?" When he returned to the front desk, he detected a faintly troubled look in her normally twinkling eyes. Worry wrinkled her forehead, and her smile seemed forced when she asked, "Did your friend find you?"

"Who, Sierra? Well, actually—"

"Dear me, no, I'm not talking about Sierra, of course. I meant the gentleman who was in here a while ago looking for you."

A chill rippled down Ben's spine. "Gentleman? What gentleman?"

Addie's smile faltered. "Very nicely dressed he was, in a dark blue three-piece suit. Dark brown hair, I believe—or was it black? And tall. Well, not *too* tall, but not too short, either. He didn't mention you by name, but when he described you, I knew right away who he was talking about. Then when I said, 'Oh, you must mean Mr. Halliday,' why, his whole face lit up with excitement! He must be a very good friend of yours. Anyway I told him you'd gone out for a spell and I didn't rightly know when to expect you back. That's when he told me he was an old friend of yours, but he wanted to surprise you, so he asked me not to... say anything. Oh, dear." Addie swallowed. "Look what I've done—gone and spoiled your friend's surprise. I'm so sorry, Mr. Halliday. Perhaps—perhaps you could *pretend* to be surprised when you see him, so your friend won't think I'm nothing but an old blabbermouth?"

The chill along Ben's spine had become a blizzard of fear. "How long ago was he in here?"

The demanding urgency in his voice flustered Addie even more. "Well, now, let me see, I didn't check my watch, so I can't say for certain, but I suppose it must have been . . . oh, now—''

"Addie, *please*." Ben closed his eyes, trying to quell the sickening maelstrom of exasperation and apprehension whirling in his stomach. "Was it more than an hour ago?"

"Oh, no, I don't believe so."

"Fifteen minutes ago?"

"Oh, longer than that." She tapped a crooked finger against her chin, considering.

Ben forced himself not to throttle her.

"If I had to guess, I'd say your friend was in here about half an hour ago. Yes, that's right," she added hastily when she saw the expression on Ben's face. "Half an hour ago." She bobbed her head firmly.

"Where did he go when he left?"

"Heavens, I've no idea! I suggested he wait in the dining room—the cook baked some simply scrumptious bread pudding this morning—but he said no, he'd come back later to meet you. Then when I asked if he cared to leave a message, he told me no, that he wanted to . . . surprise you." She patted her hair, blushing nervously.

"Don't worry about it," Ben said quickly. "The fact is, I *hate* surprises." He leaned forward and brushed a kiss on her dry, powdered cheek, making her blush even more furiously. "Thanks, Addie."

With that, he moved swiftly across the lobby and took the stairs two at a time. Friend, indeed. From Addie's vague description, it was impossible to attach a name to the man. But one fact was ominously certain: he was no friend of Ben's.

Ben hadn't told a soul he was coming here. And only one person had the motivation to track him down: Jericho. Had he sent only one emissary, or was there a whole goon squad on the way?

No matter. As Ben dashed down the hallway, he knew what he had to do. Whisk Sierra safely out of the way before anyone discovered her connection to the letter.

He restrained the urge to smash down her door and spirit her off to safety before she had a chance to argue. Better not draw attention to himself until he knew who might be watching. Instead he rapped softly on the door, ready to mumble "room service" if Sierra insisted on making sure it wasn't Ben before she opened the door.

When he got no response, he knocked louder. Damn it, if she was sitting in there sulking...

Despite his intentions Ben found himself hammering on the door with his fist. "Sierra, open up! Please! I've got to talk to you! It's important! For God's sake, I'm begging you—*please* let me in!"

A door opened partway down the hall, and a balding middle-aged man stuck his head out to see what all the ruckus was. At the sight of Ben's glowering expression, he beat a hasty retreat and slammed his door shut.

Get a grip on yourself, Ben thought. *All this racket is like shooting off cannons to announce your presence.*

He rattled the doorknob, then bent to examine the lock. Old and rusted. Probably flimsy. He hesitated. The logical move would be to go downstairs and wheedle the key out of Addie. On the other hand, Sierra played a role in this decision, so logic probably wasn't a consideration. Besides, he was in a hurry.

Bracing himself against the opposite wall, Ben lowered his shoulder and launched himself against the door.

It didn't take long for him to regret his impetuous action. "Aaargh!"

The door gave way, along with his shoulder joint. That's what it felt like, anyway. Clutching his upper arm, Ben scanned Sierra's room, ready to unlease a torrent of verbal abuse as soon as he spotted her hiding place.

Then a twinge of alarm darted through him, obliterating the pain. No sign of her. No saddlebags, no duffel bag, no clothes strewn about the room. Ben stepped quickly to the closet and flung the door open. Empty. He yanked out the dresser drawers, then ducked into the bathroom. The only evidence Sierra had even been here was the rumpled towel draped over the side of the claw-footed bathtub.

Ben returned to the bedroom, breathing rapidly. No sign of a struggle, so he could probably assume that she'd left of her own free will. If one of Jericho's men had dragged Sierra out of here kicking and screaming, surely there would be a path of destruction to rival Sherman's march to the sea. Sierra wasn't likely to have gone quietly.

So things could be worse. Not much, but a little. Ben wiped the sweat from his forehead, then charged out of the room and back downstairs. "Addie," he gasped, gripping the front desk with both hands, "where is she?"

Addie's eyes widened at the sight of Ben's agitation. "Sierra? Why, she checked out, Mr. Halliday. I meant to mention it to you earlier, but then we got talking about your friend, and it just plumb went out of my head."

"Checked out? You mean she's gone? Where did she go?"

"I wish I knew, Mr. Halliday. I don't mind telling you, I've been more than a mite worried about that child." Addie shook her head sadly. "Oh, she was in quite a mood when she left, she was. All het up about something. When I tried to find out what was bothering her, she just waved her hands around and started spouting off about snakes, rats, skunks—why, I couldn't figure out *what* had upset her so! I know she's not exactly partial to creepy crawly animals, but—"

"How long ago did she leave?" Ben interrupted, grinding his teeth. Obviously Sierra wasn't ready to forgive and forget about his little deception.

Addie drew off her glasses and tapped them against her chin. "Oh, now, I believe she was lugging her gear out the back entrance around the time that feller showed up looking for you."

The hair stood up on the back of Ben's neck. "Did my, uh, friend see her leaving?"

"That I couldn't say. There was so much confusion at the time, you see—people coming and going, Sierra all worked up about something...then she insisted on dragging Pete along with her...." Addie's ample bosom heaved in a sigh. "I do wish she hadn't kicked up such a fuss about not leaving without him. I know he was looking forward to being in your magazine article. And I must say, it was awful nice to have a man around the place again. Sometimes I think I just can't manage the hotel by myself anymore, that if I could only talk Pete into..." She turned pink. "Well, never mind, you're not interested in all that, I suppose."

Ben covered her hand with his. "I'm sure everything will work out, Addie," he said with a reassurance he was far from feeling. "But if you'll excuse me, I've got to try and catch up with them."

"Well, if you find them," she said wistfully, "you tell Pete he's always got a room here, will you?"

"I'll do it first thing," Ben promised. Well, maybe second thing. The first thing he was going to do was give a certain spoiled brat the spanking her father should have given her years ago.

Thank God for yesterday's rain. Ben was no Davy Crockett, but the soft, damp earth yielded a trail of footprints that even Mister Magoo could have followed. After questioning several residents who'd seen the merry little band of travelers pass by, Ben had managed to pick up their trail where they'd left the main road about half a mile out of Grubstake. His childhood Boy Scout training was finally paying off. Of course, it also helped that his quarry included a plodding mule whose hooves gouged deep, muddy craters in the soggy ground that even a city kid like Ben could hardly miss.

He was surprised at how long it was taking to catch up with them. After all, Pete was eighty-three, and Charlemagne wasn't exactly Kentucky Derby material. Sierra must be cracking the whip something fierce. Amazing how a little self-righteous indignation could light a fire under some people.

Every bruised, strained muscle in his body was screaming in protest when Ben clambered atop a narrow, tree-lined ridge and finally spotted them. Spotted their campsite, anyway. In the ravine below, Charlemagne was propped against an elm tree like a lounger in a seedy piano bar, looking just as bored. Tent and saddlebags were piled in a heap nearby, so Sierra and Pete couldn't be far away, either.

Pausing to catch his breath, Ben pondered the best way to approach them. He wasn't exactly expecting a warm welcome and wanted to avoid, if possible, any more injuries to his person.

Sweat plastered his shirt to his back, and as a late-afternoon breeze fanned the top of the ridge, Ben shivered with a sudden chill. The ravine was already in shadow as he carefully scanned the tangled brush below for any clue to Sierra's whereabouts.

He'd just about decided to march boldly into camp and make himself at home when a long, terrified scream rang out.

Chapter Five

He'd recognize that scream anywhere. Sierra.

Ben hurled himself down the slope like a thunderbolt from the heavens. The ravine was steeper than it looked from above, and he half skidded, half flew down the side of the ridge, sending up a spray of dirt and pebbles and starting several miniature avalanches that helped sweep him along.

He was doing a fair job of keeping his balance, however, until a thick root snaked out in front of him. Tripping over the woody tentacle, he plunged headlong down the slope, rolling head over heels until he crashed into the tree Charlemagne was using as a scratching post.

Stars swirled around the mule's head as Ben stared dizzily up at the sky. But the lingering echo of that terrified scream cleared his head immediately. He staggered to his feet, lurching off toward the stand of trees where he thought the scream had come from.

Sierra was half-crouched in a defensive stance next to a dense cluster of bushes. In her upraised hand she clutched a rock, ready to fend off the attacker lurking behind the leaves where Ben couldn't see him.

As he sprang to her rescue, Ben couldn't help admiring what a valiant little fighter she was, what a spunky, brave soul....

He grabbed her in his arms and whisked her away from the bushes. Caught off balance, they both toppled to the ground and whirled over a couple of times before rolling to a halt with Ben's arms still securely pinned around Sierra.

"Get your paws off me," she said, "or I'll clobber you with this rock."

Flabbergasted, Ben didn't move.

"Did you hear me?" she demanded. "Are you going to let me up, or do I have to get rough?"

Any second now, her assailant was liable to pounce on them. Lifting his head, Ben quickly scanned their surroundings, maintaining a firm grip on Sierra. Whoever the guy was, he seemed to have disappeared.

"I mean it," she warned, starting to struggle. "Quit manhandling me, or you'll be sorry."

He was already starting to be sorry.

As he helped Sierra to her feet, she shook off his hand. "Would you mind telling me what that was all about?" she asked, dusting off her jeans.

Ben stared at her, wondering if he'd just entered the Twilight Zone. Maybe one of his numerous recent concussions was making him hallucinate. "You might thank me just a little," he said sarcastically, "for chasing that guy off."

Sierra had a gray smudge of dirt across her cheek when she glanced up at him. "What guy?"

Ben stabbed his finger toward the bushes. "Him! The guy who was about to jump you! I heard you scream, and then I—I—" He folded his arms. "Would you mind telling me exactly what the hell is so funny?"

Sierra, doubled over with laughter, couldn't answer right away. Ben tapped his foot impatiently, sensing that once again he'd made a fool of himself in front of her. When she finally recovered sufficiently to speak, her eyes sparkled with tears of mirth. "You—you thought someone was going to *jump* me?" Her voice choked up as she began to disintegrate into laughter again. At the sight of Ben's scowl, she sobered up. A little, anyway.

"It wasn't a mugger. It was a—a—" She giggled, then cleared her throat and did her best to straighten her smile. "It was a lizard."

Ben blinked, unfolded his arms and examined his fingernails. When he spoke, his calm voice held all the contained fury of a dormant volcano about to erupt. "A lizard?"

Sierra nodded. "Uh-huh." Her chin quivered.

Ben edged toward her. "You screamed bloody murder because you saw a lizard?"

"I didn't scream bloody murder. Besides, it was a *big* lizard."

"A *big* lizard."

"Big and ugly."

He stuffed his hands into his pockets to keep himself from wrapping them around her lovely throat.

"Don't blame *me* because you jumped to the wrong conclusion," she said. "Besides, who on earth would attack me way out here? Some escaped desperado from the state prison? A claim jumper, perhaps?"

"Look, I thought you were in trouble, all right? I didn't stop to make a list of all the possibilities."

Sierra surveyed Ben from the toes of his filthy, scuffed boots to the top of his disheveled blond head. "You were really trying to save me, huh?" She pushed a lock of hair from her face.

"Why else would I have tackled you that way?"

"Oh, I can think of a couple of reasons. Maybe you had orders to hog-tie me and carry me back to L.A. over your shoulder if I didn't come along peacefully." A coy grin lifted the corners of her mouth. "Or maybe overwhelming passion simply got the best of you."

Ben's scowl smoothed into a less-grumpy expression. "I told you before, I wasn't hired by your father. As for your second theory..." He slid his tongue slowly across his upper lip and leaned closer to her. "Time will tell."

Sierra held her ground, though she was torn between the impulse to beat a hasty retreat and the aching desire to throw herself into Ben's arms. Darn his double-dealing hide, anyway! She ought to ignore him, to devastate him with some withering remark, to send him packing back to Los Angeles with his tail between his legs.

Instead she wanted to cover his dirty, scratched face with kisses. She wanted to help him hobble back to camp with his arm draped across her shoulders. She wanted to clasp her hands and sigh, "My hero!" and pledge undying love to her knight in shining armor.

Even though *this* knight's armor wasn't exactly gleaming.

"You're a mess," she said grouchily. "Come on. I've got a first-aid kit, and you can clean up in the stream. I guess I could give you something to eat, too."

"Ever the gracious hostess," she heard him mumble as she led the way back to the clearing. She busied herself with the saddlebags while Ben stripped off his shirt and tossed it over a branch near Charlemagne. Then he apparently thought better of it and prudently hung the shirt on a different tree. Sierra waited till she heard him thrashing off toward the stream before she stole a glance in his direction. She caught sight of a broad masculine back and straight, sturdy shoulders before he disappeared into the brush.

"Hoo, boy," she muttered, fanning her face. Despite the sun's fading rays, she suddenly felt warm.

By the time Ben returned, damp hair slicked back and face clean if somewhat battle scarred, Sierra had wrestled the tent up. But not to Ben's satisfaction, if the way he rolled his eyes was any indication. He didn't say a word, though. Maybe he was learning.

"Will it violate any of your sacred principles if I light this fire with a match?" he asked, dumping an armload of sticks on the ground.

"Suit yourself," she replied, trying not to stare at the glint of golden hair covering the muscular curvature of his chest. "I was collecting those rocks to put around the fire when I spotted that lizard. That very *dangerous* lizard," she added when Ben grimaced. "I picked up a rock and there he was, big as a dinosaur, practically. Ugh."

Ben arranged the rocks in a circle around the stack of wood. "Sierra," he said, pushing himself to his feet with a muffled groan, "don't take this the wrong way, but are you sure you know what you're doing?" He limped over to his shirt and fished a matchbook out of the pocket.

"You're the one who can't start a fire without matches, not me."

"That's not what I'm talking about." Kneeling, Ben struck a match and held it to the kindling until the flame caught. Sierra watched his hands with fascination. Twilight shadows and the fire's glow played across his face, casting its planes and angles into bold relief like a bronze sculpture of some ancient god.

When he scooted next to her, Sierra didn't move away. "I was referring to...everything," Ben finished helplessly, waving his arm around the clearing. "I mean, that tent's not much of a shelter *now*, let alone when winter comes. I've yet to see you actually start a fire. And you haven't found any gold yet, have you?"

Her only reply was a narrowing of her eyes and an upward thrust of her chin.

"No, I didn't think so. And you're scared to death of a *lizard*, for Pete's sake! What if it had been a rattlesnake, or a mountain lion, or a grizzly bear—"

"There aren't any grizzly bears in this part of the country," she said reasonably.

Ben sighed. "You're deliberately missing my point."

"Which is?"

He raised his hands in a placating gesture. "All I'm asking is, are you sure you haven't bitten off more than you can chew?"

"Speaking of food, I'm starved. Let's eat."

"Sierra—"

"Hold it right there," she said, holding up a warning finger. "If you and I are going to carry on a civilized conversation, we're going to follow some rules. We will *not* discuss the pros and cons of my chosen lifestyle. We will *not* debate the possibility of my going back to Los Angeles, because that subject is not debatable, as far as I'm concerned. And we will *not* mention Sloane Enterprises. Understand?''

A muscle flickered along Ben's jaw. "Fine."

"Good. Here's the first-aid kit." She lobbed the canvas bundle into his lap. "You look like you could use it."

"You're a regular Florence Nightingale, aren't you?"

"Oh, don't be such a big baby. Here, I'll help you, all right?"

As Sierra yanked out bandages, tweezers, snake antivenom and assorted pills and bottles, Ben glanced around and asked, "Where's Pete?"

She tossed the antivenom aside. "He took off on his own. Seems while we were wasting all that time in town, he heard some rumor about an undiscovered gold strike farther up Bitterroot Creek." She nodded toward the stream.

"How can anyone hear about a strike that hasn't been discovered yet?"

"Go figure." Sierra shook her head in disgust. "I've told Pete time and time again that twentieth-century prospectors have to approach mining scientifically." She doused a cotton ball in rubbing alcohol and began to swab a cut on Ben's chin. "You've got to calculate where the gold deposits are most apt to be, like in a gravel bar along the inside curve of a stream or downstream of a big boulder at a spot where the stream gradient decreases."

"And why's that?"

"Hold still. Those are places where the water slows down. Gold that's being swept along will drop out of the stream when the current isn't fast enough to suspend it anymore."

Ben arched his eyebrows. "I'm impressed."

Sierra shrugged modestly. "I learned it all—"

"From your grandfather." Ben echoed her words in unison.

She smiled at him, and for a moment she forgot what a rat he was. "Here, let me put a Band-Aid on that cut."

Ben studied the small gash at the base of his thumb. "I don't think I need one. It'll heal faster if it's exposed to air."

"Well, at least let me spray some antiseptic on it, then." She cradled his hand in hers, acutely aware of a delightful warm tingling sensation where his skin contacted hers. She met Ben's gaze, then looked down quickly, having ascertained from the gleam in his eyes that he felt something, too. He cleared his throat. "Sierra, whatever you might believe about me—"

She shook the spray bottle vigorously.

"—I want you to know that—"

She closed one eye and took aim.

"—my feelings for you— *ow!*" Ben jerked back his hand. "That stings, damn it!"

Sierra's eyes widened in innocence. "What did you expect? Didn't your mom ever spray this stuff on your skinned knees when you were a kid?"

"Well, yeah. But I don't remember it hurting this much."

"Oh, come on, be a big brave boy, and I'll give you a lollipop when we're through. Now, give me your other hand."

"Forget it. I'll risk the germs."

Sierra groaned. "It's your life. Are you going to leave that nasty sliver in your finger, too?"

"Hmm. Maybe not. Do you suppose you could—?"

She snatched his hand back and went to work with the tweezers.

"Hey, go easy, will you? Ouch! What are you trying to do, amputate the whole finger?"

With a final triumphant twist, Sierra plucked out the sliver and held it up for Ben to see. "Wow! Look at the size of this! I bet it hurt like the dickens."

"Not until you gouged it out," Ben grumbled, inspecting his finger.

"Quit bellyaching." On impulse Sierra grabbed his hand and kissed the sore spot. "There! Is that better?"

His eyes glowed with a strange incandescence. "Much better." He extended his other hand, and she brushed her lips against the small cut. Wordlessly Ben pointed to a graze on his cheek. As if hypnotized, Sierra leaned forward and kissed the scraped skin ever so gently.

Ben touched his lower lip.

"There's nothing wrong with your mouth," Sierra whispered.

"Humor me."

His words were muffled by the melding of their lips as he trapped her mouth with his, tangling his fingers through her hair and pulling her hard against him.

Sierra tumbled into his arms, feeling as if she were sailing over Niagara Falls without a barrel. Instinctively she responded to the smoldering urgency of Ben's embrace, wrapping her arms around his lean waist, falling backward to lie cradled in his arms.

He kissed her over and over again—long, leisurely, determined kisses that barely allowed her to breathe, much less get a word in edgewise. Not that she could think of much to say right now, anyway. The insistent yet tender pressure on her mouth…the way Ben slipped his tongue between her lips to twine lazily with hers...filled Sierra with an exquisite floating sensation and emptied her head of any words. The incoherent moans welling up in her throat reflected the confusing, intoxicating effect of Ben's lips, his hands, his heartbeat thudding so close to her ear.

Tentatively Sierra lifted her hand and lightly skimmed his chest, exploring its bristly surface with her fingertips. As Ben dragged his lips from her mouth and buried his face in the sensitive flesh of her throat, she slid her hand to the side of his neck and marveled at the rapid pulse beat her fingers encountered.

Now he was muttering words in her ear, so close, so muffled that she could only catch one here and there. "Precious...sweet...so lovely...ah, Sierra, if only..."

A whipcord of desire, inextricably interwoven with some aching, bittersweet emotion, lashed through her. She arched her back, pressing herself closer against the warm, heaving wall of his chest. Ben wrapped one of his arms even more securely around her, freeing his other hand to roam slowly across the curve of her hip, around her narrow waist, up over the lush swell of her breasts.

Even as a voice inside her head cried a warning, Sierra knew that it was too late. Before she'd fully recognized the danger, Ben Halliday had woven his sensual, irresistible web around her. Now she was as neatly, helplessly trapped as a butterfly in a net. No matter how hard or how fast she beat her wings, Ben had her right where he wanted: completely under his spell. Knowing that his dizzying caresses and wonderful whispered words were bankrolled by her father should have rendered Sierra immune to them. But it didn't.

"Ah, Ben," she mumbled in a half sigh, half groan. "You no-good, sneaky, rotten..."

"Flattery will get you everywhere," he responded with a throaty chuckle. His breath tickled her earlobe, making her shiver and snuggle even more cozily into his arms.

With a practiced touch, she noted wistfully, Ben plucked open the buttons of her shirt and eased his hand beneath the velvety flannel. His hands were cool against Sierra's heated skin, and she tensed a bit at the first contact.

"Easy," he crooned. "That's it . . . relax . . . we'll go nice and slow . . . I promise I won't do anything you're not ready for. . . ."

He'd mistaken her slight flinch as nervousness about his increasingly bold forays beneath her clothing. In truth every fiber, cell and nerve ending in Sierra's body was clamoring for Ben's touch, yearning for the rapturous fulfillment of the sweet, anguished longings he aroused. Her eyelids drifted shut as she surrendered herself to his lead, knowing she was slipping into a dangerous oblivion of ecstasy she would later regret . . . and not caring in the least.

Ben sensed the last strands of Sierra's resistance ebbing away, and experienced a brief surge of satisfied pleasure. God, she felt wonderful! Her skin was like silk sliding beneath his fingers; her gossamer kisses were like a healing balm to his battered face and bruised ego. Surely her opinion of him couldn't be *too* low, not the way she curled her slim, soft body around him; not the way she purred deep in her throat when he flicked his tongue across her dainty, shell-like ear; not the way she sucked in her breath with a gentle gasp when he molded his hand around the luscious mound of her breast.

She smelled like grass and fresh air and mountain flowers after a spring rain. Conflicting desires tore at

Ben. He wanted to ravish her, to take advantage of her temporarily befuddled state and possess her with the reckless, almost-savage passion that boiled through his bloodstream.

At the same time a ferocious protectiveness flooded him, intensely poignant and totally unknown in his previous experiences with women. Had this overwhelming, unfamiliar instinct seized him simply because Sierra was so out of her element, so in need of his competent masculine protection?

Hardly. Sierra might never earn any wilderness survival badges, but deep down inside, Ben suspected that when push came to shove, she could take care of herself perfectly well without help from him or anyone else.

No, this crazy impulse to shelter her, to do everything in his power to take care of her and make her life easy had its roots in far more disturbing soil. And Ben knew he'd feel the same protective urge whether Sierra was white-water rafting down the Amazon or safely ensconced at the head of the table in some corporate boardroom.

Yet here he was, entangling her deeper in the complicated mess of his life, exposing her to ever-greater peril as the emotional and physical bonds between them drew tighter. Like a noose around her neck.

Christ, there must be *some* way to destroy Quentin Jericho without endangering this fragile, increasingly precious woman in his arms!

But damned if he could come up with an alternative.

A wave of self-loathing engulfed Ben, magnified by the trusting capitulation apparent in every pliant curve, every trembling response of Sierra's body. When she fluttered her lashes half-open to gaze up at him, the

dreamy gloss of anticipation in those translucent brown
eyes struck him like an accusing slap in the face.

Ben withdrew his hand from beneath her shirt and
pulled Sierra against his chest, tucking her head beneath his chin. After a long moment, during which he
concentrated on slowing his breathing and pulse, he
drew back and kissed her forehead. Shakily he brushed
his thumb across the delicate arch of her cheekbone.
"Smudge of dirt," he whispered with a fond smile.
Then he puckered his lips and planted a playful kiss on
the tip of her freckle-dusted nose.

As she trailed her fingers down his bare chest, Ben
closed his eyes with an involuntary shudder. He clasped
his hand over hers, unsure how long he could retain his
control if she kept touching him like that. Resolutely he
began to rebutton her shirt. His fingers felt thick and
clumsy, as if they were asleep. As he fumbled with the
buttons, he could feel Sierra's eyes focused on him, wide
open now, glinting with bewilderment and suspicion.

Finally she swept his hand aside and closed the remaining buttons herself, shifting into a sitting position. Her hair fell across her face like a shield,
glimmering with coppery highlights cast by the fire.

Ben reached out and draped her hair back as if peering through a curtain. "Sweetheart—?"

She jerked her head impatiently, tossing her curls
back. When she'd finished with the last button, she met
his inquiring, apologetic gaze head-on. Her kiss-swollen
lips were clamped together in exasperation. "You'd
think I'd have learned my lesson by now, wouldn't
you?"

Ben hesitated. "I'm not sure I understand what
you—"

"I mean, I *know* darn good and well why you're doing this. Good grief, what does it take, a sledgehammer to pound some sense into me?" She shook her head. "I always considered myself a quick study, but where you're concerned I seem to have some kind of mental block."

"Sierra, I can explain—"

"Oh, you don't need to explain! I know perfectly well that this—this—advance-and-retreat, advance-and-retreat business is simply part of your strategy. Well, let me congratulate you. It's certainly working well. Although I guess I don't need to tell you that." She levered herself to her feet from her cross-legged position.

"Will you please let me—"

"God, what a fool I am! What a pushover! One kiss from those magic lips, one peek at that fabulous bare chest, and I'm a goner! Pride, self-respect, self-control—they all go flying out the window. You must think I'm a person of rather easy virtue, but I assure you I'm not. Not till now, anyway. I'm sure my father thought you'd have a much tougher time of winning me over. He'll probably be furious with himself for overpaying you, once he finds out what quick work you made of conquering my resistance."

Unable to squeeze a word in edgewise, Ben watched Sierra pace back and forth in front of the fire, waving her hands in the air, gnashing her teeth and throwing anguished looks at the night sky. More than anything, he wanted to grab her again, to smother her ridiculous rantings with kisses and smooth away her agitation with his caressing hands.

But that would only make matters worse. Ben pushed himself to his feet, barely noticing the aching protest of his muscles. Jamming his hands into the back pockets of his jeans, he vowed to keep a prudent distance from Sierra.

"Are you ready to listen yet? Or haven't you finished your monologue?" he asked.

"I'll tell you what's finished," she retorted. "You and me—*that's* what's finished."

Ben counted slowly to ten. "Okay, since it's all over, can I say just one thing?"

She folded her arms and tapped her foot. "I guess so. But make it snappy."

"Thank you," he said with exaggerated gratitude. "And I'd appreciate it if you'd let me say my piece without interrupting."

She waved her hand in a royal gesture. "Fine. Go ahead."

Ben studied her for a moment as she stood outlined against the fire. He couldn't see her face too clearly against the blazing backdrop, but he could read that defiant stance all too well. He exhaled a drawn-out sigh.

"How do you expect me to make love to you when you think I'm some kind of con man?"

His blunt question drew a faint gasp from Sierra, but she recovered quickly. "I don't *expect* you to make love to me at all," she shot back. "Don't flatter yourself."

"Liar."

She recoiled as if he'd struck her. "I beg your—"

"You accuse me of deceiving you, of pretending to be something or someone I'm not. Then you turn right around and lie not only to me, but to yourself."

He'd caught her off guard for once, and was quick to press his advantage. "Let's both be honest, shall we, Sierra?" He closed the distance between them and grasped her elbows, forgetting his resolution not to touch her again. "Something powerful, something incredible was happening between us just now. Admit it. You wanted me to make love to you." She swallowed, staring up at him with enormous, coffee-colored eyes. Ben thrust his face close to hers, and said through gritted teeth, "You wanted me as much as I wanted you. Don't bother denying it."

Her expression was frozen, only her lips moving as she whispered, "Then . . . why?"

Ben raised his hand, feathering it lightly over her eyebrows, her cheekbones, her mouth, like a blind man seeking an image of her face. "I won't make love to you as long as you're convinced I have some ulterior motive. What's happening between us is real, sweetheart. It's not a game—it's not make-believe. Until you realize that, I have no intention of trying to seduce you. I've never had to trick a woman to get her into my bed, and I'm not about to start with you." He tapped the tip of her nose. "Especially not you."

The words had tumbled out of Ben without effort, without conscious planning. Yet as he spoke them, he realized they were true. He was no longer capable of using Sierra, of taking advantage of their mutual attraction to get the letter back. Maybe he never had been.

Ben had no intention of giving up his search. But he'd been tested this evening. Lines had been drawn, bluffs had been called, and now he knew there was a limit to how far he would go in his quest for revenge. When pushed to the brink, he hadn't been able to cross that final line, to exploit Sierra's passion and emotions to achieve his goal. Tonight she'd offered him the most precious gift imaginable: herself.

And after passing self-judgment, Ben had decreed himself unworthy to accept it.

Sierra's eyes were still locked on his, radiating uncertainty. Somehow he'd managed to render her speechless, but even this amazing feat brought Ben no satisfaction. Their encounter had left him with a bitter taste in his mouth and a throbbing ache in his loins. He longed with a sharp, startling intensity to possess her, but he had no intention of making love to Sierra as long as she suspected him of some hidden motive.

Yet he couldn't tell her the truth without endangering her life.

God, what a convoluted mess this was turning into! *Oh, what a tangled web we weave,* Ben thought. He was certain of one thing, though. When he and Sierra finally came together heart, body and soul, it would be with complete openness, sharing and honesty. Sierra deserved it. And Ben would settle for nothing less.

"You're hurting my elbows," she said at last.

Instantly Ben released her. "Sorry. Guess I got carried away."

"Hmm. Seems to be a nasty habit we've both developed lately." The words were flippant, but her combative fire seemed to have died down. The way she was rubbing her elbows made it appear as if she were hugging herself. Almost absently she continued, "It's too late for you to start back for town. You can bed down out here." She ducked her head into the tent, poked around and emerged with a threadbare green army blanket. "Here," she said, avoiding his eyes as she shoved the blanket at him. "I hope you don't snore."

Ben grinned. "You won't hear it inside the tent."

"I wasn't worried about me. Charlemagne's a very light sleeper."

Was she serious? Or was she gently kidding Ben in an effort to mend the breach between them? With Sierra he was never sure. "I'll try to keep the racket down," he assured her.

"Well. Good. G'night, then." She nodded her head once, hesitating as if about to say something more. Then she pivoted on her heel and disappeared into the tent.

"Pleasant dreams," Ben called after her. He retrieved his shirt from the tree branch, rolled it up and stuffed it beneath his head to use as a pillow. Dragging the worn blanket over his creaking joints, he stretched himself out on the rock-hard ground next to the dying campfire.

With a muffled oath, he rolled onto his side and scrabbled behind him for the sharp pebble digging into his back. Pitching the stone into the darkness, he eased himself back down again. Before long the autumn chill was seeping through the thin blanket into his stiff limbs. He tossed from side to side, searching in vain for a comfortable position that would minimize his physical discomfort and soothe his turbulent thoughts.

Somewhere during the hours after midnight he must have dropped off, because all at once he snapped awake, muscles taut as bowstrings, alert to some new presence nearby. The remaining embers from the fire cast only a feeble glow, but suddenly a dark shape blocked out the stars overhead.

Ben hurled himself to one side, scrambling for a stick, a rock, *something* to use as a weapon.

"Hey, it's only me," came a puzzled, faintly amused voice through the darkness.

Ben froze, blood thudding in his ears. Then he flopped back to the ground with a moan, flinging one arm across his eyes.

"Sorry," Sierra said. "I forgot how jumpy you are."

"Forget it," Ben said thickly. "Was there something you wanted?"

"Well, yeah." She crawled over and seated herself cross-legged next to him. "I couldn't sleep."

"So you decided to share the experience?"

"Oops," she said meekly. "Were you asleep?"

Ben shrugged. "It's something I sometimes do at night. Kind of a hobby."

"Oh. Well, sorry." He noticed Sierra was getting better at apologizing. "I won't disturb you for long, then. I just—I just wanted to say...um..." She cleared her throat. "Thanks."

Ben lifted his arm and peered at her with one eye. Without a moon overhead, the darkness was thick as molasses, but that *was* Sierra over there, all right. "Thanks . . . for what?" he asked cautiously.

He sensed rather than saw her shoulders rise, then drop. "Thanks for . . . you know. Stopping. Earlier tonight. When I—when we—well, you know."

Ben toyed with the idea of making her elaborate further, then relented and decided to go easy on her. "Sure. But what changed your mind? I thought you were mad at me."

"I am. I *was*, I mean. Until I started thinking about what you said, about how I wasn't being honest. You were right." He heard her draw in a long, quavering breath. "I wanted you to make love to me, Ben. Even though I knew why you were doing it—"

He pushed himself up on one elbow. "Sierra—"

"No, stay there. Let me finish." She swallowed. "Please."

Ben waited.

"You were right. When two people make love, it has to be with openness and honesty, or it isn't worth anything. I guess I forgot that in the...heat of the moment." She sighed. "Thank you for reminding me."

"No problem." Ben reached up and wrapped one of her curls around his finger. "You see, I kind of forgot that, too. I was reminding myself, as well."

"Anyway." She fiddled with her hands. "That was all I wanted to say. I'll let you go back to sleep now."

Ben watched her slim, shadowy outline as she rose to her feet. "See you in the morning," he said quietly.

Sierra paused, then knelt and tugged the rumpled blanket up over his chest. "See you in the morning," she echoed, her breath a gentle puff of warm air against his skin.

With iron self-control Ben stopped himself from following her back to the tent.

Long after Sierra left, he gazed wide-eyed at the canopy of stars winking above. Only now he had more than the concretelike ground and bone-numbing chill to prevent him from sleeping. The tender, disturbing images of Sierra whirling through Ben's brain also kept him awake.

That...and the loud, sloppy, rat-a-tat snoring of that damn mule.

Chapter Six

Sierra peeked surreptitiously at Ben's motionless form.
When she was certain he was still asleep, she whipped
out a matchbook from behind her back, struck a flame
and lit the pile of sticks she'd just arranged. In no time
at all the fire was burning cheerfully, banishing the crisp
nip in the air. Soon the pungent, mingled aroma of
pine, coffee and burning wood filled the campsite.

She settled herself on the ground next to the fire,
drawing up her knees and wrapping her arms around
them while she watched Charlemagne breakfasting a
short distance away on a tasty clump of foliage.

Inevitably Sierra's gaze drifted back to her slumber-
ing companion. She watched the steady rise and fall
beneath the blanket as she thought about last night and
how close she'd come to giving herself to a man she
knew was a liar and a phony.

It was no use trying to analyze the reasons why she'd been so eager to throw away her principles for the sake of one wild, passionate encounter. The complicated tangle of emotions she felt toward Ben defied logical analysis.

With a sigh Sierra pushed the sleeves of her navy blue sweatshirt up over her elbows. Just when she thought she had Ben pegged as an unscrupulous heel, he had to go and do something nice. Like refusing to take advantage of her temporary insanity last night.

Who *was* Ben Halliday, anyway? Were any of the things he'd told her about himself true? Or were his stories about a plane crash and his mother's recent death merely ploys to gain her sympathy and make her more vulnerable to his advances?

But then why—*why* had he withdrawn last night, right when he had Sierra in the palm of his hand?

Maybe she didn't have him totally figured out yet. But she intended to remedy that situation. Pronto.

"Good morning, sleepyhead!" she sang out gaily when the blanket-covered lump began to move. A muffled grumbling was her only reply.

"Coffee's almost ready. Time to rise and shine!"

Ben opened one eye and peeked at her over the edge of the blanket. "Are you always this cheerful first thing in the morning?" His voice sounded as if he were speaking underwater.

"Heavens, are you always this grouchy when you first wake up?"

"Only when I've been kept awake all night by someone's snoring."

"I beg your pardon! I'll have you know, I do *not* snore."

"Not you." He craned his head around and nodded in Charlemagne's direction. "That—that poor excuse for a—"

"Shh! You'll hurt his feelings. Char's very sensitive."

"Hmm, yes. I can tell by the way he's chowing down those weeds that he's a mule of very refined tastes."

"For goodness' sake, have some coffee. Maybe it'll improve your disposition." Sierra pulled one sleeve down over her hand, using it as a pot holder to lift the coffeepot off the fire. "I've only got one cup, so we'll have to share." She filled a dented tin mug and handed it to Ben. "You can go first," she said generously.

He groped his way into a sitting position, squinting as the sun's low-angled rays hit him head-on. Really, the way that little blond cowlick stuck up on the back of his tousled head was just cute as could be. The blanket fell away to reveal his golden chest, sending a little thrill down Sierra's spine that curled her toes.

"Thanks," Ben muttered, taking the mug from her. His fingers twined with hers for an instant, and now *all* of Sierra's extremities were tingling. As he raised the cup to his lips, she was jolted by a vivid recollection of how those lips had felt on hers. She sucked in a quick breath and turned away.

An instant later a sputtering noise made her look back. "Aaargh!" Ben wiped his mouth on the back of his hand. His normally handsome features were screwed into a picturesque expression of disgust. He inspected the contents of the cup like something left too long in the refrigerator. "What the hell kind of coffee *is* this?"

"Cowboy coffee, what else? You toss in a handful of grounds and boil it up good and strong."

Ben made a disdainful smacking sound with his tongue. "Tastes like some cowboy soaked his boots in it."

"Well, excuse me, but I don't have a long-enough extension cord to plug in my fancy filter-drip coffee maker way out here."

"*You* try it! Don't tell me you think this stuff tastes good."

Sierra snatched back the cup and swallowed with gusto. A big mistake. Somehow she managed to choke down the mouthful of coffee, but not convincingly enough to make Ben believe she'd enjoyed it. "I guess it *is* a little strong," she admitted grudgingly.

"*Strong?* It's scorched! You could mix the ashes from that fire into water, and it would taste better."

"Okay, okay, you've made your—"

"Don't toss it on the ground, for God's sake! You'll kill all the plant life within a ten-foot radius and bring the forest service down on our necks."

"Very amusing." The corner of Sierra's mouth twitched in spite of her annoyance. One thing about her association with Ben Halliday: it was never dull. Infuriating, yes. Disorienting, on occasion. And tempting...always. But dull? Never.

"How about some breakfast?" she asked, scrambling to her feet.

Ben cocked a wary eyebrow. "You're not going to try to cook pancakes or anything, are you?"

"Ha! Don't you wish? But no, that takes too long. The morning's half-gone already, and I've got lots of work to do today." She crawled into the tent and grabbed a bright yellow box from her replenished store of food. She backed out of the tent on hands and knees. "How about a delicious Yummee Coconut-Creme Cake for breakfast?'' She wiggled the box at a tantalizing distance from Ben.

To her amazement, the color drained from his face. Sierra's smile wavered as Ben stared at the box in her hand with a look of pure revulsion. ''Where—where did you get that?'' he asked in a strangely flat tone. ''I don't recall seeing it with your other supplies from the general store.''

Sierra blinked. ''I picked it up on the way out of town yesterday. See, I was sort of, um, depressed, because of our little . . . fight, and when I'm depressed I kind of, well, pig out on junk food. I bought tons of this stuff— Yummee Coconut-Creme Cakes, Yummee Nut-Butters, Yummee Chocolate Eclairs— hey, are you all right?'' she broke off in genuine consternation. Ben was definitely looking a little green around the gills.

His mouth formed a crooked smile. ''Yeah. I'm fine. Really.''

''Are you sure? 'Cause you don't look so hot, if you don't mind my saying so. Your eyes look a little . . . glazed.''

''It's nothing. I just felt queasy for a second.'' He raked his hair back from his forehead and inhaled deeply. ''I'm feeling better already.''

Sierra frowned. ''Gosh, I'm really sorry. This is all my fault. I should have guessed you were the type of person who'd get nauseous at the sight of junk food first thing in the morning. If only I'd—''

''Hey, forget it. It's no big deal.'' The color was returning to Ben's face, making him more incredibly attractive than ever. ''I think I sat up too fast, that's all. Made me dizzy for a minute.'' He grasped Sierra's hand and briefly pressed her fingers to his lips. ''I'm fine. Honest.''

Distracted by the delightful, lingering sensation of his mouth on her skin, she stammered, "I could, uh, make pancakes or something. Eggs? I think I have some powdered eggs around here somewhere..."

Ben made a face. "Now, that really *would* make me queasy." He threw off the blanket and climbed to his feet. Sierra glued her attention to his straining biceps and his sculpted, hair-matted chest as he arched his back, stretching his arms over his head with a huge, jaw-cracking yawn. "Tell you what," he said, scratching his ribs. "What if *I* cook breakfast this morning? It's the least I can do after—well, after everything I've put you through."

"Sure." Sierra's mouth was dry. "I'll have eggs Benedict, an almond croissant and fruit compote." *With you for dessert,* she thought, licking her lips.

Ben's lazy smile made her mouth water. "Coming right up, madam. Would you care for a champagne cocktail while you wait?"

"Make it a Bloody Mary, would you? And keep 'em coming."

Ben could have used a drink himself. The unexpected appearance of that all-too-familiar, lemon-colored box in Sierra's hand had unsettled him like a magnitude-eight earthquake. He slipped inside the tent and, as he pawed through Sierra's cache for breakfast supplies, he came across practically the entire Yummee product line—cookies, cupcakes, doughnuts, pastries. A veritable treasure trove of sugar, flour, butter, cream and chemical preservatives, guaranteed to raise your blood-sugar and cholesterol levels, harden your arteries and deposit an inner tube of extra pounds around your middle. Sierra must have been planning to eat herself out of a depression and into a stupor.

One undisputable fact about Yummee Foods, though. They all tasted delicious. That was one reason the company had grown from a three-person bakery operating out of a ramshackle Grass Valley storefront into the largest retail purveyor of snack foods in the country.

The other reason was the wholesome family image that Yummee Foods' advertising department so carefully cultivated. In countless magazine ads and television commercials throughout the country, freckle-faced, freshly scrubbed kids in baseball caps and pigtails washed down Yummee Tastee-Bars with foamy glasses of milk that left white mustaches over their upper lips. Perfect storybook families romped at the beach or the neighborhood park with Yummee Fudge Tarts spilling from their picnic baskets. Adorable munchkins brought their mothers breakfast in bed, their little tongues poking out in concentration as they carefully balanced a tray holding a bud vase and a Yummee Banana Cupcake with a birthday candle stuck in it. Yummee Foods was as wholesome, as all-American as Mom and apple pie, baseball and the Fourth of July all rolled into one.

And Ben was intimately acquainted with every gooey confection, every sappy smile that greeted the prospect of sinking one's teeth into a scrumptious Yummee whatever. Because Ben himself had approved many of those ads when he'd been Yummee Foods' director of marketing for the entire West Coast.

And that wholesome, respectable, carefully cultivated public image was the cornerstone of Ben's plan to ruin the man who was cofounder, chairman of the board and the very personification of Yummee Foods.

Quentin Jericho.

See how many hospitals would invite Jericho to cut the ribbon at the opening of their new children's wing once Ben exposed him for the cheating bastard he really was.

See how many charitable foundations would ask Jericho to be the keynote speaker at their thousand-dollar-a-plate fund-raisers after the news media got their hands on that incriminating letter.

See how many mothers would keep plunking those bright yellow Yummee Food boxes into their shopping carts when the tabloids at the checkout stand screamed that Jericho was nothing but a conniving sleazeball.

A back-stabbing, blackmailing, definitely *unwholesome* sleazeball.

Civic groups would organize consumer boycotts, and sales of Yummee Foods would drop off. Stores would panic and reduce the shelf space devoted to Yummee products, sending sales plummeting even further. The price of Yummee Foods stock would tumble right off the profit-and-loss charts. The sprawling corporate empire that Quentin Jericho had built on betrayal and broken dreams would disintegrate and collapse. Jericho would be a pariah—scorned by the wealthy, powerful influence makers, society's movers and shakers, the very same elite he had fought so ruthlessly to join.

He wouldn't die penniless; he was too clever for that. But the public admiration, the respect of his business peers and his jealously guarded image as a benevolent, kindly philanthropist would be blown to smithereens.

Jericho's public disgrace wouldn't bring back Ben's father. It wouldn't make up for his mother's lifetime of unhappiness. But it was the best Ben could do. And the least he could do. He owed it to their memories.

He'd had plenty of time during his lengthy convalescence after the plane crash to work out his plan. At first he'd hoped to find proof of Jericho's criminal wrongdoing. Jail seemed too lenient a sentence if the theory Ben had pieced together were true, but any punishment was preferable to letting Jericho go scot-free.

Unfortunately Ben's hopes of seeing Jericho behind bars evaporated the day he was released from the hospital. He'd made straight for corporate headquarters in Los Angeles after disguising his voice, phoning Jericho's office and learning from his secretary that Jericho would be tied up in a meeting for the next hour.

Once inside the building, Ben had headed quickly for the basement storeroom where all the old company records were kept. Apparently Jericho hadn't issued any orders barring him from the premises, because the young woman behind the counter was most helpful, showing Ben exactly where the old account books from the company's sixth year of business were shelved.

Ben scanned the row of dusty ledgers with a sinking heart. Once again Jericho had been one step ahead of him. But he had to make sure.

"Jennifer? Could you come back here for a second, please?" The woman's high heels clicked on the floor as she walked down the aisle to where Ben stood with a frown on his face.

"What is it, Mr. Halliday?"

"I can't seem to find the volume for the year I want. Maybe you could double-check for me. It's probably right in front of my eyes, and I'm just not seeing it."

She scanned the shelf, then pushed her owllike glasses more securely onto her nose and looked again. "Gee, Mr. Halliday, I don't see it, either."

"Could someone have borrowed it?"

She tapped a pencil against her chin. "Not that I recall, but let me check."

Ben followed her back to the front desk, knowing what she would tell him before she said it. "I can't find any record of someone checking it out." Her eyes were locked on the computer screen, fingers poised above the keyboard.

"Maybe sometime while you stepped out to go to the, uh, ladies' room . . ."

She gave him a slightly offended look over the tops of her glasses. "No one removes anything from here without my permission, Mr. Halliday. When I'm not here, the place is locked up." Then her stern expression wavered. "The funny thing is," she mused, "I could swear that volume was there last month when I did the annual inventory, making sure all the records were in their proper places and so forth." She snapped her fingers. "I'm positive it was there."

Ben knew who'd stolen the set of records. And he was willing to bet the book was now nothing but ashes in some incinerator somewhere.

A tide of hopelessness engulfed him, drowning even his anger and frustration. Those records had been the only surviving physical evidence linking Jericho to that long-ago crime. Only someone who suspected foul play—like himself—might have found discrepancies. Now Ben would never be able to prove that Jericho had framed his father and indirectly killed him.

Now there was only one surviving document with the power to bring Jericho to some kind of justice.

The letter.

Somewhere in the Sierra Nevada wandered an old prospector Ben had been forced to entrust with the only way left to avenge his parents.

He had to find Caleb Murphy. He had to get that letter back.

Ben hadn't found Murphy, of course. But seeing those damn yellow boxes of Yummee Macaroons and Yummee Caramel Nuggets and Yummee Jellee Donuts had renewed his determination to find the letter.

Which was why he had no qualms about searching every square inch of Sierra's tent while she waited outside for him to cook breakfast.

He rooted through her duffel bag, the saddlebags, every nook and cranny of that tottering tent without finding so much as a postage stamp. Either Murphy had stashed the letter in some woodpecker's nest somewhere, or Sierra was carrying it on her person.

Ben couldn't avoid a rueful grin at that second possibility. He'd explored enough of Sierra's clothing to be fairly certain the letter wasn't hidden in a pocket or someplace more intimate. But the first possibility sobered him up. Had the secret of the letter's location died with Murphy? Or had he passed it along as part of his bequest to Sierra?

Ben cursed under his breath. He couldn't simply come right out and ask her about it—not without telling her the whole story and making her a target for Jericho's henchmen. And last night had proven that Ben could never bring himself to cajole the truth from her by cold-blooded seduction.

To make matters worse, time was running out. Thanks to Addie Winslow's gift of gab, Ben knew at least one of Jericho's hired guns was hot on his trail. Sierra might already be in danger if Jericho had discovered her romantic involvement with Ben. And if that were the case, the only way to ensure her safety was by finding the letter and delivering it to the press. Once the whole world knew Jericho's sordid secret, Sierra would no longer pose any particular threat to him.

"Hey, what's taking so long? Are you raising the chickens to lay the eggs for our breakfast?" A blinding halo of sunlight surrounded Sierra as she flung back the tent flap and stuck her head inside. "Forget the eggs Benedict. I'll settle for burned biscuits at this point."

"Ah, but *I'm* the one cooking breakfast, remember?"

She drew herself up on her knees and gave Ben a haughty glare. "Are you implying that *I* would burn the biscuits?"

"Let's just say Smokey the Bear has enough to do without rushing over to investigate any charred smells coming from our neck of the woods."

"You ingrate! After I let you camp out here last night, then made you coffee this morning—"

"Let's not bring up the subject of that coffee, agreed? Now, scoot! Out of my way. You're about to be one of the lucky few privileged to feast upon my extra special, super-duper, award-winning blueberry pancakes."

"Those aren't blueberries—those are raisins."

"That's what makes my blueberry pancakes so unique. Now, why don't you make yourself useful and—and...let's see, you could...no, how about if you...oh, never mind. I've got a better idea." Ben pushed past Sierra, his arms full of pancake ingredients. He paused to smack a quick kiss on her pouting lips. "Why don't you plant your pretty little bottom on that log over there and just *watch* me make breakfast?"

"How about if I plant my pretty little fist in your solar plexus?" she replied sweetly. But she did as he suggested.

And she had to admit the man knew how to cook. After a fabulous, rib-sticking breakfast of pancakes, bacon and hot chocolate, Sierra craved nothing more than to kick off her boots, bask in the sun and indulge in a postprandial nap. Preferably with a certain gorgeous blond chef curled up next to her.

But she couldn't let Ben think she was losing her enthusiasm for the hardworking life of a gold miner. So, after washing the breakfast dishes, she announced her intention of hiking upstream to check out some likely prospecting sites.

As she'd expected, Ben tagged along. Hours later Sierra had to chuckle, imagining what her father would say if he could see the man he'd hired to lure her out of the backwoods actually *helping* her look for gold.

She pushed herself stiffly to her knees and swiped a swatch of curls from her forehead with the back of her wrist. Her feet were soaked, her hands gloved with mud. Well, no one ever said panning for gold was glamorous.

She stole a look at Ben, who stood across the stream, filling a pail with dirt and rocks he hacked off the steep embankment. The day had turned unseasonably warm, and he'd stripped off his shirt. Sierra found herself studying the golden sheen of his sweat-slicked back, the rippling muscles of his thick, corded arms as he plunged the small shovel into the dark, rich earth again and again....

Then Charlemagne sneezed, jolting Sierra from her trance. For a moment she'd forgotten her aching back, her dirt-encrusted hands and the icy water seeping into her boots.

For a moment she'd forgotten that Ben was nothing but a mercenary, that his feigned interest in her would last only as long as her father signed his paycheck.

Yet when he turned and waded back across the stream, something about the way the water swirled and churned around his solid thighs made Sierra catch her breath. Water droplets sparkled across his chest like diamonds, and when he shook a damp lock of hair from his face and sent her a crooked, dazzling smile, she swayed with sudden giddy happiness.

"Find any gold yet?" he called.

"Huh? Er, no, not yet." She wouldn't have believed that anything could possibly improve Ben's appearance, but a day in the sun had bronzed his face and upper torso, enhancing his rugged good looks. It figured. Why couldn't he be one of those people who broil like a lobster? Sierra could practically hear the freckles popping out across the bridge of her nose.

Ben set the bucket of damp earth at her feet and propped his hands on his lean hips. "Striking it rich seems like kind of a slow process."

Instantly Sierra was on guard for more sighs and head shaking, more pleas to give up this craziness for the sanity of civilization. But the twinkle in Ben's azure eyes seemed perfectly innocent.

"It *is* a slow process," she replied cautiously. "But once I find a spot where I can pan out some gold, I'm going to build a sluice box."

Ben made a rocking motion with his hand. "You mean one of those old wooden troughs like the forty-niners used to use?"

She nodded. "I can process a lot more material that way. But I've got to keep taking samples along the stream till I locate a gold-producing site."

"Something that's been bothering me...how's the owner of this land going to react when he hears about your bonanza?"

Kneeling, Sierra scooped a few handfuls of dirt from Ben's pail into her dented metal pan. "This is public land we're on, so I should be able to stake a claim to the mineral rights once I decide where I want to mine. Usually all you have to do is post boundary markers and pay a fee to the government. Grandpa used to do it all the time."

She felt Ben's eyes upon her as she dipped the pan into the slow-moving current, swirling the pile of dirt around to float away the lighter material and allow the heavier gold to settle out.

He knelt beside her. "Would you mind if I tried that?"

She glanced sideways in surprise. "Well...sure. I mean, no—go ahead." She placed the pan in his hands, then picked out some twigs and larger rocks the current had washed clean. "Swish it around in a circle...that's right, slow and easy."

"This is kind of like the way people used to winnow grain back in the old days—tossing it up in the air and letting the wind blow away the chaff."

"Exactly," Sierra replied, tickled by the intent concentration etched in Ben's face. "You can swirl it a little faster than that. If there's any gold, it should settle into the bottom quite nicely." She flicked a handful of small pebbles into the stream.

Ben kept silent, his eyes riveted to the increasingly fine material sloshing around the pan. "I suppose your grandfather taught you how to do this," he said after a few minutes.

"Yup. I was panning gold before I even knew how to walk. My mom would bring me up here, set me on the edge of a stream and stick an aluminum pie plate in my hands."

Ben shook his head, grinning. "I can't quite picture Maxwell Sloane wading through this muck, getting his feet all wet and his clothes muddy."

Sierra tensed. "No, I don't suppose you can." Her tone was as icy as the stream.

Ben froze. "Sierra, I didn't mean that the way it sounded," he said hastily. "I don't have to know your father personally to have trouble imagining him in this environment."

"Let's change the subject, shall we?" It seemed to Sierra as if the sun had hidden behind a cloud, although the sky was still the same intense lapis-lazuli color as before. But she couldn't resist mumbling, "Besides, Daddy never came up here when Mom brought me to visit Grandpa. He was too busy with work."

"Sierra, I'm sorry—"

"Move the pan slower now. You're getting down to the fine sediment. See how black that concentrate is? That's all the iron that's sunk to the bottom."

He peered into the pan. "What do we do now?"

"Tilt out most of the water, then kind of spread the silt over the bottom so we can see if there's any gold mixed in."

Ben studied the pan as if preparing to perform brain surgery. His eyes lit up. "Gold! Hey, look, we found gold! I'll be damned—I never thought—but there it is! Gold!"

Sierra glanced at the pan's contents, then bit her lip to keep from smiling. "I hate to burst your bubble, but that isn't gold."

Ben's jaw dropped in disbelief. "Whaddya mean it isn't gold? I'd like to know what you'd call those little gold flecks, then."

Sierra folded her arms and gave him a Cheshire-cat grin. "Ever hear of fool's gold?"

"Fool's . . . gold?"

"Also known as iron or copper pyrite. Personally I've always thought 'fool's gold' a much more appropriate name. So descriptive, don't you think?"

"Ha, ha." Ben examined the glitter with mingled doubt and regret. "You're sure this isn't the real McCoy?"

"Look." Sierra pulled a Swiss Army knife from her back pocket and wrenched open the blade. "See how brittle this stuff is, how it flakes off? And gold is softer, so I'd be able to scratch it with the tip of this knife."

"Oh."

"And watch." She took the pan from him and leaned over it, positioning her body to block the sun's rays. "See? Gold glitters even when it's not in direct sunlight."

"But this stuff doesn't."

"Nope."

"So it's worthless."

"From a monetary standpoint, yes. But at least we've eliminated this spot as a likely location for any gold deposits." She rinsed the black residue back into the stream. "So we *are* making progress."

Ben's gaze followed the discarded silt as it swirled and dissipated. "I can see you need to be an optimist in this line of work."

"It helps." She shoved on her knees and rose to her feet. "It also helps to be determined."

"Stubborn, in other words."

Sierra laughed. "That's another way of putting it."

Ben unfolded himself from his sitting position. "Well, you've certainly mastered *that* part of it, anyway. And I must admit you've got a great panning technique."

"I learned from the best," she said, strapping the pan onto Charlemagne's back along with the rest of her gear. "Come on, I'm starved. Let's head back to camp and see what I can rustle up for supper."

"I can fix supper," he said quickly.

Sierra fired a withering look over her shoulder. "Just for that crack," she said, "I'm going to try out a new recipe on you."

Despite her threat, Ben whistled a cheerful tune as they plodded back to camp. Sierra dragged Charlemagne along like a child on the way to the dentist. Ben's muscles still ached, but it was the kind of good, satisfied ache he got after an afternoon of racquetball or a day spent painting the outside of his house. Nothing like good old-fashioned manual labor to work out the tension and strip away the pressures of modern living.

He barely noticed the slight stiffness in his injured leg, and the warm sun was like a heating pad on his various bumps and bruises. An entire day without any physical mishaps! Maybe his luck was finally changing. Maybe tonight he'd figure out how to get the letter back, maybe Sierra and he would—

From the corner of his eye Ben caught a flash of black-and-white darting through the underbrush just to Sierra's right. He halted in his tracks. "Hey, be careful, I think—"

Charlemagne suddenly snorted and kicked at the brush, the only abrupt movement Ben had ever seen the mule make.

Sierra whirled around. "What the heck—?"

"Duck!" Ben shouted, backpedaling for all he was worth.

"Char, what's gotten into you?"

"Sierra, watch out—"

"Uh-oh!"

"—for that—"

Sierra shrieked.

An acrid, earthy aroma filled the air.

"—skunk," Ben finished lamely.

Chapter Seven

"I don't suppose you have any tomato juice," Ben said as the merry band straggled back into camp.

"Thirsty?"

"It's the best thing for getting rid of that mule's, uh, smell."

Sierra threw him a wry look. "I *know* that. And yes, I have some. Grandpa always kept it around in case of skunk attacks." She lifted the saddlebags off Charlemagne's back, holding them at arm's length as she draped them over a tree limb.

Leaving Ben gingerly holding the mule's halter, Sierra ducked into the tent and emerged with a large, slightly rusted can of tomato juice, which she proceeded to open with the can opener on her Swiss Army knife.

Ben eyed the can dubiously. "How old is that stuff, anyway?"

"We're not going to drink it—we're going to pour it over Char."

"Better take that hat off first."

"Huh? Oh, good idea." She plucked at the knotted ribbon tying the mule's hat on. "Drat, this thing won't come loose."

"For God's sake, cut it off with your knife. I never saw such a mangy-looking hat in my life, anyway."

Sierra glared at him.

"Don't you think it makes that poor mule look just a little...undignified?" Ben asked.

"Grandpa himself put this hat on Charlemagne, and I never wanted to take it off. Okay?" At last she succeeded in working the knot loose. Pinching her nose, she also pinched the hat between thumb and forefinger and hung it on a nearby branch. "Okay, Char—hold still, now."

Charlemagne, however, wasn't about to let himself be marinated without a fight. By the time Ben and Sierra finished rubbing the mule down with tomato juice, they both looked as if they'd been thoroughly doused themselves.

"If I'd known a mule was going to shake tomato juice all over me today, I'd have brought along a change of clothing," Ben grumbled.

Sierra bestowed a sweet smile on him. "Guess you'll have to wear your birthday suit for a while after you rinse out your clothes in the stream."

"You wish."

"Don't flatter yourself."

"Didn't you save any of your grandfather's clothes?"

"What on earth for? I gave them all to Pete." She yanked on Charlemagne's halter. "Come on, you troublesome beast. Let's go dunk ourselves, shall we?" As she headed for the stream, mule in tow, she called over her shoulder, "And I don't want to see you spying on us from the bushes, either."

Ben was about to launch a nasty retort after her when a sudden thought occurred to him. A sly smile crept over his face. "What do you take me for, some kind of Peeping Tom?" he shouted after her good-naturedly.

Then he plunked himself down on the ground, drew up his knees and waited.

At the edge of the stream, Sierra did a quick reconnaissance to make sure she was unobserved. Then she stripped off her clothes and stuck her toe into the water. "Oh, Lord!" she gasped. "Char, you're not going to be too happy about this."

She temporarily forgot the frigid temperature while she struggled to drag the reluctant mule into the stream. "Come on, you ornery critter! Do you want to smell like skunk and tomato the rest of your life? What if some gorgeous lady mule comes along while you reek like this? *Then* you'll be sorry."

Somehow, with a combination of pushing, pulling, pleas and threats, Sierra managed to maneuver Charlemagne into the creek. As she scooped up handfuls of water to splash over the mule's haunches, a vivid flashback forced its way into her mind: memories of the warm, whirling Jacuzzi at her health club in Los Angeles.

She gritted her teeth and banished the image from her mind. "This is much healthier," she muttered. "Gets the old circulation pumping." For good measure she scrubbed her own arms and legs with sand, gulping in quick lungfuls of air as the freezing water swirled around her waist.

All at once Charlemagne decided he'd soaked long enough, and Sierra had to lunge for his halter as he began to thrash toward the stream bank. Somehow she lost her footing on a moss-covered rock, and before she could catch her balance she pitched forward, managing a high-pitched yelp before the icy water closed over her head.

She emerged thoroughly drenched, teeth chattering, limbs quaking from the incredible cold, just in time to see Charlemagne vanish into the trees.

"Sierra?"

With a cry of outraged protest she ducked beneath the water again, clutching her arms over her breasts. "You—you lecherous hyena! Get away from here! You promised not to peek!"

"Calm down, will you?" came Ben's amused voice from behind the bushes at the top of the embankment. "I swear my eyes are closed. But I heard you scream—"

"So of course you thought you had to come to my rescue again." She barely recognized her own voice, so distorted was it by her rattling teeth.

"Guess I was wrong. You obviously don't require any assistance. But tell me one thing—are you planning to put those same clothes right back on?"

Sierra thrust a groan through her clenched jaws. "You rat! Why didn't you remind me to bring a change of clothing down here?"

"Oh, I wouldn't presume to make suggestions," Ben replied in a voice barbed with mirth, "since you've made it quite clear you're perfectly capable of handling your own affairs without any advice from me."

Well, he had her there. Sierra's instinctive response was that she would rather freeze to death in that stream than ask Ben for help. Still, she'd probably pass out first, and he'd no doubt enjoy fishing her dripping, naked body out of the stream.

Through numb lips she squeezed out the words, "Would you *please* go back to the tent and bring me something to wear?"

His chuckle drifted down the slope, and she spent the next several minutes fantasizing about setting Ben Halliday adrift on an iceberg somewhere in the northernmost reaches of the Arctic.

"Here I come, ready or not!"

By now the only remaining feeling in Sierra's body was relief at his return. "Keep your eyes closed, you varmint!"

Ben emerged from the bushes, one hand shading his eyes while the other extended a bundle of clothing.

"Toss it on the ground right there. No, don't come any closer!"

"Oh, for Pete's sake—"

"I mean it! And quit peeking."

"I am *not*—"

"You are too! I can see your beady little eyes between your fingers."

"Hey, maybe you'd like someone else to help you instead."

"Well, if you can't behave like a gentleman for one minute—"

"Gentleman? That's a laugh! You've called me every kind of animal life from pond scum to jackal, and now you expect me to act like a gentleman?"

"Turn your back."

"This may come as a shock to you, but I *have* seen naked women before. I'm not going to lose control at the sight of your gorgeous, sexy—"

"I have absolutely no interest in the history of your love life. Now, turn your back."

Slumping his shoulders with an exaggerated sigh, Ben wheeled around. Sierra paused a moment, then darted out of the stream and scooped up the pile of clothes Ben had dropped next to his feet. In a flash she scampered uphill to the concealing shelter of a thick Douglas fir.

It took several attempts before she could stab her trembling legs into the tan corduroys, her shivering, goose-pimpled arms into the sleeves of her black pull-over sweater. Her stiffened fingers refused to cooperate, and she fumbled helplessly with the zipper of her slacks until she heard Ben call, "Need any help?"

Oh, wouldn't he love that? She finally jerked the zipper up, gathered her wits about her and stepped into the open. Ben was watching her from below, his mouth twitching in a devilish grin that made her simultaneously want to shove him into the creek…and to shed her clothes again. Slowly.

She must be suffering from exposure. Her heart was thumping a mile a minute, and her skin prickled with a strange tingling. Probably frostbite.

"Your turn," she announced.

"Whatever you say," Ben replied with a sly grin. He began to strip off his clothes immediately, never taking his eyes from Sierra's. She swallowed. "I'll just, uh, go now, and, er, let you have some…privacy."

"Don't leave on my account." His words trailed after her as she beat a hasty retreat back to camp. The next sounds she heard were a loud splash and an ear-splitting whoop.

By the time she heard Ben rustling through the bushes, Sierra had succeeded in recapturing Charlemagne and tying him up to his favorite tree. Now she was working on starting a fire. If only those matches weren't tucked into Ben's shirt pocket . . .

Bold as you please, he stepped into the clearing with nothing to shield himself but an armload of soggy clothing. Sierra sucked in her breath and quickly turned her back on him, but not before getting a tantalizing glimpse of his boldly sculpted, Norse-god-like physique.

"Haven't you one single ounce of propriety?" she mumbled.

"This was your idea, remember? And a darn clever way for you to ogle my body, too."

"Don't be ridiculous." A light-headed fog drifted over her. "Here. Cover yourself up." She snatched up the green army blanket and flung it backwards over her shoulder.

"Well, as long as you're done gawking at me, I *am* getting a mite chilly."

How peculiar. A minute ago Sierra's teeth had been chattering, but now an odd, unsettling warmth had stolen over her limbs.

"Why don't you light a fire?" Ben suggested.

"Light it yourself," she grumbled.

"Somehow I knew you were going to say that." He crouched beside her, the blanket draped around him like a toga. With a flourish he produced the matchbook. "Lucky for us I had the foresight to take this out of my pocket before washing my clothes in the stream." He pushed the scattered sticks into a pile and ignited them immediately. "I'm sorry, what did you say?"

"Nothing."

"Hmm. I could have sworn you just made some kind of nasty comment."

Ben's thigh was pressing against Sierra's, making her too vividly aware that only a couple thin layers of fabric separated them. She clambered to her feet. "I'd better hang your clothes up to dry." She felt his eyes on her as she moved away.

"I rinsed out yours, too. You left them down by the stream. Guess you were in too much of a hurry."

She ignored his amused smirk, scooping up the wet clothes and hanging them over some bushes. Why couldn't this little run-in with the skunk have happened earlier in the day, so the sun could dry the clothing quickly? An artist's palette of red, orange and lavender splashed across the western horizon, providing a breathtaking view but not much heat. It was liable to be midmorning before Ben was safely garbed in his clothes again. Until then Sierra would have to keep fending off the sensual images and disturbing desires aroused by that sleek male body moving around beneath that damn blanket.

When she returned to the campfire with two packages of freeze-dried beef stew, she seated herself on the opposite side, as far away from Ben as she could get. He arched an eyebrow at the sight of the aluminum saucepan she positioned over the flames. "Is that the same one Johnny Appleseed used to wear on his head?"

"I admit it's seen better days, but it still works. Of course, if you don't dare eat anything cooked in it, I could wolf down all this stew by myself."

"And spoil that girlish figure? I couldn't let you do that."

"Gee, thanks."

"How come you're sitting way over there? That creature squirted your mule, not me. Don't tell me I smell like eau de skunk."

"No..."

"Of course, maybe I should find out what *you* smell like before I invite you to sit next to me." He sidled around the fire and inched up next to her. Before she could dodge out of reach, he buried his face in her neck and inhaled deeply. "Mmm, you smell delicious. All clean and outdoorsy."

"Cut that out," she warned, nearly tipping the pan into the fire. "Or I'll dump this stew into your lap."

"Sierra, Sierra," Ben sighed, drawing back. "I've never met a woman with such violent tendencies. Why can't you be nice to me for even a little while?"

"Because what *you're* doing isn't very nice. Pretending to be interested in me just so you can earn a big bonus from my father."

With a groan Ben fell backward and propped himself on his elbows. "I thought we had that all straightened out. You don't still believe that ridiculous theory, do you?"

Sierra stirred furiously. "What else am I supposed to believe? You drop into my life from out of the blue, tell me a pack of lies and won't fess up when I finally figure you out."

"Look, maybe I haven't been perfectly straightforward with you—"

"Ha! *That's* an understatement."

"—but I swear to you, I've never met your father, never worked for your father, didn't even know who your father *was* when I met you."

She continued stirring, trying to scrape the burning stew off the bottom of the pan.

"Sierra? You do believe me, don't you?" Ben crooked a finger around one of her stray curls, lightly stroking the sensitive skin behind her ear.

She shivered, but didn't tilt her head away from him.

"I can't bear for you to think me some kind of...paid stud or something."

Sierra chuckled.

"Well, that's what you think, isn't it?" His low voice tickled her ear. "Let me prove you wrong." He drew his finger lightly down her backbone. "Believe me, there's no way I could fake what I feel for you. There isn't enough money in the world."

A delicious languor enveloped Sierra, radiating from the pressure of Ben's hand splayed across the base of her spine. Her eyes closed, and her head rolled back. Oh, what heaven it would be to succumb to the sweet yearnings Ben stirred inside her! How easy it would be simply to shove aside her doubts and surrender to the magic of his touch....

The smell of burning stew jarred her from her treacherous thoughts. "Yipes!" With a clatter she knocked the pan aside, nearly spilling the contents into the flames. "Ouch, darn it! I need a pot holder or something."

"Here, use this." Ben pressed a corner of the blanket into her hand, and without thinking, she pulled it forward to wrap around the pan's handle. She nearly dropped the stew again when she turned and saw how much of Ben she'd inadvertently exposed. Flickering flames and the sunset's dying glow burnished his nude male torso, emphasizing the lean, sturdy lines of his muscular build. The blanket slashed across his thighs, revealing his long, golden-haired legs and leaving very little to the imagination.

Sierra's imagination ran amok, anyway. She averted her gaze, but not before she saw the sizzling sparkle in Ben's eyes and the sexy quirk of his mouth. "Why, sweetheart, if you'd prefer me without the blanket, all you have to do is ask." He leaned forward and purred in her ear, "No need to resort to all this subterfuge."

"What I'd prefer is this camp without *you* in it," she retorted, flinching from the low rumbling vibrations that traveled along her nerve endings. "Now, shut up and eat." She slopped some stew into a tin bowl and thrust it in his direction.

She picked up the pan—thank goodness aluminum cooled off so quickly!—and raised a spoonful of stew to her lips.

"Trying to save on dishwashing detergent?" Ben asked.

She paused. "I only have one bowl."

"We could share it."

"No, thanks."

He shrugged, then sampled his stew. He chewed thoughtfully before swallowing. "Up to your usual culinary standards, I see."

Sierra smacked her lips. "Actually it tastes kind of scorched to me."

"That's what I mean."

She lifted her chin. "You can go hungry if you'd rather."

"Well, if that's the only alternative..." Ben ladled another bite into his mouth and beamed at her. "Mmm, yummy," he pronounced, licking his lips.

"And would you mind covering yourself up? There's nothing more unappetizing than staring at a hairy chest."

"Quit staring, then."

Sierra blushed to the roots of her chestnut curls, but at least Ben tugged the blanket up around his shoulders so she could finally concentrate on eating.

By the time she scraped the pan clean, Sierra's stomach was filled, but some other part of her still felt empty and unsatisfied. She tried to ignore it by bustling around the camp, rearranging their damp clothing, rinsing out their dishes in a bucket of water she fetched from the creek. All the while she sensed Ben tracking her every move like radar.

Darn him, anyway! Why couldn't he accept that the game was over, go back to the city and leave her alone? But a tiny part of her was glad Ben was so persistent, that he seemed determined to stick to her like flypaper until her father called him off.

Ye gods, he was making her nervous as a turkey on the day before Thanksgiving! She dropped the bowl on the ground, then knocked over the water bucket when she grabbed for it. Now she'd have to schlepp all the way down to the stream again, or else ask Ben to do it.

She'd rather ask Attila the Hun to buy Girl Scout cookies.

When Sierra returned after refilling the water bucket, Ben was lying on his back, hands folded behind his head, watching her. "Boy, this is the life, isn't it? A roaring campfire...a galaxy of stars overhead...the scent of wet mule wafting on the breeze...say, what's for dessert, anyway?" he asked cheerfully.

"Help yourself," she replied with a wave of her hand. "I've got a whole tent full of junk food."

"I've got a better idea," Ben said, pushing himself onto his side and letting the blanket fall across his ribs.

"I'll bet," she said, circling wide to avoid his grasp. "You're just full of suggestions, aren't you?"

"*I* was thinking about that flask of whiskey," he said, placing his hand over his heart. "What were *you* thinking about?"

"Murder," she grumbled, going over to root through the tent. "Here. Let the good times roll." She lobbed the silver flask at him.

"Aren't you going to join me?"

The evening *was* turning a bit nippy. Maybe a little swig of the ol' firewater wouldn't be such a bad idea. For strictly medicinal purposes, of course.

Sierra lowered herself next to the fire, just close enough to Ben so she could take the whiskey from his outstretched hand. As she raised the flask to her lips, she couldn't help envisioning how his mouth had closed around it moments before.

Once again she forgot to sip cautiously and nearly choked as the potent liquid seared her throat. Ben grinned at her, making her far more intoxicated than one gulp of whiskey could have.

When she handed the flask back, a shadow crossed his face. "Your fingers are ice-cold."

"My hands got wet when I refilled the water bucket."

Ben set the flask aside and scooted next to her. Before Sierra could protest, he'd imprisoned her hands between his, rubbing briskly back and forth. "Poor baby. Your fingers feel like icicles."

Actually her fingers felt pretty nice at the moment, but she didn't bother to correct him.

He slid one hand up her arm. "Good grief, it's not just your hands! You're cold all over!"

"I guess it *has* gotten kind of chilly since the sun went down...."

"It's more than that. I think you took too long a swim in the stream earlier."

"That's because I had to wait for someone to bring me my clothes."

"That's only because you forgot them yourself."

"That's only because—" A sneeze cut short her reply.

With a worried frown Ben laid his hand across her forehead. "Hmm. You don't *feel* like you're running a fever...."

"I'm fine," she insisted, batting his hand away. Then she sneezed again.

"Don't try to tell me this is your hay fever acting up all of a sudden. You're coming down with a cold, and it's no wonder—splashing around in a frigid stream all day, sitting out in the night air with nothing on but that flimsy sweater—"

"*You* picked out the sweater—"

"And I'd never forgive myself if you caught pneumonia as a result. Come here." Ben unwrapped his blanket from one shoulder.

"*Eek!* What do you think you're—"

"Get in here where it's nice and warm."

"Ben, no!"

Before Sierra could escape, he'd bundled her into the blanket next to him.

"This is no time for modesty," he told her.

"This is no time for—for— oh, lord." Sierra gulped.

"There, isn't that much better?" Ben rubbed his hands briskly up and down her arms, igniting a delightful, tingling heat that had nothing to do with friction.

"Mmm," she responded, suddenly incapable of verbal communication.

He kneaded her back and shoulders with expert thoroughness, leaving her limp as a rag doll. Warmth invaded every cell in her body. Tension seeped away, replaced by a slowly building fire whose flames licked along her flesh wherever Ben stroked and prodded her.

"Now I know what heaven feels like," she said in a thick voice.

"Sweetheart, heaven feels a lot better than this," Ben growled in her ear. "And I'm going to prove it to you."

"Mmm..." Sierra descended into incoherent moaning again as Ben worked his hands down her spine, pushing, squeezing, massaging that fine line between pain and pleasure.

When he slipped his hands beneath her sweater, Sierra didn't utter a peep of protest. She floated lazily, suspended in a dreamlike trance that vaporized any resistance, worry or suspicion. Pure sensation. That was her only conscious awareness, and she reveled in it.

Until Ben circled her waist with his arms and slid his hands up to gently cup her breasts. "Um, Ben...just what do you think you're—"

"Shh." His whisper was a heated gust teasing the nape of her neck. "Trying to make you warm." He continued his tender massaging of her pliant flesh, molding her breasts into the hollows of his big hands like an expert sculptor working with soft clay. "Am I succeeding?"

"Hmm?"

"Are you getting warm?" He pressed a kiss into the cleft just above her collarbone.

"Yes...warm..." Her head fell back to rest against his shoulder, and his bristly jaw prickled against her cheek with delightful abrasion. A tiny pang of disappointment pricked her when he shifted his attention from her breasts to her thighs and began to rub his hands briskly back and forth over her pants.

No doubt about it, she *was* getting warm. Even a bit overheated, perhaps. Whether her rise in temperature resulted from Ben's vigorous massage or the sharing of his body heat or simply the blood-simmering excitement of his nearness, Sierra couldn't tell.

Whatever the source, she was definitely heating up. Maybe getting a little *too* hot. How else to explain this sudden overwhelming urge to strip off her clothes and bare her skin to the night air?

Ben drew her knee up so he could cradle her foot between his hands. His chin rested cozily on her shoulder while he pressed his thumbs into the arch of her foot, then twisted each of her toes between his fingers. A wonderful tingling spread up her calves as he took her other foot and continued his thorough ministrations.

"Such dainty feet," he mused, his vocal chords vibrating against her skin. "There! Have I missed a spot anyplace?"

"Mmm, no, I don't think so."

"What about . . . right here?" He lifted her curls and planted a leisurely kiss on the nape of Sierra's neck, sending a jolt of electricity zapping down her spine.

"No, I think you got that spot before . . . ."

"Then how about . . . here?" He nuzzled her temple.

"Well . . ."

"I *know* I didn't miss these." His hands skimmed beneath her sweater and found her breasts again. He flicked his thumbs across the hardened peaks.

"Oh, God," she moaned.

"Sierra . . ." Ben's voice was muffled as he buried his face in her hair. With one swift, sure motion he spanned her waist with his strong hands and twisted her around to lie across his lap. The blanket fell away, exposing his torso as he cradled her in his arms and gazed down at her. Sierra could see the rapid flutter of his heartbeat as his chest rose and fell.

She wasn't conscious of holding her breath as Ben lowered his head to hers, eyes glowing like fiery cobalt, until his face blocked out the stars and he seized her lips with a passionate urgency that threatened to drive all the air from her lungs.

Dizzy, she clung to him while the constellations reeled overhead. She locked her arms around his neck, weaving her fingers through his coarse golden hair. Ben was her only anchor in the explosive, tumultuous upheaval of her universe, and Sierra hung on to him for dear life. He *was* her life, wasn't he? But no, wait, how could that be? Ben was a double-dealing, unscrupulous scoundrel . . . wasn't he?

Then why did she feel at this moment that she'd gladly, willingly follow him to the ends of the earth, no matter what his reasons for leading her there?

Could it possibly be she was in *love* with this double-dealing, unscrupulous scoundrel?

Instantly Sierra shoved the thought aside as too horrible to contemplate. Because if it were true that she'd somehow fallen in love with Ben, she was in big, big trouble.

But she couldn't so easily ignore the insistent, eager pressure of his mouth on hers, not when he stroked so languidly into the deepest recesses of her mouth before twining his tongue deliciously with hers. Not when the musky male scent of him filled her senses and the caress of his hands on her body sent her soaring into orbit.

Not when every molecule in her body was clamoring for his touch, straining toward him with agonizing, rapturous anticipation.

When Ben finally raised his head, his lips glistened with moisture, his eyes flared with wild, urgent intensity. His breath came in ragged gusts. "Sweetheart," he gasped, placing his hand alongside her face. His fingers trembled slightly. "Sierra, you feel so wonderful, you're so warm and sweet. . . ." A shadow of regret or sorrow drifted across his handsome, tormented face. "Ah, darling, if only. . . if only. . ."

The rest of his words were smothered between their lips as he bent his head to hers for another earth-shattering, heart-wrenching kiss. Then, almost before Sierra realized it, Ben had loosened her clothing and cast it aside like a handful of leaves. He caressed her with wandering hands that trailed a path of shimmering desire in their wake. He was like the prince in the Sleeping Beauty fairy tale, only instead of waking her instantly with one kiss, he brought her gradually to life, inch by square inch over every new place he touched her.

Somehow the blanket became entangled around their limbs, and when Ben tugged it impatiently aside to free their movements, Sierra felt the hard, pulsating evidence of his desire. With a slight gasp, she tensed. Ben paused, a look of grim yet tender understanding softening the edges of his features.

"I won't pressure you into anything you aren't ready for," he said in a voice harsh with yearning. "Say the word, and we'll stop." He brushed her chin, then trailed one finger down her throat, along the valley between her breasts, across her belly to the quivering juncture of her thighs. He waited.

Sierra's eyes expanded into dark, wavering pools of excitement and uncertainty. Ben was leaving the decision up to her. Not exactly fair, after he'd spent what seemed an eternity stoking her internal fires to the brink of spontaneous combustion.

She wanted Ben with an aching urgency that consumed her in towering flames, nearly blinding her to the consequences of such reckless indulgence. Yet he hadn't taken advantage of her obvious weakness. Surely that meant that somewhere inside, Ben Halliday possessed at least a spark of integrity, a flicker of decency.

Maybe he wasn't rotten to the core, after all. Maybe he was even a man... worth loving.

It was that possibility more than any other consideration that decided for her. Sierra refused to believe that she could have fallen so completely under the spell of a man with absolutely no redeeming qualities. Something fundamentally honest about Ben, something basically good and honorable and true beckoned her.

Her lips barely moved as she whispered, "Don't stop, Ben. Don't... stop."

Joy, relief, expectation flared in his eyes. "Never," he replied, shifting his arm beneath her shoulders to lay her gently on the blanket. "I'll never, ever stop...." His face blurred into a kaleidoscope of whirling sensations, desires and emotions as he lowered himself on top of Sierra. He entwined his legs with hers, and she surrendered to the delirious pleasure of his long, hard body pressed against her heated flesh.

She clutched handfuls of his hair when he dropped his mouth to her breasts and drew moist, lazy circles with his tongue. When he flicked teasingly across her taut, straining nipples, she couldn't stifle the cry that erupted from her throat.

She writhed against him, seeking release for the smoldering pressure building up in her abdomen. Only Ben could free her from this maddening, desperate desire and send her soaring to heights of pleasure she could barely begin to imagine....

Then, with a groan of anguish, Ben pushed himself off Sierra and rolled away. "I can't do it," he said in a strangled voice. "Damn it, it's not right! I just can't do it." He buried his face in his hands, shaking his head. A smothered stream of curses escaped through his fingers.

Sierra stared at him with mounting horror and humiliation. After she'd practically begged him to make love to her, he was spurning her rash, foolish surrender! What an idiot she'd been, what a lovesick, passion-besotted—

"I'm sorry." Ben smoothed back his tousled hair and looked at her. Suddenly Sierra realized she was stark naked, and the idea didn't hold nearly the same appeal it had moments ago. "Sierra, the thing is—"

She grabbed the blanket and flung it around herself as she jumped to her feet.

"Hey, wait a second! Where are you going? *I* need that blanket!"

Sierra was about to shoot a scornful reply over her shoulder when she saw Ben scrambling after her. The prospect of being pursued by six feet of lean, naked masculinity was more than she could deal with at the moment.

Quickly she unwrapped the blanket and hurled it at his head, hoping to block his vision while she scooped up her sweater and pants. By the time Ben finished thrashing around and emerged from the scratchy folds, Sierra was backing toward the tent, covering herself as best she could with her hastily retrieved bundle of clothing.

"You keep away from me, Ben Halliday, you—you slinking weasel! You slithering snake! You—you—slimy barracuda!"

"Barracuda?"

"I mean it! Stay back! Don't come any closer!"

"Sierra, for God's sake, you have to let me explain—"

"I don't have to let you do anything!" Her backward retreat came to a temporary halt when she bumped into the tent.

"Sweetheart, there's a perfectly reasonable explanation for this, if you'll only stand still and listen—"

"Don't you 'sweetheart' me. I'm warning you, Ben Halliday, I've got Pete's shotgun around here someplace, and I know how to use it!" She ducked her head and backed into the tent. The vision of Ben clutching the green blanket around his waist like a hula skirt would have struck Sierra as vastly humorous under any other circumstances. But right now she was too unnerved by the determined slant of his brow, the exasperated scowl on his face.

"Don't you dare follow me in here! Get out! Get out, I tell you!"

Ben kept advancing with the relentlessness of a bulldozer. Sierra licked her lips, darting her eyes from side to side as she searched frantically for an escape route out of this trap.

Then she tripped over an open box of Yummee Cocoa Crunches and toppled backward, arms cartwheeling through the air, clothes flying in all directions. She landed with a jarring thud that knocked the breath out of her.

Ben dove on top of her, pinning her wrists to the ground and imprisoning her with the unyielding length of his body. A muscle rippled along his clenched jaw, and when he spoke, his breath rustled the wisps of hair curling at her temples.

"For once—just *once*!—I'm going to talk and you're going to listen. Got that? *I* talk, *you* listen. Think you can remember that?"

Sierra glowered at him. "What choice do I—"

"Ah-ah-ah . . . no talking."

Even without words the glare she aimed at Ben certainly got her message across. She chafed under the handcuffs of his fingers, squirming beneath the oppressive weight of his body. When even Sierra had to admit there would be no escape until she allowed Ben to say his piece, she collapsed in surrender.

A temporary truce, however. Because as soon as Ben released her, Sierra was going to kick his scurvy hide out of these mountains, back to Los Angeles and all the way into the Pacific Ocean.

"Okay," she said. "Talk."

Chapter Eight

The tip of Ben's nose itched, but he didn't dare scratch it. If he freed even one of Sierra's wrists, she was likely to take a swing at him.

Now that she'd grudgingly agreed to let him explain why he'd stopped making love to her, Ben hadn't the faintest idea what to say. He wasn't sure he understood it himself. All he knew was that he'd never taken a woman to bed under false pretenses, and he wasn't about to start now. Not with Sierra. She was far too special to him.

For an instant Ben considered spilling out the whole story—the letter, his parents, his crusade for revenge against Quentin Jericho—all of it.

Then he remembered the stark terror of those moments before the plane crash. He remembered the ruthless, evil glint in Jericho's eyes when Ben had confronted him at the funeral and threatened to expose him. And he remembered Addie's innocent warning that at least one of Jericho's thugs was hot on their trail.

Telling Sierra the truth might be the same as signing her death warrant.

She wouldn't be completely out of danger until Ben reached the news media with proof of Jericho's sleazy past. Until then, the less Sierra knew, the better her chances for emerging unscathed from this whole mess.

"The reason I stopped making love to you," Ben said, "is because you don't trust me."

"Why on earth *should* I trust you?" Sierra replied. "You've done nothing but lie to me from the very beginning. Pretending you were looking for my grandfather, then handing me that cockamamy story about being a journalist."

"You're right," he admitted. Sierra's eyebrows flew up in amazement. "I *have* lied to you all along."

"I knew it," she said. But her voice was strangely devoid of triumph or gloating. In fact she sounded rather unhappy. "My father *is* paying you to lure me back to Sloane Enterprises."

"No!" The word came out louder than Ben had intended, startling them both. "That much of what I told you is true. Your father didn't hire me, I've never met the man, and I'm not part of one of his schemes."

Sierra's lips curved into a skeptical frown. "Then just who exactly are you, Ben Halliday, and what the hell are you doing here?"

"I can't tell you."

"Oh, for God's sake." She began to struggle again. "Let me up, damn it. I've heard enough of your double-talk. You must be some kind of politician. Is that it? You're trying to establish personal contact with each of your constituents?"

"I'm not letting you go until I've finished what I have to say." Ben clamped down more firmly on her wrists. Astounding how much stronger Sierra was than she looked.

"But you haven't said *anything*! All you've done is hand me a bunch of gobbledygook, accusing me of not trusting you, then in the next breath admitting you're a liar."

Ben blew a lock of hair out of his eyes. Or tried to, anyway. It fell immediately in front of his face again. "Look, no more lies, okay? I promise."

Sierra smiled angelically. "Okay. You've convinced me. I'm not mad anymore. You can get off me now."

"Oh, no, you don't!"

She batted her long lashes at him. "Why, whatever do you mean? You asked me to let you explain, and I did. You want me to believe you, and I do. What's the problem?"

"The problem is that you still don't believe me, and you're still mad!" he nearly shouted.

She blinked. "Gee, sounds to me like *you're* the one who's mad."

"Mad as a hatter," he mumbled under his breath, "for trying to reason with you."

"I beg your pardon?"

"Nothing. Never mind." Inhaling deeply, Ben tried again. "I *did* come here looking for your grandfather, but not to write a story about him. We had a...business deal of sorts."

"You and *Grandpa*?" Suspicion laced her voice. "What kind of deal? Buying the Brooklyn Bridge? Swampland in Florida?"

"That's between your grandfather and me." Surprisingly Sierra seemed to accept this. Maybe there was still a bit of Fortune 500 left inside her. "The last time I saw Caleb was back in March. I didn't know he...had passed away."

Sierra's throat convulsed slightly as she swallowed.

Ben rushed on, trying to ignore the glitter of moisture in her eyes. "I'm asking you to take my word that I can't reveal any more about our deal than I already have. Believe me, if I could tell you, I would. I'm not going to lie to you anymore, Sierra. What I've told you is the absolute truth, even though it's incomplete."

Her only response was a forlorn sniffle.

"And the other thing I want to make absolutely clear is that I am *not* being paid to trick you, or seduce you, or— oh, sweetheart, don't! Please don't cry!"

The tear leaking from the corner of Sierra's eye and trickling down her temple finally got to Ben. Without hesitation he released her and pulled her into his embrace. When she linked her arms around his neck and pressed her cheek against his shoulder, a profound, protective tenderness surged through Ben, sweeping aside any thought but to comfort her, to keep her safe and make her happy.

Her thin, fragile body quivered against him like a willow tree in the wind. He patted her shoulder, pressed a kiss on her forehead, feeling helpless and strong and happy and sad all at the same time. "There, there," he crooned over and over—meaningless words that soothed more by tone than content.

"I'm sorry," she finally choked into the side of his neck. "I don't usually lose control like that, but I just miss Grandpa so darn much, and sometimes—sometimes when I look at the mess I've made of things, I wonder what he'd say if he could see me now, how he'd shake his head in disgust and—"

Ben drew back to study her tearstained face in surprise. "What are you talking about, sweetie? What mess?"

"Oh . . . you know. You've pointed it out yourself on more than one occasion." She flung her arm around the tent. "Look at this place! We're lucky it doesn't collapse on our heads. I've been scrambling around these mountains for two months, and I haven't found one speck of gold yet. I don't like sleeping on the ground and I hate bugs and snakes and taking baths in the stream and eating crummy freeze-dried backpacking food and I—I can't even start a fire!"

Ben chuckled, drawing her head under his chin again. "Sweetheart, that's not true! Why, only this morning, when I woke up—"

"I used a match!" she wailed. "I snuck one out of your pocket while you were—were sleeping!" Her voice disintegrated into a fresh storm of sobs.

Ben's laughter rumbled deep in his chest. A second later Sierra punched him in the ribs. "What's so funny?" she demanded, indignation vanquishing her sorrow.

"You are," he said, gasping. "I've never in my life met anyone as determined, as obstinate as you are."

"You haven't met my father," she muttered.

Ben didn't miss the significance of that statement, but he wasn't about to be sidetracked. "It's one thing to be a little...inept about living up here, but you don't even *like* roughing it! Why can't you admit this hasn't worked out and go back where you belong? Not necessarily to Sloane Enterprises, or even Los Angeles," he said, whisking a finger across her lips to forestall her outraged protest. "You could move someplace else and start over, find some new career that's more suitable, more enjoyable than slogging around in an icy creek all day sifting through mud.''

Sierra giggled. "You're making it sound more glamorous than it really is.''

"Well, there you are. Something to consider at least, isn't it?''

A frown creased her brow. "I don't know. I absolutely hate—and I mean *hate*!—the idea of being a quitter, of slinking back to Mom and Daddy with my tail between my legs—"

"Sierra, for Pete's sake, they're your parents! They're not going to say, 'We told you so.' And even if they *do*—" he continued when she gave him an oh-yeah look "—who cares? You can't let other people's opinions dictate how you run your life.''

Ben shifted her so she sat on the ground facing him. "Sierra, you have to live your own life. Not your grandfather's.''

"But he left everything to me.''

"Because he loved you, not because he wanted to trap you into a miserable existence.''

She twisted her hands together. "I feel like I'd be letting him down again. I neglected him during his last years, and this seems the least I can do to make up for it.''

"Sierra, how is being unhappy going to make up for the past? And I'm sure you didn't neglect your grandfather as much as you think. Didn't you see him on holidays?''

"Well, yes, but—"

"Did you write to him?''

"Writing's not the same as—"

"Did you always remember his birthday?''

"Of course, but—"

"Sierra." Ben clasped her hands in his. "Your grandfather struck me as an intelligent, perceptive man. Even behind that long shaggy beard of his, I sensed that the moment we met. I bet he understood that when human beings grow up, they inevitably grow away from the people they depended on as children. That's simply a fact of life."

Reluctant agreement was gradually displacing the doubt in Sierra's expression.

"Do you think your grandfather wanted to chain you to a way of life you simply aren't cut out for? Do you think it would make him happy to see you suffer?"

"Don't be silly."

"Well, then. Maybe you should rethink some of your decisions."

She chewed on her lip and stared at the floor. In a moment she shrugged one shoulder. "Maybe."

Ben squeezed her hands. "Good. That's all I ask."

She peered at him from beneath knitted eyebrows. "You know, if I didn't know better, I'd think you had some financial stake in persuading me to give all this up."

"Scout's honor." Ben raised three fingers in the Boy Scout salute. With the other hand he made an X across his chest. "Cross my heart. My interest in your well-being has nothing to do with financial gain."

"No? Then what *does* it involve?" she asked with an impish grin.

"Let's just say my interest in you is strictly... personal." He raked her with an appreciative glance. In all the commotion she'd forgotten about modesty, but under Ben's admiring scrutiny, her skin turned pink and she made a grab for the blanket.

"No, don't," he said in a low voice, catching her by the wrist. "Let me look at you."

"Ben," she said helplessly.

He caressed the side of her face, and she tilted her head into his hand, closing her eyes. Releasing her wrist, he traced the outline of her smooth shoulders, her waist, her hips. She was so slender, yet so soft....

When he lifted his hand to her breast, her eyes opened wide and she trembled slightly. As Ben continued to fondle her, Sierra kept her eyes focused on his, her expression transforming from cautious uncertainty to quickening desire. Her eyelids lowered with sultry heaviness; her rosy lips parted slightly as her breath came faster.

Excitement boiled up inside Ben as he kneaded and stroked the creamy mounds, rasping his thumbs across her nipples, reveling in the shivers that racked her body under his touch. His own body responded with a flood of quick, hot passion, and he could barely restrain himself from dragging her down to the ground and taking her with wild, desperate urgency.

Instead he slowly guided Sierra's hand to the hard evidence of his desire, lowering himself to lie beside her. Her eyes brimmed with wonder and longing and secret satisfaction. As she stroked him, hesitantly at first, then with growing confidence, a surge of incredible aching rapture swept through Ben, obliterating the last remnant of his self-control.

Almost the last remnant. As he arched himself above her, Ben paused and managed to grind out, "You do believe me, don't you, darling? That the reason I'm making love to you is because I . . . care about you? Because I want to share these feelings with you?"

A welter of emotions riffled through Sierra's eyes like a shuffled deck of cards. Blood thundered in Ben's ears as he scanned her face for the only answer he could accept, the only response that would allow him to merge his heart, mind and body with hers.

Sierra felt as if she were poised on tiptoe at the brink of a towering cliff. She knew in her heart that if she made love with Ben, her life would never be the same afterward. If he were lying to her again, if he betrayed her after she gave herself so eagerly, so trustingly...

She searched his eyes for a clue to the truth. Would a man who was only using her for some secret purpose hold himself in check as Ben was now? The anguish of overwhelming desire was scrawled plainly across the bold, straining planes and angles of his face. She could see how much his restraint was costing him by the taut cords in his neck and the flickering muscles along his clenched jaw.

What could Ben possibly have to gain by such effort unless what he said was true—that his feelings for her were genuine, his motives so pure that he refused to tarnish them by making love to a woman who didn't trust him?

In Ben's tormented eyes Sierra saw many things, but dishonesty wasn't one of them. As she lifted her fingers to graze his whiskery cheek, she realized with heart-stopping certainty that whatever else Ben Halliday cared about, he cared about her, too.

"Yes," she whispered. "Oh, yes...I believe you, Ben."

His body shuddered as he released a deep breath. He closed his eyes in relief, turning his head to brand a searing kiss into her palm. As he lowered himself toward her, he hesitated one last time. "And you want this as much as I do?"

"As much as you do," she echoed. *More*, she thought. *I love you, Ben.*

Then she forgot this wistful realization as Ben eased himself inside her. She gasped sharply, clutching at his shoulders. His muscles were like taut steel cables beneath her fingers, his heart a thudding, rhythmic accompaniment to her own.

As Ben's hardness filled the soft, molten core of her being, the shared pleasure and fulfillment reflected in his eyes filled an aching void in Sierra's heart—a void she hadn't even known existed before. Somehow the connection of their bodies had also bridged some gaping emotional chasm, astounding Sierra with its profound intimacy and intensity. She sensed what a person born and raised in total isolation from the rest of the world might feel upon first contact with another human being.

She hadn't known what being lonely was until she wasn't alone anymore.

Ben touched his fingers to her face, a brief smile shimmering across the distorted passion of his features before he bent his head to seize her mouth with his. Sierra arched into the curve of his body, matching her movements to his accelerating tempo, marveling at the perfect synchronization of their bodies' responses. Somehow Ben knew the exact moment to be gentle, to pause, to resume his throbbing, thrusting strokes with ever-increasing vigor.

"Sweetheart," he gasped, his breath hot against her ear. "Sierra, this feels so good . . . so right. . . ."

"Oh, yes," she whispered. "Yes . . ."

Whatever doubts she might once have had about the wisdom of their entanglement were banished by the pulsing, smoldering fire building inside her. No matter what the ultimate price for this encounter, she knew the indescribable, unimaginable ecstasy of this moment would be worth it.

Sierra dragged her fingers down the solid, straining wall of Ben's back, familiarizing herself with every square inch of him. When her hands swept across his thigh, she felt a web of scar tissue splayed across his upper leg. As she traced the faint ridges with her fingertips, she remembered Ben's accident and was suddenly possessed by a crazy determination to shield him from any more plane crashes or suffering or sadness.

Then the onslaught of his sensual caresses drove all other awareness from her mind. His hands were everywhere upon her body at once, tangling in her hair, cupping her breasts, skimming across her belly.

Sierra flung back her head as a tortured moan welled up from the very depths of her soul. Ben growled with satisfaction, sliding his hands beneath her hips and pulling her even closer, more intimately against him. "Go ahead and scream," he rasped. "There's no one around to hear us. I want to hear you scream my name...."

His mouth blazed a path of exquisite, soul-shattering delight over her lips, her eyelids, her breasts. As the pace of their lovemaking increased, Sierra felt like a pulsating star on the verge of a supernova, spinning out of control through the galaxy, throbbing, temperature rising, incredible pressure building.

At the exact moment the critical balance was attained, she exploded across the heavens in a blinding conflagration of white-hot, radiant embers. And then she *did* call Ben's name, over and over again, dimly aware that he was shouting her name, too. The agonized rapture warping his chiseled features mirrored her own dazzling ascent into a part of the universe she'd never known existed before.

Together they careened slowly back to earth like two shooting stars falling from the night sky, landing with passions dimmed and cooled, but no less real now that they were stilled.

Sierra lay with her head against Ben's shoulder, listening to the gradual slowing of his breath and the fading thunder of his heartbeat. He turned his head to smile lazily at her as he brushed a damp curl from her forehead. "Comfortable?"

"Mmm, yes. The cold, hard ground never felt so good."

His chuckle rumbled through his chest, vibrating against her ear. "I guess it would have been better in a thick, plush feather bed."

"Nope." She snuggled into the crook of his arm. "It couldn't possibly have been any better."

He kissed her temple. "You're a love, you know that?"

The word stirred something sweet and tender and kind of scary inside Sierra. She took refuge in her usual flippancy. "I'll make you eat those words the next time we're fighting about something."

Ben laughed briefly, but then grew serious. "I don't want to fight with you anymore, Sierra."

"What? And undermine the very foundation of our relationship?"

"Is that what our relationship is based on? Fighting? Arguing? Being constantly at cross-purposes?"

"No..." she said slowly. "But you have to admit, that does spice things up a bit."

Ben groaned. "Any more spice, and my ulcers will flare up again."

She craned her neck to peer at him in surprise. "You have ulcers?"

"Used to. I had a pretty high-pressure job, and I'm afraid I wasn't in the habit of stopping to smell the roses, as they say." He shifted his hold around her shoulders, and she stretched her arm to rest lazily across his chest. "While I was hospitalized after the plane crash, they managed to patch up my ulcers along with the rest of me."

Absently Sierra drew one fingertip in circles through his chest hair. "What kind of high-pressure job did you have?"

She really hadn't intended to trick him into revealing more about himself, but his entire body stiffened. Warily he replied, "Let's not talk about that right now, okay?"

"Ben, I didn't mean—"

"Forget it."

"But I don't want you to think that I was trying to—"

"Sierra, I promise, as soon as it's safe, I'll tell you everything about me. You'll probably get sick of hearing me talk about myself."

"What do you mean, as soon as it's safe?"

He cursed under his breath. "Never mind. Can we change the subject now, please?"

"Uh-oh," she sighed, rolling away from him and folding her arms over her breasts. "Here comes another fight."

Ben's hand sneaked out, and his fingers crawled spiderlike down the curve of her waist. "The only thing I want to fight about," he said, "is who's hogging the blanket."

Sierra flinched as if he'd stuck an ice cube on her skin. "Cut that out!"

"Oho, so we're a bit ticklish, are we?"

"No, *we're* not. I don't know about you, but I am definitely *not* ticklish, so— Ben, stop it! Knock it off!"

"Hmm, ticklish here... and here... and here... and how about there?"

Sierra shrieked. "Enough, already! I told you, I'm not—"

Ben rolled on top of her and imprisoned her body with his while he continued his maddening assault. "Admit it! Tell me you're ticklish! I won't stop till you say it!"

"Never!" Dissolving in a fit of hysterical giggles, Sierra resolved to die laughing before she'd surrender. Ben's eyes sparkled with amused determination, and his quick reflexes parried her every attempt to escape. "Okay!" she gasped finally. "I give up! I'm ticklish!"

"What? I can't hear you."

"I'm ticklish!" she howled.

Instantly he rolled off her and propped himself on one elbow to observe her with casual scrutiny. "I thought so," he said.

She thumped him on the shoulder. "You monster! Don't you know that tickling is a form of torture?"

"In that case, let me make it up to you. Come here." With that, he reached across her to grasp the edge of the blanket, using it to pull her into his embrace.

As the scratchy folds enveloped Sierra, joyful laughter bubbled up inside her. She wrapped her arms around Ben and sank eagerly into bliss.

She awoke nestled in Ben's arms, the blanket wrapped around them both like a fuzzy cocoon. The first gray light of dawn allowed her to study the way sleep altered his face, blurring the sharp angles so he appeared younger, more relaxed, but definitely just as handsome.

Fondly she ruffled his hair and whispered, "At least you don't snore."

Without opening his eyes, Ben mumbled, "Wish I could say the same about you."

She pinched his nose. "How unchivalrous! Positively ungallant, if you ask me." She sniffed, then resumed her observation of him with bright-eyed interest. "So, what's the routine here? Am I supposed to fix you breakfast or something?"

He pried open one eye. "Well," he said in a gravelly voice, "if you were any other woman, I'd insist upon it. But considering it's you..."

"Monster," she replied good-naturedly. She snaked one arm out from beneath the blanket's warmth and fumbled through the stash of supplies piled behind her. One after another she picked up a box, brought it in front of her eyes and tossed it aside. "Aha! Here we go!"

She plucked a Yummee Macaroon out of its bright yellow box, took a bite and offered the rest to Ben. His eyes were closed again, so she nudged the savory morsel between his lips.

Ben quickly plucked the macaroon from his lips in disgust. "Isn't it a little early for junk food? What time is it, anyway?'' He groped for his watch, then squinted blearily at it. "Good lord, it's still the middle of the night!''

"In Hawaii, maybe. Here it's time to rise and shine.''

He sank back with a groan. "I hardly slept at all last night.''

Sierra pushed herself up on her elbow and poked a finger into his stomach. "And whose fault is that?''

"Oof!'' His muscles knotted in reflex as he cocked one roguish eyebrow at her. "Yours.''

She pressed her hand against her chest. "*My* fault?''

"Yes, *your* fault.'' Ben snatched her and nuzzled his face in her neck. "How the hell was I supposed to get any sleep while you were cuddling your sexy, gorgeous body against me?''

"Hmm. You know, *I* didn't get much sleep, either, if you recall.''

His low, lascivious chuckle sent delicious shivers zipping down her spine. "Oh, I recall,'' he said. "I recall quite well, as a matter of fact. But just so I don't forget, maybe you'd better give me a refresher course.''

She wedged her hands between the two of them and shoved. "Business before pleasure. And I don't mean monkey business,'' she warned as Ben made a grab for her again. She dusted her hands, propped them on her hips and gazed down at him with affectionate disgust. "You can catch up on your beauty sleep while I make coffee.''

"Sounds good to me,'' he said with a yawn, turning over and burying his face in his arms. As she retrieved her scattered clothing, Ben said, "Hey, Sierra?''

She poked her head through the neck of her sweater. "Yes?''

His voice was garbled. "The matches are tucked under one of the rocks around the fire."

She threw a grateful glance at his back as she crawled by on her way out of the tent. "Thanks."

"Don't mention it."

Seeing the ashes of last night's fire made Sierra blush as she recalled how the flames had leaped and crackled while Ben removed her clothes. She could still feel his hands roaming over her body, stirring to life something wonderful and exciting within her. As the sun peeked over the tops of the tallest pines, spilling a golden glow over the campsite, the world seemed like . . . well, like a pretty terrific place.

Sierra shut her eyes, threw back her head and spun around and around in circles, reaching up to the sky, reaching out to grasp all of life's fantastic, thrilling possibilities. Laughter flowed from her throat, a sound as light and lilting as the chirping of the finch perched in a nearby cedar.

The smile illuminating her face was like dawn spreading across the mountains. Hugging herself in delight, Sierra reveled in this totally unfamiliar, totally exhilarating flood of deep, fulfilling joy.

She didn't need a treasure map to show her the source of her happiness. At this very moment the source was less than twenty feet from her, well-muscled limbs sprawled across a scratchy green army blanket.

With a heavy sigh of contentment, Sierra gave herself one final hug before kneeling to tackle the task at hand. It seemed a particularly good omen when the fire ignited immediately, flaring to life with a cheery crackle. In no time at all the heavenly aroma of coffee filled the clearing.

Sierra sat cross-legged in front of the blaze, enjoying the time alone, but anticipating the moment when Ben would emerge from the tent and join her. The flames reminded her of the golden glints in his hair; the heat stirred memories of how warm his skin felt against hers. The soft whisper of the burning wood almost sounded like his voice murmuring in her ear.

"Oh, brother," she said, rolling her eyes. "Boy, have *you* got it bad, kiddo!" She pushed herself to her feet, shaking her head. "What do you think, Char?" She untied the mule from his tree. "Am I a hopeless case, or what?"

As she led Charlemagne down to the creek for a morning drink, Sierra couldn't suppress the dart of hope that ricocheted through her heart whenever she thought of Ben. At last their rocky relationship seemed to be on a steady, smoother course. No more sidetracking lies, no more deceptive detours. The barriers of deceit and distrust between them were toppling down. Maybe she didn't know the whole truth about Ben, but she'd learned the most important truth: he cared about her. Maybe he wasn't in love with her the way—she swallowed—the way she was in love with him, but it was a start, wasn't it?

As for the rest of Ben's mysterious past, well, Sierra didn't want to probe that too closely yet. Best not to ask too many questions right now. She had a sneaking suspicion she might not like some of the answers.

"Char, will you hurry it up? I left the pot on the fire, and if that coffee scorches, I'll never hear the end of it." She wrestled the mule back to the clearing, tying him to his tree in case he decided to repeat yesterday's disappearing act.

Stepping back, she frowned. "Something's wrong with this picture." Her forehead cleared. "That's it!" She snapped her fingers. "I forgot to give you back your hat. Hang on a second."

She retrieved the mule's straw hat from its branch, then wrinkled her nose in disgust. "*Phew!* I hate to tell you this, Char, but that skunk really did a number on your hat. I know Grandpa gave it to you, but I'm afraid you're going to have to buy yourself a new one." Pinching the brim between two fingers, she glanced toward the woods, wondering if a straw hat was biodegradable or if it would litter the landscape for generations to come.

Well, straw was a plant, wasn't it? Sort of? She shifted her eyes from side to side, satisfying herself that no forest ranger lurked nearby, ready to pounce on her and haul her off into custody.

Then she grasped the hat like a Frisbee and prepared to sail it off into the brush. At the last second something caught her eye.

Tucked beneath the ribbon that wound around the inside of the hat before dangling through two slits in the brim was a piece of paper. A dirty, crinkled, folded-up piece of paper, to be exact. Sierra wiggled it from underneath the ribbon and turned it over in her hands.

What on earth?

She unfolded it gingerly so the thin, worn paper wouldn't tear. It was a letter. A very *old* letter, from the looks of it. "My dear Margaret," it began. Sierra's eyebrows furrowed in puzzlement. Who was Margaret, anyway? Some long-lost love of her grandfather's?

Her eyes skipped to the bottom of the page. No, the letter was signed by someone named Quentin. "Curiouser and curiouser," she mused, sinking onto a fallen log and crossing one leg over the other. Absently she tossed the straw hat aside.

Then, smoothing out the wrinkled paper, Sierra began to read.

Chapter Nine

A bundle of clothing slammed Ben square in the face when he crawled out of the tent.

As he scrambled to his feet, his confused gaze fell on Sierra—clenched fists pressed to her sides, feet planted firmly apart, brown eyes blazing. "You lousy, conniving, lying snake," she said quietly.

Ben's heart sank. "Darling, I don't know what you're—"

"Don't 'darling' me, you weasel. I see right through your two-faced sweet talk. It took me long enough, but I've finally wised up to you."

Ben swallowed. "Sierra, whatever it is, I'm sure there's a logical—"

"Oh, there's an explanation, all right. The explanation is that you lied to me. Again." She threw up her hands in exasperation. "I guess I should be getting used to it by now, but after last night . . ." Her chin trembled

as her eyes brimmed with tears. "Oh, Ben," she qua-
vered, "how could you? How *could* you?" Without
waiting for a reply, she pivoted on her heel and fled into
the trees.

Ben started after her, then realized that prancing
through the woods without wearing a stitch of clothing
was probably not the swiftest move he could make. He
scooped up his clothes and hopped after her, bouncing
up and down on one foot while he tried to insert his
other leg into his jeans. "Sierra, wait! Come back!"

Naturally she did neither. Ben couldn't imagine what
had lit her fuse this time, but surely it was all a misun-
derstanding. He fully intended to keep his promise to
tell her the truth from now on—at least as much of the
truth as was safe. Stumbling after her, he racked his
brain for some stray lie that had come back to haunt
him, some loose end he'd forgotten to tie up.

What on earth could have happened between the time
Sierra was lazily offering him a macaroon and the moment she hurled his clothes at his head?

Ben caught a glimpse of her up ahead, the sun glinting bright copper off her dark curls. Thank God all this
outdoor living had strengthened his leg, or he'd never
have caught up with her. Not with fury propelling her
like a booster rocket.

Vaulting over a fallen log, Ben closed the distance
between them and captured her wrist. Immediately she
shook him off and whirled to face him like a cornered
animal. "Leave me alone," she snarled.

"Not until I find out what the hell has upset you so
much."

"What are you going to do, tickle me until I tell you?
Wrestle me to the ground and refuse to let me up? Those
are your usual tactics, aren't they?"

Ben closed his eyes and counted to ten. "Sierra," he said in a calm, reasonable voice, "I'm not going to force you to do anything. But don't you think you owe me an explanation?"

"Me?" She smacked her palm against her chest. "Owe *you* an explanation?"

He tried again. "After last night I thought—"

"After last night I thought a lot of things, too. All of them wrong." She banged the heel of her hand against the side of her head. "What a gullible fool I was! Oh, when will I ever learn?" She shook her head in disgust.

Not for the first time, Ben wondered what it was about Sierra that stirred up such violent tendencies inside him. He was basically a peace-loving man who rejected brute force as a matter of principle. But right now he wanted to shake Sierra silly.

Instead he decided to try a new tactic. Shrugging, he said, "All right, if you don't want to tell me what's wrong, fine. I respect your right to keep secrets." He slid his hands into his pockets and turned back toward camp, whistling a tuneless refrain.

His strategy worked. "Secrets?" she shouted after him, her voice teeming with outrage. "You dare to accuse *me* of keeping secrets?"

Ben heard the rustle of dried leaves as she tagged after him. He kept walking.

"You're the one with all the secrets, Ben Halliday. Compared to you, *my* life's an open book."

He sauntered along, tilting back his head to study the sky. Looked like it was going to be a pretty nice day.

"Just who are Margaret and Quentin, anyway?"

She might as well have clobbered him with a two-by-four. All the air whooshed out of Ben's lungs; his legs simply stopped functioning, as if they'd suddenly turned to lead. In slow motion he wheeled around and stared at her. "What did you say?" His voice sounded hollow, as if he were speaking into a concrete tunnel.

At the look on his face, some of her indignation faded. "I said, who are Margaret and Quentin?" Now she looked uncertain, like a mischievous child who suddenly realized she'd gone too far.

Ben took one faltering step toward her. "Where did you hear those names?" he asked hoarsely.

Her lower lip pushed forward with slight defiance. "I didn't hear them. I read them."

Ben's heart thumped like a timpani drum. Dear God, could it be? Was it possible—? He moved a step closer. "Where?" he said. "Where did you read those names?"

Sierra studied him for a moment, as if considering whether or not to prolong this interesting inquisition. Then she shrugged, extracted a folded-up piece of paper from her back pocket and held it out to Ben. "Here," she said offhandedly, as if the matter were no longer of much interest to her. "I read the names in this letter. You're mentioned in there, too."

The letter.

As Ben reached for it, his hand seemed disembodied, as if it had absolutely no connection with the rest of him. Shock and disbelief gave time a dreamlike quality, and the seconds before his fingers actually touched the paper seemed to stretch out into eternity.

Amazingly his hand remained steady as he unfolded the letter, scanned it with unseeing eyes and tucked it into his shirt pocket. This one piece of paper had cost him so much, had given him so much. Without the letter Ben would have no chance to avenge his parents' memory.

And if it weren't for the letter, he would never have met Sierra.

Now that he actually had the letter in his possession, Ben found himself somewhat at a loss. He ought to be shouting for joy, punching the air in triumph. Instead all he could focus on was the sad disillusionment on Sierra's face. Her anger had apparently dissipated, leaving her as deflated as a limp balloon. With a sigh she slumped back against a tree trunk, folded her arms and stared unhappily off into the distance.

"Sweetheart," he said in what he hoped was a soothing tone, "I still don't understand why this letter upset you so much."

She refused to meet his eyes. "It's pretty obvious, isn't it?"

"If it were obvious, I wouldn't be asking."

"You're going to make me say it, aren't you?" she asked in a flat voice. "All right, then. Have it your way." She turned her enormous dark eyes on him, and the hurt accusation Ben saw there nearly broke his heart.

"You were only after that letter," she said. "I don't know why it's so important to you, but it was important enough that you were willing to lie to me, to trick me, to use me." She gulped. "You thought that by making love to me, you could somehow get the letter back. Well, I guess your plan worked, didn't it?"

"Sweetheart—"

"Although it's rather ironic, because I only came across it by accident. I had no idea it even existed before I found it hidden away inside Charlemagne's hat this morning."

Ben's jaw dropped. "You mean to tell me that all this time, that crotchety old mule—"

"—had it stashed inside his hat." She peered at him from beneath her long lashes. "I presume Grandpa must have hidden it there?"

"I gave it to him for safekeeping after my plane crashed."

Her eyes widened in surprise. "Your plane crashed around *here* someplace? And Grandpa saw it?"

"He was the first one to find me. Or actually—" Ben scratched his jaw "—Charlemagne was."

That brought a glimmer of a smile to her troubled face. "In the Alps people get rescued by Saint Bernards. In the Sierra Nevada they get saved by mules." Then her forehead furrowed again. "What do you mean, you gave that letter to Grandpa for safekeeping? Safekeeping from what? Or whom?"

For a moment Ben wavered, sorely tempted to tell her everything. He was so close now . . . so close to the day when the truth about Quentin Jericho would be blazoned across every newspaper in the country. He was sick and tired of lying to Sierra. She deserved better than that.

The whole story welled up inside Ben's chest, ready to burst from his throat. Then, in a brutal flash he recalled his confrontation with Jericho right before his mother's funeral service began. His memory dredged up with sickening clarity the pure malevolence, the ruthless determination seared on Jericho's face when he discovered the letter hadn't been destroyed years ago, after all.

Ben shuddered, reliving the wave of shock and revulsion that had swept over him when he saw for the first time what evil his "Uncle Quent" concealed behind his good-natured, benevolent mask.

Ben had to keep protecting Sierra for just a little while longer, until he could rip away that mask in front of the whole world.

"I can't tell you anything about the letter," he said finally.

She eyed him skeptically. "Can't? Or won't?"

He paused. "Won't."

She threw up her arms. "Well, this is a switch! How come you don't just dream up another phony story to satisfy me? Or are all these lies getting to be too exhausting?"

"I swore I wouldn't lie to you anymore, and I meant it." Ben tipped her chin up, forcing her to meet his eyes. "But I can't tell you the whole truth right now. Not yet. It's too dangerous."

She swatted his hand away. "There, that's more like it! I was starting to worry I wouldn't get to hear another one of your fairy tales. Dangerous, indeed."

"It happens to be the truth," he said quietly.

"The truth, huh?" She probed her cheek with her tongue. "Let's see, which version of the truth are we up to now? Version three? Four? Goodness, I've heard so many versions of the truth from you I've simply lost count."

"Sierra..."

She clamped her hands over her ears. "Please, no more, all right? I don't want to end this relationship with one last lie. Although that would certainly be appropriate, wouldn't it? God knows, that's what this whole relationship has been based on."

Ben clenched and unclenched his fists. "I had to hide the truth from you for your sake."

"For *my* sake?" She dropped her hands. "Hey, don't do me any more favors, okay? *My* sake. Too dangerous. Oh, that's priceless," she scoffed. "What on earth could be so dangerous about an old letter?"

Before Ben could reply, Sierra narrowed her eyes and tapped her finger against her chin. "Are Margaret and Quentin your parents?"

"No!" The very idea struck Ben as so horrific, he spit out a denial before he realized that Sierra had just managed to pry another chunk of information from him.

"Then Margaret and this Tom mentioned in the letter must be your parents. And apparently this Quentin person tried to blackmail Margaret into dumping Tom and marrying him. He says in the letter he'll drop the embezzlement charges against Tom if Margaret will leave him. And he urges her to think about poor little Ben, how awful it would be for him to grow up with a father in prison."

Ben groaned inwardly. Sierra nearly had the whole thing figured out, all right. Except for one key piece of information: she didn't realize who Quentin was.

Fresh urgency seized him. He had to get to Los Angeles and contact the press. Fast. Sierra was too smart for her own good sometimes.

Her smug look of triumph melted in sympathy. "Did your father spend time in prison, then? Is that why you hid the truth from me? Because you were ashamed?" She laid her hand on his arm and spoke with earnest intensity. "You don't have to be ashamed, Ben. Your father made a mistake, but he paid for it. And it was all so long ago...."

He focused his eyes where her hand rested on his arm. "You don't understand," he said in a low voice. "My father didn't do anything wrong. The only mistake he made was trusting that bastard Quentin Jer—"

Ben broke off in horror. His resentment and anger had made him reckless, pushing him to the brink of revealing everything and thrusting Sierra even deeper into danger.

But her eyes, searching his face in bewilderment, showed no sign that she'd detected his near slip. Relief washed over him, and with a swift, abrupt movement he pulled Sierra into his arms and buried his face in her hair. He felt her arms slide slowly, cautiously around his waist.

Ben inhaled deeply, wanting to absorb the clean, woodsy scent of her, to imprint on his brain the memory of her small, fragile body cradled against him. Soon, very soon he would have to leave her. He didn't know for how long, or what kind of reception would await him when he returned to set things right with her.

This might be his last chance for a long time to hold Sierra, to touch her. The knowledge made their imminent parting even more bittersweet.

No sense prolonging the agony. The sooner Ben accomplished his mission, the sooner he could return to Sierra. Drawing back, he traced his thumb across the lush, sensual fullness of her lips. Then he pressed his mouth against hers and kissed her gently. "I have to go," he said at last, brushing one of her reddish brown curls off her temple.

Her arms, loosely clasped around him, tensed. A look of startled disappointment dashed across her delicate features, chased by an expression of pained acceptance. She skittered away and stood with her back to Ben. Unhappiness and resignation were written in every line of her posture.

"So that's it, huh?" she said in a dull voice. "You found what you were looking for, and now you're leaving."

Ben stepped closer, intending to grasp her shoulders and turn her toward him. At the last second he paused, then dropped his hands limply to his sides. "I'll be back," he said in a strained voice. "But I have something to do first. Something important. Something that can't wait."

She spun around quickly, and for an instant he saw the naked hurt in her eyes before her anger and resentment disguised it. "But you expect *me* to wait."

"I don't expect it. But I'm *asking* you to wait, yes. Just for a little while longer. Then I'll come back and explain everything to you."

She searched his face with a mixture of hope and frustration. Then something in her eyes flickered and died. Whatever she'd been searching for, she hadn't found it. "You're not coming back at all, are you?" she said softly.

Ben seized both her hands and pressed his lips against her knuckles. "I'll be back, Sierra. I swear it."

She continued as if she hadn't heard him. "Now I finally know the real reason why you pursued me, why you pretended to care for me, why you—" she nearly choked on the words "—made love to me."

Ben shook his head wildly. "You've got it all wrong, sweetheart!" Her anguish was like a knife stabbing him through the chest. "I never *pretended* to care for you! I didn't make love to you just so you'd help me find the letter! Those things I said, my feelings for you—all that was real, Sierra. It was the truth." He gripped her hands even tighter. "I *do* care for you, darling, and I *will* come back. You've got to believe me!"

Tears glittered in her eyes. "Oh, Ben," she said with a strangled sob, "how can I believe you, after all the lies you've told me?"

Then she wrenched away from him and stumbled off into the woods, pressing her hand to her mouth.

"Sierra, please! You've got to give me a chance...you've got to let me...oh, hell." Ben pulled up short and watched her disappear into the trees. Desperation gnawed at his stomach, but his instincts warned him that letting Sierra go was the only way to win her back. Trying to reason with her now would be pointless. He could hardly blame her for not believing a word he said anymore. Now he knew how the boy who cried "Wolf!" once too often must have felt.

But after she'd had a chance to cool off and calm down, Sierra would surely realize Ben hadn't been cold-bloodedly using her. And when he came back from Los Angeles, that would prove to Sierra that he truly cared for her, wouldn't it?

That's what Ben was counting on, anyway. Because he couldn't bear to consider any other outcome.

He removed the letter from his pocket and turned it over in his hands. Then he looked up at the spot where Sierra had disappeared. This letter was their life-insurance policy. Neither of them would be safe from Jericho until the letter was exposed to the blinding spotlight of public scrutiny.

There was no time to waste. Ben hated like hell to leave Sierra without straightening out this mess, but he'd have to postpone that until later, after their lives were out of danger. And he somehow suspected Sierra wasn't exactly in the mood to listen to him, anyway.

Nevertheless, he was still torn by the urgency of getting the letter to L.A. and his reluctance to let Sierra think the worst of him.

But protecting her from Jericho's hired killers had to be his first priority.

That, and avenging his parents, of course. Ben blinked as if coming out of a trance. For a moment he'd almost forgotten his original purpose for retrieving the letter. He studied the paper in his hands. Funny. He'd imagined this moment so many times—the moment when he finally recovered the weapon that would wreak vengeance on Quentin Jericho.

Except in his imagination he'd felt a surge of fierce joy, a dizzying flood of triumph.

Now all he felt was weary relief that his difficult task was almost complete. In place of triumphant joy was a hollow ache, a nagging suspicion that he faced an even more difficult, more desperate challenge ahead: winning Sierra back.

But first he had to see *this* matter through to its conclusion. Ben stuffed the letter into his jeans pocket and ran down a mental checklist. He couldn't think of anything he'd left at Sierra's camp, so there was really no need to swing by there before heading back to town.

Besides, he had a feeling that avoiding Sierra for a while would be a wise move.

Casting one final look of regret over his shoulder, Ben turned and began the long trudge back to Grubstake.

Spiky branches snatched at her hair and clawed her face as Sierra floundered through the woods. The only sounds were the crackle of sticks and leaves underfoot, the harsh rasp of her breathing and the hammering thud of her heart.

She wanted to keep running forever, away from the pain, the lies, the memory of Ben's face hovering so close to hers while they made love. "Stop it!" she shouted, squeezing her eyes shut as if that could somehow banish his taunting image.

Instead she tripped over a gnarled tree-root and pitched headfirst into a prickly snarl of bushes. Once imprisoned in their thorny clutches, she simply couldn't muster the energy to fight her way free, and lay sprawled there, tears stinging the scratches on her hands.

At last, disgusted with her unaccustomed bout of self-pity, she disentangled herself and scrambled to her feet. With one final sniffle, she wiped her eyes with the sleeve of her sweater and pushed her hair out of her face. "Well, that's the end of it," she told herself. "We met, I fell in love, he broke my heart, I went boo-hoo. Now it's over. End of chapter, end of book. *Fini.*"

As she brushed dirt and leaves off her slacks, her lower lip trembled. But she held up her head, gritted her teeth and headed back to camp—at a slower pace this time. Despite her resolve to wash her hands of Ben once and for all, her ears were keenly alert for the sound of his pursuit.

She tried not to be too disappointed when he didn't catch up with her. By the time Sierra arrived back at camp, she realized he was probably gone for good this time. Well, what reason did he have to stick around, anyway? He'd got what he'd come for.

The only problem was, he'd taken away a lot more than that stupid letter.

Sierra fought back her tears, cursing herself for being an idiot. Obviously Ben Halliday wasn't at all the man she thought she'd fallen in love with.

So why did her heart feel like it had been plowed over by a bulldozer?

Damn him, anyway! Now that he'd got his mysterious letter back, he couldn't even be bothered to keep up a pretense. He simply refused to tell her *anything*, even another one of his outlandish stories.

Sierra's harsh laughter snagged in her throat. Who would have thought she'd ever look back on Ben's lies with sentimental longing?

Yet somehow his indifference was even harder to bear. At least he'd needed her before, if only for some secret, sinister purpose. But now Ben had no use for her. No use for her, at all.

Another shaft of grief plunged into Sierra, making her gasp with its intensity. She tossed her head back. Well, who needed Ben Halliday, anyway? Who needed his devastating blond looks, his smooth-talking charm, his arousing, passionate embraces?

With a convulsive swallow, she dammed back a new flood of tears. Then she crawled into the tent and liberated a box of Yummee Coconut-Creme Cakes. But her first bite of the sweet, mushy confection only aggravated her already-churning stomach.

Eyeing the bright yellow box with disgust, she scooted back out of the tent and accosted Charlemagne. "Here," she said, sticking the gooey cake under the mule's nose. "Live it up. You can eat the whole darn box if you want to."

At such a tempting invitation, Charlemagne shook off his usual lethargy. He wolfed down the partially eaten morsel with gusto, then hopefully nuzzled his nose into the yellow box.

Sierra absently fed him seconds. "I guess you were right about Ben all along, Char. You knew from the very beginning he wasn't to be trusted. Here, have another one." She sighed, trying to dislodge the heavy weight compressing her chest. "I should have listened to you in the first place. Everyone knows what good instincts animals have about people."

Charlemagne brayed indignantly.

"Oops! I didn't mean to lump you in with a bunch of animals, Char. Forgive me? Look, here's another coconut-cream cake. Are we still friends?"

After a moment Sierra sighed again. "I *want* to believe that he cares about me, Char. I *want* to believe he'll come back. But I just can't. Dealing with that man is like peeling an onion. I keep stripping away all these layers of lies, but there's always another layer underneath. The truth must be in there someplace, but I'll be darned if I can figure out what it is or how deep it's buried. And I'm sick of peeling onions. They always make me—" she sniffed "—cry."

Impatiently she dashed another tear from her cheek. Charlemagne nudged her in sympathy. With a moan of despair, Sierra dropped the box and flung her arms around the mule's neck. "You're the only friend I have in the world," she wailed. "The only person I can trust. And you're not...even...a...person!" Her voice dissolved in a fresh spate of sobs as she buried her face in Charlemagne's neck.

Charlemagne stood this undignified embrace for as long as he could. Then he snorted and tried to pull away. Sierra raised her tearstained face and wrinkled her nose. "You may be my best friend in the whole world, but as one friend to another, I gotta tell you, pal—you stink!''

She sniffed, then frowned. That peculiar smell wasn't skunk, and it wasn't coming from Charlemagne. She drew back, noting in surprise that the mule's long ears were twitching nervously. This was as close to a state of agitation as she'd ever seen him.

''What's wrong, Char? Do you smell it, too? Do you hear something?''

Then an ominous prickling slithered up Sierra's spine. Too late, she whirled. Something soft and wet clamped down over her nose and mouth before she could cry out. She tried to squirm from side to side, but a hand grabbed a fistful of her hair and yanked her head back in an iron grip.

Instinctively she tried to hold her breath, simultaneously straining to see who her captor was. If this was her father's idea of a last resort, he'd definitely gone too far this time.

Her lungs clamored for oxygen, and when she could no longer resist the overpowering urge to breathe, a sickly sweet, vaguely medicinal odor permeated her senses, seeping into every cell in her body.

Her vision clouded like a TV with poor reception. Through the swirling dots and roaring static, her last conscious thought was, *Ben*.

Then the picture snapped off, and the whole world went black.

Chapter Ten

Ben drummed his fingers impatiently on the front desk of the Grubstake Hotel. With the phone cradled between his neck and shoulder, he watched Addie Winslow bustle back and forth like a duck in a shooting gallery. The woman was upset, and she simply couldn't keep still.

Ben was the person who'd upset her, and for that he was sorry. Well, another name to add to the list of people he'd have to apologize to when this whole ordeal was over.

"Come on, come on," he muttered into the receiver. Addie darted him a nervous glance, and he forced himself to give her a reassuring smile.

No wonder she was nervous, the way Ben had come bursting into the hotel lobby an hour ago, barely taking time to toss a greeting over his shoulder before he dashed up the stairs two at a time.

Exactly four minutes later he'd clunked his hastily packed suitcase down beside the front desk, told Addie he was checking out and asked if he could use the phone to make a few quick calls.

He'd seen the questions spinning through her eyes like pictures in a slot machine. What was his hurry? Where was he going? And, most important of all, what about Sierra?

Addie had had high hopes for their romance, and now here was Ben, fleeing like a refugee from a war zone without so much as mentioning Sierra's name.

No wonder Addie looked so disappointed.

Ben wished he could reassure her and explain that his relationship with Sierra was just alive and well. But he could have used some reassurance himself on that score. He'd hurt Sierra badly, and could only pray she'd give him a chance to make it up to her.

But she'd looked so damn fed up the last time he saw her. What if she'd pulled up stakes by the time he got back, and moved on to someplace where Ben couldn't find her?

The thought set his stomach seething with worry, and he wondered briefly if his ulcers were coming back. He smothered a groan. Sparring with Sierra would give ulcers to the most easygoing man in the world.

Or maybe the unpleasant burning in the pit of his stomach was simply fear. Primitive, uncomplicated, garden-variety fear. Because as soon as he tracked down a plane to rent, Ben was going to fly again.

He'd spent the past hour on the telephone, calling all the rinky-dink airports in the vicinity, trying to find one with an extra airplane lying around. So far he'd had no luck. It was Saturday—a gorgeous, blue-skied, unseasonably warm Saturday, and apparently every pilot within a fifty-mile radius had had the same urge to take the old Cessna or Piper or Beechcraft up for a little spin today.

Ben hadn't flown since the crash, over six months ago. First had come his long recuperation, and then his all-consuming efforts to uncover exactly what had happened between his parents and Quentin Jericho twenty-seven years ago.

Now he was about to take a plane up again, and all he could think of was the overwhelming helplessness he'd felt when the controls had refused to respond . . . those tall, spiky pine trees reaching up for him . . . the terror of knowing he was about to die.

Ben shook his head once, sharply. He wiped his sweaty palms on his shirt. His fear was completely irrational. Quentin Jericho couldn't possibly know which plane Ben was going to rent. And even Jericho wouldn't sabotage every small aircraft in northern California just to be on the safe side.

Yet the thought of climbing into that cockpit, gripping that control wheel and finding nothing between himself and the ground but ten thousand feet of airspace made Ben's heart pound.

But it was a seven-hour drive from here to Los Angeles, and a lot could happen during those seven hours. A truck could run him off the road, for example. Or someone could take a shot at him from another car. All things considered, Ben would no doubt be safer airborne. Now if he could only explain that to his flip-flopping stomach.

"Hey, you still there?" At last the voice at the other end of the line returned.

"Still here," Ben replied. "Have you got something for me?"

"Yeah, we got one that's just had a major overhaul. That's what I was checking on—to see if it was finished. It's a Cessna 210. Ever fly one of those before?"

Ben flinched. A Cessna 210. The same plane he'd been flying when he'd crashed. "Yeah," he croaked. "I've flown one before."

"Great. Now, do you know how to find the airport?"

Ben placed his palm over the receiver and mouthed to Addie, "Pencil and paper?"

Her hands fluttered like nervous butterflies as she searched for something to write with.

Ben scribbled down the directions. The remote mountain airport was about an hour's drive from here, he calculated. "Okay, thanks. I'm on my way." He banged down the receiver. Addie jumped.

"Thanks for everything," he said, bending to pick up his suitcase. At the sight of her woebegone face, he relented. "By the way, I expect to be back soon."

She brightened immediately. "You do?"

Ben nodded. "I have some business to take care of first. But maybe you could keep that same room reserved for me? If it's not too much trouble, that is."

"Oh, my goodness, it's no trouble at all. I'll make a note of it right away. Let me see now, where did I put my glasses?" She located them on the chain around her neck and opened the dusty black ledger. "What day do you expect to return?" she asked, pencil hovering over the page.

Ben backed toward the door. "Gosh, Addie, I can't really say at this point. Look, you go ahead and rent that room if someone wants it, okay?"

Her face fell. "Well, all right, although this late in the year—"

"And if you see Sierra..."

"Yes?"

"Tell her I'll be back, okay?"

Her face crinkled into smiles. "I certainly will."

"Thanks, Addie." With one final glance at the lobby, Ben swung his suitcase around and pulled the door handle. As he stepped onto the front porch, he collided with Sourdough Pete.

"Whoa, slow down, buddy!" Ben exclaimed, reaching out to steady the old prospector. "What's the matter, did you finally strike it rich?"

Pete did indeed look rather dazed. "What? No. Matter of fact, I was lookin' for you, sonny."

"For me?" Ben quelled a stab of impatience. He was in a race against time, and Pete had stalled him when he was barely out of the starting blocks. "If it's about that interview for the magazine article—"

"No, no, it ain't that." He squinted at Ben from beneath his shaggy white eyebrows. "Besides, Sierra told me you weren't really a writer, anyways."

Embarrassment joined the host of uncomfortable emotions Ben seemed destined to experience today. "Look, Pete, about that magazine business—"

Pete brushed his explanation aside with one swipe of his gnarled hand. "Forget about it, sonny. I done told a lie or two myself in my day. I'm sure you had your reasons, but they ain't none of my business. Besides, I got something for you."

"Pete, I'm kind of in a hurry, so—"

"Keep your shorts on, sonny. I know it's in here someplace." Ben watched in mounting frustration as Pete rooted through the pockets of his red windbreaker. "An' that feller told me it was important, so you just hold on a second."

Dread began to inch its way up Ben's spine. "What fellow?" he asked cautiously.

"Why, the one who asked me to give you this note," Pete said, whipping out a crumpled envelope.

Once again, Ben felt the dreamy sense of unreality that had crept over him when Sierra had handed him the letter. Only this time it was edged with fear.

Willing his hands to remain steady, he tore open the envelope and drew out the paper inside. As his eyes frantically scanned the message, the envelope fluttered to the ground.

Stunned, Ben read the words a second time, as if he could somehow alter their content by knowing what they said in advance. But the same message taunted him, warned him, threatened him.

No, not him. The threat wasn't against Ben. He wasn't the one whose life hung in the balance, subject to the whims of a merciless cutthroat.

"He's got Sierra," Ben said hoarsely.

"Huh? Who?" Pete tugged on his mustache.

Ben seized his shoulders. "Who gave you this note, Pete? When? And where?"

Pete looked at Ben as if he'd gone plumb loco. "Some feller in a dark suit give it to me in front of the general store, right after I come into town for supplies. He asked if I knew who you was, then told me you was in the hotel and to bring you this note pronto. Said it was a—how did he put it? A matter of life and death."

Ben ground his teeth together. Truer words had never been spoken, unfortunately. "Listen to me, Pete. This is very important." He forced himself to release the miner when Pete stared pointedly at Ben's hands on his shoulders. "Did you see where the man went? Was he alone?"

"He was alone, and I didn't see where he went. I come straight over here to the hotel without lookin' back. Didn't see where he disappeared to."

"You didn't see Sierra anywhere, did you?"

Pete frowned. "Sierra? What's she got to do with this?"

Ben wiped the sweat from his forehead. "She's been kidnapped, Pete." God, he had to force back this panic, had to think clearly, or he wouldn't have a chance. Sierra wouldn't have a chance.

Pete's eyebrows shot skyward. "Kidnapped? What the hell are you jabberin' about, sonny?"

Ben thrust the paper at him. "This is a ransom note, Pete."

Suspicion filtered across his grimy, weather-beaten face, followed by concern and then confusion. "Well, what did that feller tell me to give *you* the note for? Sierra's daddy's the one with all the money."

"He's not after money, Pete. He wants something else. Something *I've* got."

Pete scratched his head in bewilderment. "And what might that be?"

The letter. That damn, troublesome letter that had nearly cost Ben his life and might very well end up costing Sierra hers.

But not if Ben had anything to do with it. Not while he had a breath left in his body. A tormenting vision exploded in his brain—the image of his darling, unpredictable, oh-so-vulnerable Sierra trapped in the clutches of that scoundrel. Ben could just imagine her lying chained in some dank dungeon while Quentin Jericho rubbed his hands together in evil glee.

Then, without warning, Ben's emotional dam burst and fear drenched him, leaving him cold and shivering with the bleakest, most bone-rattling terror he'd ever known.

Suddenly the letter didn't seem so important anymore.

First she heard a monotonous whooshing sound, as if a freeway were nearby. But there were no freeways up here in the mountains, were there?

Then the delicious aroma of tomato sauce and basil tantalized her nostrils. Now she *knew* there was something weird going on.

Groggily Sierra peeled open one eye, wondering who'd put the lead weights on her eyelids. The bright sunlight streaming in the window nearly blinded her. Instantly she squeezed her eye shut again.

Okay, take two.

This time she raised her hand to shade her eyes. Lifting her arm was like pulling the strings on a very heavy, uncooperative marionette. With her hand in front of her face, she opened both eyes very cautiously, squinting through her fingers.

A ceiling. Well, nothing too surprising about that, especially when she realized she was lying on her back. Nothing too informative about that ceiling, though. It couldn't tell her, for example, just where the hell she was.

Figuring *that* out was going to require more drastic action. Levering up off her elbows, Sierra swung herself into a sitting position. She regretted that move immediately.

"Aaargh," she moaned, clamping her palms against the sides of her head to still the painful throbbing inside her brain. The room spun about her like an out-of-control merry-go-round, making it even harder for

Sierra to examine her surroundings through her blurred, half-shut eyes.

This was like being in a carnival fun house. Except that it wasn't exactly what you would call fun.

Nausea swooped through her stomach, and all of a sudden that mouthwatering aroma of Italian food wasn't nearly so appetizing anymore. In fact . . .

She spotted the tray of spaghetti, salad and garlic bread on the nightstand next to the bed she was sitting on. "What, no Chianti?" she muttered. With enormous, groaning effort, she managed to lower the tray to the floor and slide it under the bed.

Drat, she could still smell it. Her stomach lurched ominously.

"Boy, I've had hangovers before," she said in a bleary voice, "but this one beats them all. And I can't even remember what I had . . . to . . . drink."

Wait a second. She hadn't drunk *anything*. She'd been at the campsite, talking to Charlemagne, when—

Chloroform. That was the cloying smell lingering in her nostrils. Someone had actually chloroformed her. And when she found out who, he was going to require some general anesthetic himself.

Turning her head slowly to minimize the little jackhammers attacking her skull, Sierra determined she was, in fact, alone in the room. Which was, in fact, somebody's rather luxurious bedroom.

But not hers. She'd never seen this place before in her life. Which would seem to rule out theory number one: that her father had sent someone to kidnap her and drag her back to her rightful place as the crown princess of Sloane Enterprises.

Time to consider theory number two. Except that Sierra didn't *have* a second theory. Pressing her fingers into her temples, she tried to remember what had happened between the moment someone had served her the chloroform cocktail and the moment she'd awoken in this strange bed with a huge bass-drum headache and a mouth that tasted like a ripe litter box.

It was no use. Her memory of that time frame was a big blackboard. A big *empty* blackboard. The only fragments she could dredge up were hazy and vague— brief flashes of men in dark suits and a glimpse of a . . . helicopter rotor whirring overhead?

Yes, for what it was worth, she was almost certain she'd been brought here in a helicopter. Wherever *here* was.

That was the next puzzle to figure out. Taking a deep gulp of air, Sierra eased herself to her feet and tiptoed to the closed door. She grasped the doorknob, turned it, then rattled it with growing annoyance.

Locked. Somehow that news flash didn't come as a surprise. Well, before she started banging her tin cup and hollering for the warden, it might be prudent to investigate other possible escape routes.

She poked her head into the adjoining bathroom. Marble fixtures, huge sunken tub, expensive tile. But no way out. Then she crossed the plush carpet to the bedroom's single window, an enormous expanse of glass she was almost certain would yield to a persuasive chair bashed into it.

What luck! The window was actually unlocked, sliding open on a well-oiled track in a very cooperative manner.

"Time to blow this scene," Sierra mumbled, hoisting one foot to the sill. "I didn't feel like eating lunch, anyway." She had one leg hanging out the window before she chanced to look down. "Whoa, Nellie!"

Just in the nick of time she refrained from heaving herself through the window...and onto the jaws of some very jagged-looking rocks a good hundred feet below. Heart thudding, she perched half in, half out of the window, pondering her newfound respect for that old adage Look Before You Leap.

So that's what that whooshing sound had been—not a freeway at all, but the rhythmic crash of ocean waves against the rocks. Sierra had to admit, her cell had a fabulous view. Gazing up and down the coast, she could see dozens of expensive homes, many of them propped against the steep shoreline cliff with massive, towering pylons—like the house in which Sierra was currently an unwilling guest.

She tsk-tsked in disgust. She'd been in many homes like this before, and could never understand why some people insisted on defying nature, the tides, coastal erosion and mud slides by constructing their houses where they required propping up, extra reinforcement, sandbagging and constant maintenance just to keep their backyards from sliding into the ocean. Maybe people just did it to prove they could afford it.

At least now she knew where she was. No mistaking one of the most exclusive neighborhoods in Malibu for anyplace else. So she'd wound up back in L.A., after all.

She had no intention of sticking around, however. Too bad the window had turned out to be such an un-satisfactory escape route. And no wonder it hadn't been locked. Dropping to the floor, Sierra strode across the room and hammered her fist against the door. "Fun and games are over," she shouted. "Now let me out of here!"

The noise made her wince, but she hadn't found a bell to ring for the butler. "I said, let me out of here," she yelled. "Unlock this door, or you'll be sorry!"

She pressed her ear to the wood, noting the door was constructed of thick, solid oak. So much for a sharp karate kick to smash it open. Not that she knew karate, anyway.

Was it her imagination, or did she hear muffled footsteps outside? Yes, she was almost positive she recognized the swish of expensive Italian-leather shoes against thick shag carpeting.

Then...nothing. She slammed her fist halfheartedly against the door a few more times, but the racket only made her headache worse, and her throat was getting sore from yelling.

Leaning back against the door, Sierra sank to the floor, crossing her arms over her upraised knees. This was really getting irritating. Not scary or anything, but definitely a drag.

Why couldn't people just leave her alone, anyway? Was that so much to ask? First her father kept pestering her to come home, then Ben chased her all over creation so he could get his stupid letter back. Now someone had shanghaied her for some incomprehensible reason.

Hmph. If that louse Ben Halliday could only see the predicament she was in now, he'd sure be sorry for the way he'd treated her.

"Oops, almost waded into a puddle of self-pity there," Sierra scolded herself. "Knock it off. He's not worth it."

She was spared further depressing thoughts by the click of a key in the lock. She sprang to her feet, stirring up a swirl of red dots in front of her eyes. By the time the door swung open, she was planted in the center of the room, hands on hips, feet set firmly apart, indignation blazing.

She couldn't have been more astounded if the Prince of Wales had strolled into the room.

She'd seen this famous, beetle-browed face countless times on the evening news, on TV talk shows, on the covers of magazines. His jet black hair, swept straight back off his prominent forehead, had always struck Sierra as a bit suspicious for a man in his sixties. His well-fed paunch, ballooning out the vest of his dark three-piece suit, evoked an image of Santa Claus that only enhanced his widespread reputation as a kindly philanthropist, a doer of good deeds.

Those twinkling black eyes had certainly never seemed ominous to Sierra. Until now.

"Quentin Jericho," she breathed.

"But of course," he said, closing the door behind him. "Whom did you expect?"

"Expect?" she squeaked. "What do you mean, expect? I didn't expect to be kidnapped in the first place, so how could I expect you or anyone else?"

He shrugged. "It shouldn't have been too hard to figure out, after everything your friend Ben Halliday told you."

His words were like a punch in the stomach. She paused a beat to catch her breath. "Ben?" she whispered. "What's he got to do with this?"

Then all the bits and pieces began to spin and slide into place, like the tumblers in a combination safe. Quentin Jericho. Quentin and Margaret. The letter. Ben.

"You," she said in a shocked voice. "*You're* the one! You tried to blackmail Ben's mother into leaving his father. You had something to do with Ben's father going to prison, didn't you?''

"Blackmail is such an ugly word, don't you think?'' Jericho pulled a gold cigarette case from his inside pocket. "And Tom Halliday was an embezzler who got what he deserved. Do you mind if I smoke?''

"Yes.''

He lit a cigarette anyway. Sierra stared at his elegantly manicured nails, trying to absorb the implications of this mind-blowing discovery. No wonder Ben had been so desperate to get that letter back. Sierra's corporate instincts were too deeply ingrained for her not to grasp immediately what the consequences would be if that letter were ever made public.

That letter was as explosive as dynamite. It would blast Quentin Jericho's Santa Claus image to smithereens. She'd hate to be the public relations director of Yummee Foods if its sordid contents ever leaked out.

And if Quentin Jericho was the kind of man who could write that letter, he was also the kind of man who wouldn't stand idly aside while his company, his fortune and his reputation were threatened.

Sierra pressed her fingertips to her forehead. So Ben *had* been trying to protect her by being so secretive. He'd been telling the truth when he warned that her life might be in danger.

And if he'd been telling the truth about *that*, maybe he'd been telling the truth about other things, as well.

A warm surge of love flooded Sierra's heart, filling her with tenderness and longing. For a moment she swayed, made dizzy by the overwhelming desire to see Ben again, to find a safe haven in the comfort and security of his arms.

First she had to figure a way out of this mess.

Coughing, she fanned her hand back and forth to dispel the noxious fumes from Jericho's cigarette. Well, they said the best defense was offense, right?

She folded her arms. "Would you mind telling me exactly how *I* fit into the picture?" she demanded.

"Simple." Jericho blew a stream of smoke at the ceiling. "Ben has something I want. Now I have something *he* wants." With an infuriating leer, he bobbed his cigarette at Sierra. "I'm going to offer him a trade."

"Me for the letter."

"Precisely." He let a gob of ash trickle to the carpet. "Ben hands over the letter—I hand over you. A simple business deal."

"You'll never get away with this, you know."

Jericho's jowly, well-tanned face creased with amusement. "You're hardly in a position to make threats, my dear."

"Oh, yeah?" Sierra had vowed never again to take advantage of her family connections, but in this extreme case she decided to make an exception. Fixing Jericho with her haughtiest sneer, she said, "My father will be furious when he finds out about this, you know."

"Your father?" He arched half of the long, dark eyebrow that ran all the way across his forehead.

"Maxwell Sloane, of course," she replied smugly.

Now both sides of Jericho's eyebrow jutted toward the ceiling. "Maxwell Sloane? You're Midas Sloane's daughter?"

"What's the matter, didn't your spies report back that bit of information?"

Anger shadowed his face, then vanished. "I can see I shall have to have a talk with my employees. But no matter." He squashed his cigarette into a crystal ashtray on the dresser. "Ben's a smart boy. He knows better than to go running to your father, the police or anyone else."

"But after I get out of here..." Sierra's eyes expanded with dawning horror. Jericho's nonchalance, his complete lack of concern about any future consequences of this dastardly deed told her everything she needed to know. More than she *wanted* to know. Jericho wasn't the least bit worried about what she might do after he let her go... because he had no intention of letting her go. Ever.

And since imprisoning her in his seaside mansion for the rest of her life seemed a bit drastic even for Jericho, that left only one possible conclusion.

With barely the briefest sideways glance, Sierra hurled herself toward the sturdy oak door. She hardly had time to register the fact that it was still unlocked before Jericho's hand clamped down on her wrist like a guillotine. With surprising strength he whipped her arm behind her back, wedging it into a painful position that made her cry out.

"That was very foolish, my dear," he said into her ear. "Not that you could have escaped, anyway, with Vincent standing guard in the hallway." His breath stank of tobacco, and his cloying after-shave reminded Sierra of the chloroform. "I'll overlook your impulsiveness this time, but I warn you—don't try my patience again with any more useless attempts to escape."

He shoved her onto the bed and, when she glared up at him again, rubbing her wrist, he was standing in the open doorway. Behind Jericho she could see a big thug with no neck and massive shoulders that stretched the seams of his business suit. You had to give Jericho credit; at least the slimy bastard insisted on a tasteful dress code for his employees.

"Don't abuse my hospitality again," he said, "or I might have to become...less hospitable." The ruby signet ring on his pinkie finger seemed to wink at Sierra like an evil eye as he shut the door and was gone.

A geyser of panic erupted inside her, and she flew across the room to pound on the door with her fists, shouting every threatening curse she'd ever heard, plus a few she made up on the spot.

After a few minutes it became obvious this strategy was not going to work. Sierra positioned her ear against the door and held her breath, listening for the slightest response.

Nothing. The damn door was probably soundproof, anyway.

Time to try a new tactic. She rushed around the room, yanking open drawers, whipping pictures off walls, dragging cushions off chairs. There had to be *something* here she could use, some clever tool she could fashion into a means of escape.

Pacing back and forth Sierra racked her brain, trying to recall every Robert Ludlum novel, every cops-and-robbers show, every movie thriller she'd ever seen. The hero *always* found a way out, *always*! All it took was some good old Yankee ingenuity, a dash of luck and nerves of steel.

So how come in real life, the only plan Sierra could conjure up was the old tying-the-bed-sheets-together routine?

She peered out the window, shuddering as a particularly dangerous-looking wave crashed against the rocks so far below. Even if she could somehow screw up the courage to lower herself out that window, she'd need a whole linen closet full of sheets to reach the rocks. And once she got there, what then? Sierra wasn't the world's greatest swimmer, and those waves looked like they could be hiding some nasty riptides. If only this house weren't so isolated from its neighbors, she could scream for help. But the thundering ocean would drown her cries as surely as it would drown *her* if she ever managed to rappel down the steep cliff somehow.

From the corner of her eye Sierra caught a glimpse of herself in the mirror of the antique dresser. Startled, she examined her reflection. Her hair looked like she'd combed it with an eggbeater, her cheeks were streaked with dirt and a lovely purple bruise adorned her left forearm. Scratches covered her face and hands, mystifying her until she remembered her earlier tumble into that prickly bush back in the mountains.

But the most unsettling, unfamiliar aspect of Sierra's appearance was her eyes. She brushed her fingertips against the mirror, then touched her lids to make sure those eyes were really hers.

How strange. Sierra had seen a lot of different emotions reflected in her brown eyes before: joy, sadness, skepticism, coy flirtation. Even suspicion and outrage.

But never had she seen such a chilling expression of primitive, naked fear in her own eyes.

It wasn't until his plane touched down at Van Nuys Airport in Los Angeles that Ben realized he'd made his first flight since the crash. His jitters about climbing into a cockpit again had been swept aside by his fears for Sierra and his guilt about landing her in this predicament.

If Jericho had harmed even one hair on her curly head, Ben would never forgive himself. But he would make Jericho pay.

Careering his rental car onto the Ventura Freeway, Ben headed for one of the winding canyon roads that cut through the Santa Monica Mountains to Malibu. No time to swing by his West Los Angeles home to change out of his bedraggled jeans and shirt. And going to Sierra's father and the police was also out of the question. If Jericho saw or heard them coming, what would stop him from killing Sierra out of pure spite? With his reputation ruined and a kidnapping charge promising a lifetime sentence in prison, the ruthless Jericho would murder Sierra for revenge against Ben—and to have the last laugh. Ben didn't dare underestimate Jericho by taking the risk.

Tires screeched as he swerved the car around the tight curves, ignoring the steep, rocky slopes that plunged away from the road. His mind was focused on one all-consuming goal that blotted out any other awareness: rescuing Sierra.

Reaching the coast, Ben swung north and within minutes was racing up the curving street leading to Jericho's mansion. He slammed on his brakes outside the discreet yet insurmountable wrought-iron gates, pausing to work out his plan of attack.

If a man's home was his castle, Jericho's was a fortress. This place had once been like a second home to Ben, but he'd never noticed before how truly impregnable it was. The front gates, monitored by video cameras, electronic sensors and an intercom, were the only entrance. The twelve-foot brick wall that wound around the border of the estate was topped with shiny coils of barbed wire. Ben recalled with a shudder the pair of vicious, slavering Dobermans that would automatically be turned loose if the sophisticated alarm system should go off.

Funny how it had never occurred to Ben before that a man so obsessed with keeping people out must have something to hide.

He inched the sedan forward and lowered the window. Instantly a red button lit up on the intercom and a flat, uninterested voice erupted from the speaker.

Ben announced his name with no further comment, and almost immediately the massive iron gates swung open. He cruised cautiously up the landscaped drive, scanning his surroundings for any inspiration as to how he could snatch Sierra out of here unscathed.

No reception committee so far. The only person in sight was the uniformed gardener who came every day to manicure the perfect green lawns and carefully trim the bright purple bougainvillea vines and orange hibiscus bushes so they looked artfully junglelike and untended.

Ben parked the car on the circular driveway, bounded up the polished granite steps and raised the heavy brass knocker, intending to bang it loud enough to wake the dead.

Before he could vent his worry and anger on Jericho's eardrums, the huge oak door swung open silently on oiled hinges. Ben recognized Vincent Stockton, one of Jericho's so-called bodyguards. Hired gun was more like it.

Wordlessly Stockton nodded, not an easy trick for someone with no neck. His beefy face conveyed no expression, but his slitted eyes revealed unmistakable gloating. For once in his life he had the upper hand over Ben Halliday, former corporation hotshot.

Stockton grunted and made a motion with his hand that Ben took to mean he was about to be frisked. Heart pounding, he raised his arms. As Stockton patted him down, Ben couldn't help noticing the man's fingers were thick as sausages. Right then and there he eliminated hand-to-hand combat as an option for rescuing Sierra.

Stockton led Ben down the hall and left him alone in Jericho's den, one wall of which was solid glass. As the minutes ticked by, Ben stared at the spectacular view of the Pacific, strode back and forth, settled onto the black leather couch and jumped to his feet again.

He recognized this ploy, of course. Keeping a visitor twiddling his thumbs in the waiting room was a common business ploy to put the visitor at a disadvantage, to give him time to get nervous.

But knowing exactly what Jericho was up to didn't make it any easier for Ben. Tension crouched inside him like a leopard ready to pounce. He wanted to lash out, to knock the expensive crystal lamps off their lacquered tables, to rampage through the mansion, busting down doors until he found Sierra.

Ben had no doubt she was hidden somewhere here on the estate. What better prison could Jericho have found for her?

That panic-laced dread began to suffocate Ben again. How the hell was he going to find her, let alone get her out of here in one piece? Jericho's oceanside villa was as secure as Fort Knox.

And Ben would gladly trade every gold bar in Fort Knox to have Sierra safely back in his arms again.

He sensed rather than heard someone enter the room. When he spun around, knotting his fists in a defensive reflex, Quentin Jericho lounged casually in the arched doorway. He lowered a cigarette from his mouth, tapped it against a cut-glass ashtray and blew a cloud of smoke in Ben's direction.

"Well, well, well," he said. "So the prodigal son returns. Or should I say, prodigal nephew?"

Ben nearly cringed at the reminder of how he'd once called this unscrupulous sleazeball Uncle Quent. "Cut the chitchat," he growled. "Where is she?"

The edges of Jericho's mouth twitched in amusement. "My dear boy, I'm disappointed. Have you forgotten the first rule of business? Never let your opponent see how desperate you are to make a deal."

Ben hadn't forgotten; he simply didn't have the stomach for such subterfuge anymore. He dug his nails into his palms. "I said, where is she?" he forced through his teeth.

Jericho inhaled one last puff from his cigarette, then stubbed it into the ashtray. He gave Ben an oily, superior smile. "I'll be more than happy to return the delightful young lady in question," he said pleasantly, holding out his palm, "as soon as you hand over that letter."

Chapter Eleven

Jericho's blunt demand hit Ben like a punch in the stomach. Even though he'd been expecting it, mention of the letter knocked the wind out of him. For an instant he was certain that Jericho could see the folded paper, tucked under Ben's heel inside his boot.

Ridiculous, of course. Jericho was a man of many talents, but X-ray vision wasn't one of them. Still, Ben couldn't shake the feeling that somehow Jericho sensed the letter was in this very room. And if something in Ben's face gave him away, neither he nor Sierra would ever walk out of this place alive.

He'd never been much of a poker player, but Ben's only choice now was to bluff. "You didn't seriously expect that I'd bring the letter with me," he said to Jericho. "What kind of fool do you think I am?"

Jericho closed his empty fingers around thin air and shrugged. "Perhaps I overestimated the young lady's importance to you. But my sources informed me the two of you were rather...close." He gave Ben a lecherous wink. "Am I to assume you don't think the lady's life is worth that ridiculous piece of paper?"

"I didn't say that." Ben was amazed at how easy the choice was. In fact there *was* no choice. If he could have actually saved Sierra's life by handing over the letter, Quentin Jericho would have torn it to bits by now.

Like a dazzling, golden dawn breaking on the horizon, Ben realized with soaring illumination that losing his last chance to even the score with Jericho was nothing compared to the horrifying prospect of losing the woman he loved.

Trapped in Jericho's lair, confronting the man who had destroyed his father and ruined his mother's life, Ben smiled. The blissful, earth-shattering, indisputable fact of his love for Sierra made everything else seem so clear. He wasn't sure how he was going to save her. But at least he knew what his priorities were.

Jericho frowned as if Ben's smile worried him. He snapped his fingers. "What's it going to be, Ben? The girl? Or the letter?"

Wheels spun furiously in Ben's brain. He knew with cold, dead certainty that Jericho had no intention of letting Sierra go once the letter was back in his possession. How could he? Even if he destroyed the letter, he'd still face kidnapping charges, at the very least.

Besides, Sierra knew too much. If Ben had a corroborating witness to confirm the contents of the letter, Jericho would have a hard time denying Ben's accusations, even without written proof.

On top of everything else, Jericho would face the wrath of Maxwell Sloane if Sierra escaped from this nightmare alive.

Handing over the letter would be the same as signing Sierra's death warrant. And then Jericho would naturally have to kill Ben, as well.

Both their lives were riding on how Ben played out this hand. He decided to stall for time.

"Tell me something," he said, folding his arms with feigned casualness. "Did my father know about this letter?"

Jericho snorted. "What the hell difference does that make?"

"If it doesn't matter, why not tell me? I'm curious, that's all."

Jericho sighed. "He wasn't supposed to, but yes, somehow he found out about it. Either he came across it by accident, or your mother showed it to him."

"How do you know that?"

"Because he came after me like a maniac, that's why!"

A long-ago incident stirred in Ben's memory. "Are you talking about the time the two of you got into that fistfight? Right before Pa went to jail?"

"I should have pressed assault charges against him. But I knew he was heading for prison, anyway."

Everything was starting to mesh, all the bits and pieces from Ben's childhood that hadn't made sense to a six-year-old boy, but that made all-too-horrible sense now. He'd always wondered what had provoked an easygoing, nonviolent man like his father to attack his best friend and business partner.

"You framed Pa on those embezzlement charges, didn't you? You set him up." Ben cut off Jericho's denial. "You might as well tell me. You know damn good and well I don't have any proof. It'd only be my word against yours."

Jericho moved to the teak liquor cabinet, pulled out a bottle of Scotch and poured himself a drink. "Would you like one?"

Ben shook his head.

Jericho swirled the whiskey around his glass before taking a small sip and smacking his lips appreciatively. "In answer to your question, yes, I did 'set your father up,' as you so quaintly put it."

"Just so you could blackmail my mother into leaving him for you."

"Your mother should have belonged to me."

"So you created a set of phony books, opened a secret bank account in my father's name and made it look like he was channeling money into it."

Jericho smiled modestly. "Simple, yet effective."

Cold rage congealed in the pit of Ben's stomach. "And you kept the records, figuring if anyone ever came poking around after my father died in prison, the books would still prove my father's guilt."

"Ah, but you didn't find them, did you?" Jericho asked, wagging his finger. "As soon as I realized you intended to make this unfortunate matter a personal crusade, I removed the book from the company archives myself. I know what a smart boy you are—you might have found something I'd overlooked." He took another swallow of whiskey and smiled. "I can personally assure you, the records have been destroyed."

His triumphant smirk got under Ben's skin like fingernails raked down a blackboard. Although he knew that provoking Jericho was as dangerous as jabbing a stick at a wounded grizzly, he couldn't resist the temptation to take him down a peg or two. "Seems to me you made a big mistake by writing that letter in the first place."

Jericho's face didn't change, but his manicured nails turned white as he clenched his glass. "Yes," he said, "that was a serious mistake." He tossed back the rest of his Scotch. "Chalk it up to the foolish impetuousness of youth. Margaret refused to see me or speak to me after the first time I made my little proposition to her." He spoke into the bottom of his glass, as if watching those distant events playing themselves out once more. "The letter was one last effort to persuade her to see reason."

With a sudden violent gesture, Jericho flung his glass across the room. The expensive, well-crafted glass bounced off the wall without breaking, leaving a trail of liquor to dribble down the paneling. "She told me that letter had been destroyed!" he shouted. He rubbed his hand over his face. "We had a deal. Margaret swore never to use that letter against me, and in return I promised to pay for your education, get you a good job after college, see that you never wanted for anything financially." Jericho's face was a boiled-lobster shade. "I always suspected she kept that damn letter. That's why I sent Vincent to search her house the day of the funeral." His mouth twisted into a sneer. "I should have known better than to believe her when she told me the letter had been destroyed."

"Ma kept her promise," Ben said in a deadly calm voice. "She swore she'd never use the letter against you. She never promised that *I* wouldn't."

"Oh, you were both very clever, weren't you?" Jericho took another glass from the cabinet, filled it, then gulped down more Scotch. "But in the end I'm going to win. Because you're going to give me that letter."

"Let me see Sierra first."

Jericho shook his head. "Not a chance, boy."

"How do I know you haven't—that she's all right?"

"You'll just have to take my word for it." He swayed drunkenly toward Ben. "After all, what choice do you have?"

What choice, indeed? Ben had to admit Jericho had won this round. But the game wasn't over yet.

Not by a long shot.

"All right," he said. "I'll go get the letter. But if I'm followed, the deal's off, understand?" He had to maintain the pretense that he believed Jericho actually intended to trade Sierra's life for the letter.

Jericho waved his hand expansively. "Why should I bother having you followed when I know you'll be back to deliver the letter yourself?"

Ben didn't bother to reply. He pushed past Jericho and strode toward the front door. The *only* door to the outside. And somehow he had to figure out a way to sneak back in past the Incredible Hulk standing guard.

He hated like hell to leave Sierra behind, but he needed time to formulate a rescue plan if he were to have even a slight chance of getting her out alive. Once again his palms went sweaty and his heart thudded painfully as he thought about how scared she must be right now.

Ben had got Sierra into this mess. He had to get her out. Even if she never forgave him.

As he drove through the towering iron gates into the street, he had an idea. A desperate, crazy, reckless idea. But one that just might work....

Once out of sight of the mansion, Ben pulled over to the curb, leaped out of the car and opened the trunk. Then he threw open the car's hood and spent a minute hooking things up. Back inside he rooted through the glove compartment, found a flashlight that would serve his purpose quite nicely and settled back to wait. His eyes never left the rearview mirror.

Perhaps twenty minutes later the vehicle he'd been waiting for appeared. He'd known it would, sooner or later, since this was the only route back to the main road, but relief washed over him nonetheless.

Hopping out of the car, Ben stationed himself in the middle of the street and waved his arms back and forth like a contestant on a game show. The gardener's van skidded to a reluctant stop.

Ben approached the window. "Say, buddy, can you give me a jump? My battery's dead."

The gardener, a middle-aged man in a baseball cap and a khaki jumpsuit, chomped on his cigar and scowled. "I'm in a hurry, bub. Got a schedule to keep."

"Aw, come on, it'll only take a second. I got the jumper cables already hooked up and everything."

"Look, Mac, wouldja mind gettin' outta my way? I told you, I'm in a hurry. Flag down the next guy, huh?"

Life in the big city, Ben thought in disgust. "Look, I'll pay you, all right?" He pulled out his wallet. "Here's ten bucks, okay?"

The gardener shifted the wet cigar to the other side of his mouth and chewed thoughtfully. "Make it twenty, and you got a deal."

"Fine, twenty it is." Ben handed the man a bill and stepped to the front of the rental car while the van pulled alongside. He took the ends of the jumper cables and pretended to be attaching them to the van's battery.

"Hey, come on, what's the holdup?" the gardener yelled, sticking his head out the window.

"I can't seem to get these things connected right," Ben said. "Do you suppose you could have a look?"

"Oh, for Chrissake," he grumbled, climbing out of the van.

Ben stepped aside.

"For cryin' out loud, what's the matter with you? Can't you—"

Ben jammed the flashlight into the gardener's back. "Don't move, don't turn around and don't say a word."

The man froze.

"Throw those cables out of the way and close the hood. Now, very slowly, walk to the back of the van and get inside. Don't try anything funny, or you're history, got it?" The words spilled from Ben's mouth as if he were an actor in some corny gangster movie. He would have felt embarrassed if he weren't so nervous.

He had to stay behind the gardener so the man wouldn't see he was being threatened with a flashlight. Ben followed him into the van. "Now climb into the front seat, but *don't* turn around."

"Afraid I'll see you ain't got a real gun?" the gardener muttered.

"If you turn around, you'll find out for sure how real the gun is. But I don't want you to get a good look at me. If I figure you can identify me later, I'll have to kill you. Got that?"

"Whatever you say, mister. Now what?"

With the gardener at the wheel, they drove back to Jericho's mansion, and while Ben hid behind the front seat, the gardener spoke into the intercom. "It's me again. I forgot a pair of clippers I need."

The gate swung open.

Ben wrapped a rag around the flashlight to conceal it, then directed the gardener to park behind a stand of eucalyptus trees on the far side of the estate. "Now, climb back here and take off that uniform."

"Hey, what the hell is this?"

"Shut up and take it off."

"I bet that ain't even a gun you got there."

"Want to take that gamble? Feeling lucky? Now hurry up, before I pump you full of lead." Ben closed his eyes. Good lord, what cliché was going to come out of his mouth next?

After what seemed an eternity but was probably only a few minutes, the gardener was bound hand and foot with twine and gagged with another rag Ben found. Ben hastily donned the gardener's jumpsuit over his own clothes. Not a perfect fit by any means, but it would have to do. As a final touch he tugged the man's baseball cap down over his eyes.

So far so good. Now if he only had the foggiest idea what to do next.

Sierra held her handiwork at arm's length. Using a tube of toothpaste she'd found in the bathroom, she'd laboriously spelled out the word Help across one of the bed sheets.

As she inspected the results, she shivered. The toothpaste was of the red-gel variety, and the wiggly letters looked as if they'd been scrawled in blood.

After hanging the sheet out the window, she propped her elbows on the sill and stared morosely out at the ocean. The only possible rescuer who could see her makeshift banner from here would be a ship or sailboat passing by. Or maybe a very intelligent seagull.

Well, what other way did she have to attract attention? No one would hear her screaming. A note in a bottle would take too long. Besides, she didn't have a bottle. And considering her success rate at starting fires, smoke signals were definitely out of the question.

How long had she been locked up in here, anyway? When she'd thrown away her career in the rat race, she'd also thrown away her watch. Judging from the sun's low position above the horizon, it must be five or six o'clock in the evening.

As if in confirmation, Sierra's stomach rumbled, reminding her she hadn't eaten since early this morning when she'd gobbled down the Yummee Macaroon that Ben had refused. Of course, now she understood why her supply of goodies disgusted him.

Her heart gave a queer lurch. Goodness, was that only this morning? A million years seemed to have passed since then. She'd awakened in the cozy rapture of Ben's arms, only to face a day full of lies, betrayal and kidnapping.

"I should have read today's horoscope," she mumbled. "I'd never have gotten out of bed."

Although it went against Sierra's grain to sit tight and wait for someone to rescue her—Daddy? Ben?—she couldn't think of a more productive action to take at the moment.

Well, there was *one* problem she could alleviate. Kneeling next to the bed, she reached underneath and pulled out the plate of spaghetti. As she forked cold noodles and sauce into her mouth, she crinkled her nose. Next time she was kidnapped, she would definitely demand a microwave oven in her cell.

Sierra chewed mechanically, watching the sun sink into the sea. Would this be the last sunset she ever saw? She swallowed hard as the food stuck in her throat.

Ben, she thought, *where are you?*

With one final burst of exertion, Ben dragged himself onto the roof and lay there, panting. Using a combination of rope, muscles and a conveniently located jacaranda tree, he'd somehow managed to scale the side of Jericho's mansion. Thank goodness the sprawling, multileveled house was only one story high in this secluded corner.

He'd have made faster progress if he hadn't strained his bum leg again. But a setback in his recuperation was the least of Ben's worries right now.

His immediate problem was figuring out where the hell Jericho was keeping Sierra. Chances were good he'd lock her up somewhere in the back portion of the house, facing the ocean and as far away from the front door as possible.

Shifting himself into a sitting position, Ben raked his hair off his forehead and yanked off his boots. Then he rose cautiously to his feet and started tiptoeing across the flat, shingled roof, crouching as low as he could to avoid being seen from below.

He reached the far edge of the roof and peeked over. Hastily he pulled back. Amazing how far down that rocky shoreline seemed from up here!

Once again he inched his head over the roof eaves, hoping to spot an open window he might be able to climb through—even though the idea of shimmying down the side of the house while dangling over those crashing waves and menacing rocks seemed sheer madness.

Desperate times call for desperate measures, Ben assured himself. But he didn't feel too reassured.

Then he spied something below and off to his left, something flapping in the breeze. He frowned. What on earth?

He sidled closer to get a better look at the strange apparition. The wind refused to cooperate for a minute, but then, in one glorious gust, the breeze billowed out what Ben now saw was a sheet.

By cocking his head he could make out the upside-down letters: Help.

A relieved grin spread across his face. "That's my girl," he whispered.

He fumbled with his coil of rope, unwinding it so one end swung like a pendulum in front of the window. He didn't want to signal her with a noise if he could help it.

Moments later a headful of chestnut curls poked out the window and twisted to look up at him. Ben grinned down at Sierra and waved.

A whole deck of emotions shuffled across her face: surprise, relief, amusement and a profoundly tender expression that reached up and tugged at Ben's heart. But all she said was, "It's about time you showed up."

Ben slanted a finger across his lips as a warning to keep quiet. Sierra formed a circle with her thumb and forefinger to show him she understood. But when he lowered the rope farther, she stared at it blankly.

"Tie it in a loop under your arms," he called softly, hating to raise his voice to be heard over the waves. "I'll pull you up."

Sierra's chin jutted out as she shook her head wildly. "Not on your life, buster." She looked down, then back up at Ben. "You're kidding, right?"

"It's the only way." He jiggled the rope impatiently. "Come on, do you think I'd drop you?"

She sent him a doubtful look. "Well, maybe not intentionally..."

"Sierra, for God's sake, we don't have much time! Tie the damn rope around yourself, climb onto the windowsill, close your eyes, and I'll take care of the rest."

She glanced down again, then swallowed. "Did I ever mention that I'm afraid of heights?"

Ben tried to stem a rising tide of panic. "If you don't give this a try, you're going to wind up at the bottom of the ocean, anyway. Wearing a pair of concrete overshoes." Another line from a gangster movie. If he and Sierra ever got out of this mess, maybe he should try writing for Hollywood.

Sierra appeared to be wavering. Then she asked, "Why don't you just give Jericho the stupid letter?"

That familiar exasperation rose in Ben's chest. "Don't you think I would if I thought he'd really let you go?"

Her expression softened. "You would? You'd really do that for me?"

Ben shut his eyes. "Yes," he replied through grating teeth. "I would. But the question's academic, since Jericho intends to kill us both, either way."

That convinced her. Reluctantly she grasped the end of the rope and disappeared inside the house. Ben played out more rope as Sierra wound it around herself. Finally she crawled onto the windowsill, perching there as if Ben had commanded her to fly and she didn't hold out much hope for success.

"Is that knot secure?" he called.

"I hope so. But I should warn you, I flunked out of knot-tying in Girl Scouts."

"Why doesn't that surprise me?" he said under his breath. "Okay, reach up and loop the rope around each of your hands. Hang on. Ready? Here we go."

Ben braced his feet, took a deep breath and sent up a quick prayer. Then slowly, slowly, he increased the tension on the rope until he felt Sierra swing clear of the window. He shoved aside his awareness of the terror she must be feeling right now, and concentrated every muscle, fiber and tendon in his body on pulling…pulling at a slow, steady rate…refusing to let his imagination picture the woman he loved dangling a hundred feet above certain death.

Sierra's eyes were pinched so tightly shut she wondered wildly whether she'd ever be able to open them again. Her hands were so slick with sweat she could barely keep a grip on the rope. The lower half of her body swayed freely in midair, and although she tried not to think about how high up she was, terrifying images forced their way into her mind, anyway.

Inch by inch she felt herself rising, and with each inch she fully expected to find herself plummeting straight down onto the rocks. She had absolutely no concept of how far Ben had pulled her or how far she had to go— and she wasn't about to take a peek.

Dear God, she *must* be almost there! It seemed as if she'd been hanging forever with this sickening free-fall sensation. The rope cut into her hands and exerted a painful, nearly unbearable pressure around her ribs. When her body wasn't swinging out over thin air, it was scraping against the splintery shingles covering the side of the house.

Then, in one horrible split second, Sierra's worst nightmare came true and she felt herself plunging downward. Her eyes flew open, and her throat constricted with terror, strangling the scream trying to burst from her lungs.

The rapid descent probably lasted no longer than half a second, but to Sierra it felt like half a lifetime. Then, with an agonizing jerk she was suspended in midair again. After another eternal moment, she began to inch upward once more.

Cautiously she dared to look up, fastening her gaze on the edge of the roof less than four feet away...three feet...two feet...one...

Then somehow, miraculously, she was scrambling over the edge, numbly clawing her nails into the roof, struggling to bring her knee up so she could lever the weight of her body onto a solid surface at last.

The world spun around as she collapsed, trying to catch her breath and regain some feeling in her extremities. Then a strong pair of hands dragged Sierra to her feet, and all of a sudden she was in Ben's arms, laughing, crying, sagging against him as if she'd never have the strength to move away from him again.

Ben plastered her tangled hair with kisses, then cradled her face between his palms and kissed her forehead, her eyelids, her cheeks. "Thank God you're all right," he murmured over and over. Then he grasped her shoulders and held her at arm's length. As he scrutinized Sierra from head to toe, his relieved expression hardened into a grim, dangerous scowl. "My God," he breathed, "what have they done to you?"

"Huh?" Sierra blinked in confusion.

"Your face, your clothes..."

She held up her arms for inspection, seeing the scratches, the bruises, the torn sleeves. She could just imagine what her face must look like. "Oh, that," she said, smiling sheepishly. "I had a close encounter with a brier bush this morning. Jericho and his men didn't lay a hand on me. Honest," she insisted when Ben continued to fume.

"They didn't hurt you?" he asked suspiciously.

"Just my dignity."

He enveloped her in his arms again, and Sierra could have sworn she felt him tremble. She tugged at the lapel of his jumpsuit. "What is this, some kind of para-trooper uniform?"

"Not exactly."

"And what's with the baseball cap?"

"Never mind. I'll explain later. Right now we've got to get out of here."

"For once we're in complete agreement," she said. "Will wonders never cease?"

"Come on. No, wait—take off your boots first." Leaning against him, Sierra complied.

They tiptoed back across the roof. "Oh, no—more acrobatics?" Sierra groaned when they reached the far edge. "My mother didn't raise me to be a trapeze artist."

"Will you pipe down?" Ben whispered. "Come on, it's easy. Didn't you ever climb a tree as a kid?"

"I don't think trees were this tall when I was a kid."

"Here's what it boils down to," Ben said as they both put their boots back on. "Climb down that tree . . . or else."

"Well, when you put it in *those* terms," Sierra grumbled, stretching precariously for the nearest branch.

Somehow they both managed to make it to the ground with only a few additional scrapes to show for it. Ben grabbed Sierra's hand and drew her along behind him in a zigzag course, making sure to keep a tree or hedge between them and the house at all times. Sierra felt like a resistance fighter fleeing through enemy territory.

Ben pulled her down into a crouch, and she noticed a brown van parked behind some eucalyptus trees on the other side of an open stretch of lawn. Ben scanned the area for a moment, then squeezed her hand. "We've got to make a dash for that van," he said. "You run around and get in the passenger side while I'm starting the engine. Then hang on tight. Understand?"

"Sure." Sierra gnawed on her lower lip. "I just have one question."

Ben sighed. "What?"

"Who's that angry-looking man in his underwear running toward the house like his shorts are on fire?"

Ben whipped his head around. "No. Oh, no." He yanked Sierra to her feet. "Come on, sweetheart—run!"

She didn't have much choice in the matter, not with Ben practically pulling her arm out of its socket. She stumbled after him, her free arm pinwheeling in an attempt to keep her balance. They raced toward the van, and Sierra flung herself into the passenger seat just as the engine roared into life. Ben floored the accelerator and cranked the steering wheel, nearly flinging Sierra out of the van. As they sped across the estate, tearing through flower beds and plowing up the manicured lawn, she managed to slam the door shut.

"How are we going to get through those gates up ahead?" she asked through chattering teeth.

Keeping his eyes focused straight ahead, Ben said, "There's a release lever that visitors can pull to let themselves out." As if to demonstrate, he screeched to a halt next to a tastefully concealed metal post about thirty yards from the gates. Cranking furiously, he rolled down the window and speared out his arm to pull the lever. Sierra snapped back in her seat as the van flew into motion again.

"The only problem," Ben said as the imposing iron gates began to slowly swing open, "is that there's an override control inside the house, so if our friend in his underwear has had time to sound the alarm—''

Right on cue the gates hesitated, then began to close like a monstrous set of jaws.

Sierra gripped the edge of her seat when Ben stomped his foot to the floorboard. As the distance to freedom narrowed, so did the gap between the two gates.

She squinched her eyes shut, then peeled open one eyelid. ''Ben,'' she said in a choked voice, ''Ben, we're not going to make it!''

''Duck your head,'' he said sharply. ''I mean it! Get down!''

As Sierra dove for the floor, she caught a quick glimpse of Ben's white knuckles gripping the steering wheel. The engine roar filled her ears, and an oily, scorching odor assailed her nostrils. When the horrendous grating shriek of metal on metal splintered the air and the van lurched like an animal caught in a trap, she was sure they were goners.

Then all of a sudden they were flying forward like a stone from a slingshot, tires screaming, rubber burning. With shaking hands, Sierra climbed up to peer cautiously over the dashboard.

''Not that I'm complaining,'' she said, ''but do you suppose on our next date we could just go to the movies or something?''

Chapter Twelve

Sierra aimed the remote control like a laser gun and zapped off the television.

She had no need and not the slightest desire to watch yet another replay of the taped interview currently filling airwaves all over the country. She'd seen and heard it dozens of times during the past forty-eight hours. Every last detail was painfully etched into her memory.

Sierra tossed the remote control aside, hoisted herself out of the deep, overstuffed cushions of the cream-colored couch and crossed the Aubusson rug to the French windows of her parents' living room. Pushing open the glass doors, she stepped onto the flagstone terrace overlooking the vast metropolitan sprawl of Los Angeles.

The Santa Ana winds were paying their usual late-September visit to southern California, lowering the humidity, raising the temperature and whisking away the grayish brown curtain of smog that frequently hung over the city. Today was what Los Angelenos called a Chamber of Commerce day—one of the rare interludes when pristine cobalt skies formed a dazzling backdrop to the soaring skyscrapers and towering palm trees. Photographers would be out in droves today, snapping as many postcard and tourist-brochure pictures as possible before the smog settled in again.

The glorious day was a mocking contrast to Sierra's bleak mood. As she propped her elbows on the terrace railing, she scarcely noticed the fabulous view from the hills of Bel Air. The hot breeze whipped her curls into a froth around her head, while the sun beat down on her bare arms and legs.

Sierra shivered with unhappiness.

She really had nothing to be depressed about, did she? After all, at least she was alive, and two days ago she'd been wondering if she'd live to see another sunset.

But that damn videotape kept playing itself over and over in her head, tormenting her with those riveting blue eyes, that tousled blond hair, those handsomely chiseled features.

And those devastating, heart-shattering words in response to the reporter's question: "There is absolutely nothing personal going on between Ms. Sloane and myself. Ms. Sloane was simply an innocent bystander in all this, and I can't tell you how sorry I am that she had to get involved."

Innocent bystander, indeed. Sierra snorted. Ben made it sound like she'd been a witness to a traffic accident or something. He'd better hope she never spotted him crossing the street while she was driving, or people would be shaking their heads in dismay and calling *him* an innocent bystander.

"Absolutely nothing personal between Ms. Sloane and myself . . . sorry she had to get involved."

Sierra clamped her fists over her ears as the taunting refrain echoed through her head again. Bad enough to find out that Ben didn't care for her, after all, but why did she have to learn it from the evening news?

The hours immediately following their narrow escape from Quentin Jericho's mansion had passed in a mad blur of confusion. The clearest images Sierra could single out were the harsh glare of spotlights, the rapid-fire clicking of cameras, the forest of microphones thrust in front of her face when the news media converged on the police station like pigeons flocking to scattered crumbs.

The police, naturally, had been rather dumbfounded when Ben and Sierra, looking like bedraggled survivors from a garbage-scow explosion, had rushed into the station. Their initial skepticism about the wild tale of blackmail and abduction had changed to grudging belief when the desk sergeant, shutting one eye as if to blot out the dirt and scratches adorning Sierra's face, had announced, "Geez, Lieutenant, I can't be a hundred percent positive, but she sure *looks* like the picture of Midas Sloane's daughter in all those celebrity magazines my wife reads."

The desk sergeant scratched his head in mild amazement as he gave Sierra another once-over. "Geez, famous people sure look different in person, don't they?"

Once the police-beat reporters discovered that prominent businessman Maxwell Sloane's daughter was accusing equally prominent businessman Quentin Jericho of kidnapping her, the police station soon resembled the floor of a political convention. Ben hadn't needed to call a press conference, after all.

Less than fifteen minutes after the Sloanes' housekeeper, Hannah, let out a scream at the sight of Sierra's face airing live on the six o'clock news, Maxwell and Rosemary Sloane had marched into the police station and hauled off their daughter.

All the late-evening news programs had broadcast the scandal as their lead story, and by bedtime people all across the country could talk of nothing but the letter, the kidnapping and how years ago Quentin Jericho had framed an innocent man who was later killed in a prison knife fight.

Those who somehow missed hearing the story could open their Sunday-morning newspapers and read all the details over their omelets and blueberry muffins.

The police had nabbed Quentin Jericho as he was scrambling aboard his private Lear jet. The pilot had filed a flight plan for Rio de Janeiro. Vincent Stockton and another of Jericho's henchmen were arrested and charged with kidnapping Sierra and sabotaging Ben's airplane.

So the tragic saga of the Halliday family, begun over a quarter of a century ago, had finally reached its conclusion. Not exactly a happy ending, Sierra mused, since nothing could bring back Ben's father or erase his mother's years of suffering. But maybe the Hallidays would rest easier, now that their son had finally brought Quentin Jericho to justice.

Too bad the saga of Ben and Sierra wouldn't have a happy ending, either. Another sad tide of regret welled up inside Sierra as she gazed unseeing at the lengthening shadows. She swallowed, but the pain lodged firmly in her chest. Would she ever be rid of this hurtful, suf-focating pressure?

Not until she could banish the memory of Ben tell-ing the entire world that there was nothing, absolutely *nothing* personal between them.

And though she'd managed to fall in love with Ben in near-record time, Sierra suspected that falling out of love with Ben was going to be a very lengthy process indeed. She wouldn't be the least bit surprised if it took the rest of her life.

A sigh wrenched itself from the bottom of her soul as she turned from the terrace railing and reentered her parents' elegant home.

Funny. She'd never thought of it as her *parents'* home before. Sierra had grown up in this house, so of course she'd always considered it *her* home, as well, even after she'd moved into her own place. But during the months since she'd left Los Angeles, some emotional link had been severed. Now she saw this house with a new de-tachment, as if she were outside looking in, instead of the opposite.

The realization only confirmed Sierra's previous de-cision to jump off the corporate ladder, to exit the fast lane. She was more convinced than ever that she didn't belong in Los Angeles anymore.

The only problem was, she had no idea where she *did* belong. Panning for gold wasn't turning out to be the life she was destined for. And she obviously didn't be-long with Ben, either.

Yet facing the future without him made Sierra feel like a rudderless boat adrift on a sea of pointless choices. What did it matter where she lived or how she made her living, as long as Ben wasn't part of her life?

She collapsed into the puffy sofa cushions, then guiltily yanked her sneakered feet off the top of the glass coffee table as her parents entered the room.

Rosemary Sloane, a grayer, less-freckled version of Sierra, perched next to her daughter. "How do you feel, dear?" she asked, concern lacing her soft voice as she curved her slim, cool hand against Sierra's forehead.

Sierra mustered a smile. "I'm fine, Mom. Really."

Rosemary frowned as if she didn't quite believe her. "You've been through a terrible ordeal. I still think Dr. Hendricks should examine you."

"Mom, I've been telling you for two days—I'm fine."

"But those scratches, those bruises—"

"Are healing quite nicely, thank you. A couple days from now, and I'll be good as new—ready to battle ruthless evildoers again." She touched the sleeve of her mother's tailored suit. "Mom, I'm only teasing. Wipe that worried look off your face. Daddy, tell her I'm just kidding, will you?"

Maxwell Sloane had a worried look of his own creasing his distinguished features. Distractedly he ran a hand over his expensively barbered, salt-and-pepper hair. "I still can't believe that Quentin Jericho—my God, I've sat next to the man at banquets...once I even presented him with some damn award or other...and he has the audacity, the unmitigated *gall* to *kidnap* my only child—"

Sierra groaned. "Both of you are making too much of this."

"Too *much*?" her parents chorused. They gave each other a what-are-we-going-to-do-with-her glance.

"Dear, if that nice Mr. Halliday hadn't rescued you from that awful man's house—"

"Hey, Mom, what's this damsel-in-distress nonsense? I was well on my way to escaping by the time Ben showed up. I'd have gotten out of there *without* his help. Eventually." Sierra tossed her head and jumped to her feet. "Who needs that grandstander, anyway? Have you seen the way he's been spouting off all over the news? What a publicity hound. Then *you* give him credit for saving my life. Good grief, he was the one who put me in danger in the first place! Now you talk about him like he's some kind of saint or something."

Rosemary's startled look of bewilderment finally registered in Sierra's brain. She stopped pacing and threw her hands into the air. "Oh, what's the use? I'm sorry. I didn't mean to hop up on a soapbox like that."

Rosemary took Sierra's hand between hers. "We're concerned about you, dear."

"I appreciate that, Mom, but I told you—I'm fine. In fact I'm thinking about changing careers again and becoming a stuntwoman. Just kidding, Daddy," she said quickly in response to the flash of alarm in her father's face.

Her mother smothered a smile, but then her forehead wrinkled again. "You may be fine physically, Sierra, but that's not what I'm talking about."

"Oh, no, are we going to start this stuff again? Mom, I thought you were on *my* side! I thought you understood that I wasn't happy at Sloane Enterprises, that I have to live my own life—"

Rosemary hushed her. "I'm not talking about that, either. I'm referring to the way you've been moping around here for two days. You don't smile, you won't eat, and I hear you roaming around the house in the middle of the night." She brushed Sierra's cheek.

"Dear, you seem so unhappy. Won't you tell us what's wrong?"

For an instant Sierra was possessed by the nearly uncontrollable urge to burst into tears and fling herself into her mother's arms. But her problem was more serious than a skinned knee or a broken toy this time. She was an adult now, and was just beginning to realize how much she craved her parents' respect. How could she let them know what a fool she'd been, falling in love with a man who was so transparently using her?

Her parents would still think of her as a child if she confessed her schoolgirl crush, her naive mistake.

She forced down the truth. "Mom, you're sweet to worry about me—*both* of you." She threw her father an affectionate glance. "But it isn't necessary. If I'm a little down in the dumps—it's probably just some silly subconscious reaction to my recent . . . adventure."

Her mother blew a dainty puff of air between her lips and looked unconvinced. "Well, all right, dear. If you say so." She looked pointedly at her husband. "And as long as the subject has come up, your father has something to say to you."

Maxwell Sloane fiddled with his watchband.

"What is it, Daddy?" Sierra asked, bracing herself for another argument.

He snapped his fingers. "Did you hear the bottom fell out of Yummee Foods when the stock market opened this morning?"

"Now darling, that's not what you were going to tell her, and you know it," Rosemary scolded.

Maxwell Sloane sighed and gazed at the ceiling. "What your mother means—what *I* mean, is that if you still don't want to come back . . . that is, if you're still bound and determined to pursue this crazy—"

"Maxwell..." Rosemary warned.

"What I'm trying to say..." He gripped Sierra by the shoulders. "Honey, I promise that from now on I'm going to quit nagging you to come back to Sloane Enterprises." His words were surprising enough, but to her everlasting amazement, Sierra detected a damp sheen in her father's gray eyes. "After all that's happened—after we nearly...lost you—" her father swallowed "—I realize the only thing that matters is your happiness and well-being."

"Oh, Daddy..."

"And if tromping around the mountains looking for gold, or joining the Marines or becoming a damn *stuntwoman* is what makes you happy, then that's what I want you to do, baby."

Sierra flung her arms around her father and buried her face in his lapel. She couldn't remember the last time she'd hugged him, and the familiar, reassuring smell of his bay rum made her feel about six years old. But it was a nice feeling. "Thank you, Daddy," she choked.

Half laughing, half crying, she finally drew back and rubbed her fingers across his smudged lapel. "Oops, I'm getting your nice suit all wet."

"Never mind," he said gruffly, giving her a squeeze. "I've got plenty of suits. But I've only got one daughter."

"Oh, Daddy, that's the sweetest thing you've ever said...." Her voice climbed to a squeak as a fresh spate of happy tears gushed forth. Maxwell Sloane pulled a monogrammed linen handkerchief from his pocket and handed it to Sierra. She blew her nose with a loud honk.

How ironic, she thought. Her father had finally given her his blessing to follow whatever dream would make her happy. And now the one man who could make her happy wanted nothing more to do with her.

Maxwell Sloane patted his daughter helplessly on the shoulder as she continued sniffling. Only they weren't tears of happiness anymore.

The weather had changed abruptly in just the few short days Sierra had been away from the mountains. As she knelt on the edge of Bitterroot Creek, swirling her gold pan, a harsh wind swooped down the ravine and sliced right through her layered blouse, sweatshirt and windbreaker.

Her hands and feet were numb from the freezing water, her back ached and for about the thousandth time that afternoon, she wondered what on earth had possessed her to come back here.

"Well, where else was I supposed to go?" she said as if Charlemagne had asked the question. Inspecting a clump of weeds at the top of the stream bank, the mule made no rejoinder.

"I mean, I've decided L.A. isn't where I want to live anymore. Besides, that town isn't big enough for both Ben Halliday and me." She plucked a handful of pebbles from her pan and pitched them aside with an impatient gesture. "At least here I've got friends—Pete, Addie . . . you. Maybe Addie will put us up this winter until I decide what to do next." She frowned. "Of course, now that Pete's decided to stay on and help Addie run the hotel . . . well, you know what they say about three being a crowd."

Swishing most of the black dirt from her pan, Sierra halfheartedly spread the residue over the bottom. "Hmm, too bad there's no market for fool's gold. I'd be a millionaire." She was about to rinse the worthless contents into the stream when she pictured how disgusted her grandfather would be if he could see her sloppy mining practices. She sighed.

With stiff fingers she wriggled her Swiss Army knife from her hip pocket. "Maybe I ought to join the French foreign legion," she mused. "Or sign up for the first manned mission to Mars." She flicked open the blade and poked listlessly at the shiny flecks. "I wonder if they need workers down in Antarctica. Gee, that's weird." She bent closer over her gold pan, shading the glittering specks from the sun. "If I didn't know any better, I'd swear that . . ."

She scratched the tiny flakes with the tip of her knife. Stunned, she rolled back on her heels and sat right down in two feet of icy water. "Well, I'll be a son of a gun," she breathed, staring into the pan.

A shadow fell across her from behind. "Char, you're not going to believe this," she said, "but we just struck gold."

"Honest-to-goodness gold? You really found it?"

Sierra spun around so fast she nearly dumped her precious find into the stream. She didn't know which shocked her more: discovering gold after all this time, or finding Ben leaning over her, sunlight forming a halo around his blond head.

He extended a hand and—when she gripped it in a daze—pulled Sierra to her feet. She stood there dripping, clutching her gold pan, staring at him. He stuffed his hands into the pockets of his leather jacket and gave her a lazy grin. "Aren't you going to come out of the water?"

"What? Oh, er, sure." She waded out of the creek, holding the pan in both hands like a serving tray. "Look what I found."

"So that's the real McCoy, huh?" When Ben lowered his head for a closer view, Sierra inhaled the heady masculine fragrance of leather and denim. His fingers closed over hers to hold the pan steady, but the tantalizing pressure of his touch only made her hand tremble more.

She pried the pan away and stepped back. "What the hell are you doing here?" she demanded.

His eyes flickered with amusement. "I wanted to deliver a present," he said.

"I don't want any presents from you, Ben Halliday, so you can just take your bouquet of flowers or your box of chocolates and—"

"I didn't say the present was for you."

"Oh." She snapped her mouth shut.

"I brought a present for Charlemagne."

"For—but you don't even *like* Charlemagne."

Ben shifted his weight from one long, lean leg to the other. "I think Charlemagne and I got off on the wrong foot, that's all. So I brought him a peace offering." He smiled sheepishly. "Besides, it's the least I could do after he kept the letter safe and sound all those months."

"Hmph." Sierra shoved a cluster of curls from her face. "So where *is* this so-called present, anyway?"

Ben bowed his head in the mule's direction, and when Sierra turned, she spied a brand-new straw hat dangling from a tree branch by a bright red ribbon. "*You* can tie the hat on him," Ben said. "Even though your mule and I are embarking on a new era of peaceful relations, I decided not to press my luck."

"Wise decision," Sierra muttered. "Charlemagne's been known to hold a grudge."

"What about you?" Ben shaded his eyes to study her closely.

"What about me what?"

"Do *you* hold a grudge?"

Her eyes raked him from the toes of his boots to the top of his gorgeous head. "Have you done something for me to hold a grudge about?" Her haughty expression managed to convey both innocence and disdain.

"One or two things. Like lying to you. Using you. Nearly getting you killed. Some people might hold those things against me."

Sierra took a deep breath. "Let's cut to the chase, all right? You didn't come all the way back here just to play milliner to a mule." Her chin inched up a fraction. "Why don't you tell me what you *really* want?"

"Fair enough. As long as *you* quit pretending that nothing's wrong between us."

"Seems to me *you're* the expert on pretending."

"Okay, okay." Ben held up his hands in surrender. "I deserve that. But I also think you deserve an explanation."

"Don't do me any favors."

Ben hissed a long breath through his teeth. Plowing his fingers through his hair, he said, "When I left you here the day you were kidnapped, I promised to come back and explain everything. I'm trying to keep my promise."

Who the hell am I kidding? Ben taunted himself. He'd returned to the mountains with only one purpose in mind: to win Sierra back. And if his success so far was any indication, he had quite a struggle ahead of him.

By bargaining for Sierra's life, Quentin Jericho had inadvertently done Ben a big favor by making him realize how important Sierra was to him. Now he was desperate. He *had* to convince her to give him one more chance.

They faced each other like gunslingers at a showdown. All at once Sierra's anger and defiance seemed to melt away. She carefully set down the pan, then lowered herself to the ground and drew her knees up to her chin. "You don't need to explain," she said quietly, sounding as forlorn as she looked. "I read all the papers and heard all the TV reports. Jericho framed your father for embezzlement, then tried to blackmail your mother into leaving him. She refused, and your father went to prison. He was accidentally killed during a fight between two other inmates." Her dark brown eyes clouded with sadness. "You were only six years old," she whispered.

Ben eased himself onto the stream bank next to Sierra. She brushed her hand against his sleeve. "I'm so sorry, Ben. I can't begin to imagine what you and your mother must have endured."

He captured her fingers and held them where they rested on his forearm. His gaze traveled across the stream, but the scenes he envisioned had taken place long ago. "The three of them grew up together in Grass Valley," he told her. "Jericho and my father were rivals for my mother's hand. She picked my father."

"And Jericho, being the sore loser he was, never accepted her decision."

Ben shook his head. "Who could have suspected the bitterness that lay festering all those years? On the surface, my father and Jericho remained best friends. They even went into business together, starting a small-town bakery that eventually became Yummee Foods." He picked up a small stone and rolled it between his fingers before lobbing it into the creek. "Then, after the company grew so big they had to move operations to Los Angeles, Jericho figured out a way to get even.''

"One thing I'm not clear about," Sierra said. "Why didn't your parents expose Jericho when he first wrote that letter?"

Ben shrugged. "You've read the letter yourself, so you know Jericho didn't admit in so many words that he'd framed my father. The letter didn't prove any criminal act."

"Yes, but it would have shown people what a despicable louse Jericho was."

"It wouldn't have mattered back then." Ben picked up a twig and examined it absently. "Yummee Foods was just starting out. No one had ever heard of Quentin Jericho. The letter wouldn't have been the effective weapon it became after Jericho got famous."

"But surely your mother could have revealed the letter years ago."

Ben shook his head. "She made a bargain with Jericho. He swore to take me under his wing and provide me with a good education, a job with a future...all the financial advantages I never would have had otherwise—if Ma would keep the letter secret." He gave a harsh laugh. "But she never promised that *I* wouldn't use the letter against him."

"So you grew up believing that the man responsible for your father's death was your benefactor."

Ben leaped to his feet and hurled the twig aside. "Pretty ironic, huh? Good old Uncle Quent. He was like a father to me after Pa died. God, I actually worshipped that man! He was so good to my mother and me...." Ben slammed his fist into his palm, waiting for the usual surge of bitterness to choke him.

Surprisingly the familiar bile didn't rise up this time. Maybe he didn't need to hate anymore, now that he'd avenged his parents by showing the world Jericho's true colors.

But Ben's usual anger was replaced by a raw, aching emptiness. He'd lost three of the people who were most important to him: his mother and father and the man who'd been an uncle to him.

And he'd be damned if he'd lose the woman he loved, as well.

Grasping Sierra's hands, Ben pulled her to her feet. He slid his hand along her cheek, weaving his fingers through her curls. "Sierra," he pleaded in a husky voice, "I want to make up for all the lies, all the deception." He stroked his thumb over the lush fullness of her lips. "Will you give me one more chance? Please?"

Her gaze was locked on his as if she were mesmerized. Then a shutter clicked into place, and she backed away from him. "Don't play games with me, Ben."

"Sweetheart, I swear I have no intention—"

"What is it you *want* from me?" she asked, her voice rising. "My forgiveness? Fine, you've got it. I accept your apology for involving me in this whole crazy episode. You're absolved of all guilt, okay?"

"That's not exactly what I had in mind."

"That's what you said on TV! 'I can't tell you how sorry I am that she had to get involved.' Well, now you've made your apologies, so why don't you go away and leave me alone?" she cried.

She angled her head so the wind blew her curls across her face. Ben clutched her arm and pushed her tangle of hair aside. "Is that what all this is about?" he demanded. "That damn television interview?"

"You said—and I quote—that there is 'absolutely nothing personal' between us."

Ben cradled her face between his hands. "Sierra, that didn't mean anything!"

"You announced it to the whole world, buster! I'd say that means something!"

Ben flung up his arms. "What was I *supposed* to say to those reporters? My God, we'd just been through a nightmare…I didn't have a chance to talk to you alone afterward, what with the police and then the press swarming all over the place. Then your parents showed up and hustled you away before I knew what was happening. How was I supposed to know how you felt about me? For all I knew, you never wanted to see me again. I wasn't about to tell the whole world I loved you, for Pete's sake!"

Sierra blinked. "What did you say?"

"I said I love you, for Pete's sake!"

The words stunned her as sharply the second time she heard them. A wild flame of joy ignited deep inside her, but was quickly doused by caution. She'd been burned once too often.

"You've said a lot of things to me before that weren't true," Sierra pointed out, trying to keep her voice steady. "Why should I believe you now?"

"I don't blame you for not believing me," Ben said. "But I intend to spend the rest of my life proving it to you."

Sierra gulped. "What do you mean?" she asked slowly.

Ben stepped forward to grasp her shoulders. He slid his hands all the way down her arms to twine her fingers with his. Her eyes flared open as he slanted his head to press a gentle, incredibly tender kiss against her lips.

"Marry me, Sierra," he said, his mouth a mere half-inch from hers.

She caught her breath and staggered back a step, wanting desperately to accept Ben's proposal at face value. She scanned his eyes for some evidence, some proof that he *did* love her, after all, that this wasn't merely the next phase of some secret scheme of his.

In the past Sierra had always been able to tell when Ben was lying to her, even when she hadn't been able to figure out what the truth actually was. And now, incredibly, she saw love blazing in the depths of his eyes, written in every crease and crinkle in his handsome face. The truth shone forth with a powerful, blinding beacon that dazzled her with its miraculous promise.

Despite their muddled, mixed-up history of lies and deception, Sierra was flooded with the crystal-clear certainty that this time Ben wasn't lying, that he'd never lie to her again....

"Never, ever," she whispered with a dreamy smile.

Ben's fingers tightened convulsively around hers as a startled, worried frown crashed over his face. "Sierra, you can't mean that! I know you're still angry, but—"

"Huh? What you are talking about?"

"Don't you think 'never' is too strong a word? Maybe I caught you off guard, maybe if I gave you some more time to think about it . . ."

Her brows knit together in puzzlement. "Think about what?"

Ben's jaw fell open. Dropping Sierra's hands, he dashed the sweat from his forehead and folded his arms. "Excuse me, did I miss something here? I asked you to marry me, and you said—"

"Oh, that." She waved her hand. "Of course I'll marry you."

"You—you will? But then why did you say—what were you—oh, hell, never mind!" Ben grabbed her by the waist and lifted her into the air, whirling her around so fast that the trees kept spinning even after he set her down.

"You won't be sorry, sweetheart...we're going to be incredibly happy together...."

That was putting it mildly, Sierra reflected, if the next few moments were a foretaste of things to come. If she lived to be a thousand, she would never forget the indescribable rapture that spread through her body like wildfire when Ben wrapped her in his arms and kissed her with a fierce passion that made her dizzy.

For the rest of her life the scent of pine would evoke the rushing sound of the creek, the sight of red autumn leaves fluttering to the ground and the exquisite sensation of Ben's eager, possessive lips communicating far more than mere words ever could.

Nestled in Ben's embrace, Sierra knew at last where she belonged.

Eventually she nudged him away. "Give a girl a chance to breathe, would you?" As Ben drew back reluctantly, the wind swept between their bodies, making Sierra gasp as it made contact with her wet clothing. "Oh, my gosh, Ben—now *you're* soaked, too! You shouldn't have hugged me. Didn't you realize I'm all wet?"

He bundled her into his arms again as his laughter echoed across the ravine. "Hold still, will you? Now that I've finally got you back in my arms, I'm never letting you go."

"Well, that could certainly prove awkward in certain situations," she said, giving him a playful poke in the ribs. "By the way..." She circled her arms around his neck and gazed tenderly into his eyes. "Have I forgotten to mention that I love you, too, Ben Halliday?"

He cocked one eyebrow and considered. "Well...now that you mention it, I do believe it's slipped your mind until now." He kissed the tip of her freckled nose. "But I suspected as much, anyway."

"Pretty sure of yourself, were you?"

"Well...yes and no. But after I talked to your mom, I decided I had a pretty good chance of persuading you to spend the rest of your life with me."

Sierra stared at him. "You talked to my *mom*? When?"

"When I came looking for you, of course. After I finally shook off all those reporters, I made a beeline for your parents' house. Pretty swanky digs, by the way."

"If you think we're going to live there after we're married, forget it."

"I assure you, that's the furthest thing from my mind." He nuzzled her neck. "I don't think your father likes me, anyway."

"No? What did you do, break a lamp or something?"

"Let's just say your father was a little reluctant to tell me where you'd disappeared to. I think he's still mad at me for embroiling you in our whole unfortunate escapade. For which I don't blame him at all."

Sierra fidgeted from one foot to the other. "Get to the part where you talked to Mom."

"Oh, yes, your mother. Charming woman. I think she likes me. At least that's the impression I got when she hauled me out of your father's earshot and told me you'd gone back to the mountains. She was awfully concerned about the way you'd been moping around lately. Seemed to think it might have had something to do with me."

"You big egomaniac, you."

"Well? That *is* why you were depressed, isn't it? Because of that stupid remark I made on TV?"

"Ha! That's what you think. I was depressed because the price of gold's fallen off during the last week."

"Is that it? Well, in that case I'm glad I wasn't aware of it. I might not have had the nerve to propose if I hadn't thought you were pining away for me."

"Speaking of marriage, what are we going to do after we're married?"

Ben winked. "Sweetheart, if you don't already know, I'll be more than happy to show you."

She slapped his chest. "I'm not talking about *that*! I mean, where are we going to live? How are we going to make a living? After all, we're both unemployed at the moment."

"Not exactly an auspicious start for a marriage, is it? Maybe we should wait until we're both established in new careers...."

"Forget it."

Ben kissed her soundly. "My sentiments exactly." When he pulled her head against his chest, Sierra could hear the low rumble of his voice. "To tell the truth, I haven't the faintest idea where we'll go or what we'll do. The only thing that matters is that we'll be doing it together."

"Maybe we could open a wilderness survival school."

Pause. "As I said, the only thing that matters—"

"Become acrobats in the circus?"

"—is that we'll be—"

"—together," they finished in unison.

Ben rested his chin on top of her head. "Sweetheart, I know how attached you are to that mule...."

"Say no more." Sierra pressed her finger over his mouth. "I'm sure Addie and Pete will be glad to adopt him."

"You won't miss him too much?"

"I'll miss him like crazy, but I think Charlemagne's earned his retirement. Besides, three's a crowd."

Ben grinned. "For now, anyway."

Sierra beamed in agreement. "For now."

Ben squeezed her tight, then ruffled her curls. Flicking a glance at the gold pan, he teased, "Are you really sure you want to give up your mining career to marry me, now that you've finally found gold? You might be passing up your big chance to strike it rich."

"I've got news for you," Sierra said, stretching up on tiptoe and cupping her hand to whisper in his ear. "I already have."

*   *   *   *   *

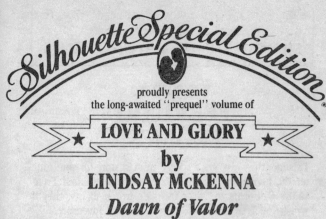

Silhouette Special Edition

proudly presents
the long-awaited "prequel" volume of

★ LOVE AND GLORY ★

by
LINDSAY McKENNA
Dawn of Valor

In the summer of '89, Silhouette Special Edition premiered three novels celebrating America's men and women in uniform: LOVE AND GLORY, by bestselling author Lindsay McKenna. Featured were the proud Trayherns, a military family as bold and patriotic as the American flag—three siblings valiantly battling the threat of dishonor, determined to triumph . . . in love and glory.

Now, discover the roots of the Trayhern brand of courage, as parents Chase and Rachel relive their earliest heartstopping experiences of survival and indomitable love, in

Dawn of Valor, Silhouette Special Edition #649

This month, experience the thrill of LOVE AND GLORY—from the very beginning!

Silhouette Books

DV-1A

SILHOUETTE·INTIMATE·MOMENTS®

WELCOME TO
FEBRUARY FROLICS!

This month, we've got a special treat in store for you: four terrific books written by four brand-new authors! From sunny California to North Dakota's frozen plains, they'll whisk you away to a world of romance and adventure.

Look for

L.A. HEAT (IM #369) by Rebecca Daniels
AN OFFICER AND A GENTLEMAN (IM #370) by Rachel Lee
HUNTER'S WAY (IM #371) by Justine Davis
DANGEROUS BARGAIN (IM #372) by Kathryn Stewart

They're all part of February Frolics, available now from Silhouette Intimate Moments—where life is exciting and dreams do come true.

You'll flip ... your pages won't!
Read paperbacks *hands-free* with

Book Mate · I

The perfect "mate" for all your romance paperbacks

**Traveling • Vacationing • At Work • In Bed • Studying
• Cooking • Eating**

Perfect size for all standard paperbacks, this wonderful invention makes reading a pure pleasure! Ingenious design holds paperback books OPEN and FLAT so even wind can't ruffle pages – leaves your hands free to do other things. Reinforced, wipe-clean vinyl-covered holder flexes to let you turn pages without undoing the strap...supports paperbacks so well, they have the strength of hardcovers!

Pages turn WITHOUT opening the strap

SEE-THROUGH STRAP

Reinforced back stays flat

Built in bookmark

BOOK MARK

BACK COVER HOLDING STRIP

10 x 7¼ opened
Snaps closed for easy carrying. too

SILHOUETTE·INTIMATE·MOMENTS®

NORA ROBERTS
Night Shadow

People all over the city of Urbana were asking, Who was that masked man?

Assistant district attorney Deborah O'Roarke was the first to learn his secret identity . . . and her life would never be the same.

The stories of the lives and loves of the O'Roarke sisters began in January 1991 with NIGHT SHIFT, Silhouette Intimate Moments #365. And if you want to know more about Deborah and the man behind the mask, look for NIGHT SHADOW, Silhouette Intimate Moments #373, available in March at your favorite retail outlet.

NITE-1

 *Silhouette Books*®